My Sardinian Summer

Michaël Uras

Michaël Uras was born in 1977. With Sardinian origins through his father, he grew up in Saône-et-Loire, western France, and now teaches French literature in Burgundy. *My Sardinian Summer* is his fourth novel.

My Sardinian Summer

MICHAËL URAS

Translated from the French
by Adriana Hunter

HODDER

First published in the French language as *La Maison à droite de celle de ma grand-mère* by Librairie Générale Française in 2018

First published in Great Britain in 2020 by Hodder & Stoughton
An Hachette UK company

This paperback edition published in 2020

2

A CIP catalogue record for this title is available from the British Library

B format ISBN 9781529351613
eBook ISBN 9781529351637

Typeset in Plantin Light by
Palimpsest Book Production Ltd, Falkirk, Stirlingshire

Printed and bound in Great Britain by Clays Ltd, Elcograf S.p.A.

Hodder & Stoughton policy is to use papers that are natural, renewable
and recyclable products and made from wood grown in sustainable forests.
The logging and manufacturing processes are expected to conform
to the environmental regulations of the country of origin.

Hodder & Stoughton Ltd
Carmelite House
50 Victoria Embankment
London EC4Y 0DZ

www.hodder.co.uk

To Angéla and her smile

From my village I see as much of the universe as can be
    seen
from the earth,
And so my village is as large as any town,
For I am the size of what I see
And not the size of my height . . .

Fernando Pessoa, *A Little Larger Than the
Entire Universe: Selected Poems*, translated
by Richard Zenith, Penguin, 2006

On this wondrous sea – sailing silently –
Ho! Pilot! Ho!
Knowest thou the shore
Where no breakers roar –
Where the storm is o'er?

Emily Dickinson, *Emily Dickinson's
Poems: As She Preserved Them*,
Harvard University Press, 2016

The house to the right of my grandma's is red, the one on the left is blue. The house opposite is yellow. Ours is green. Walking down the street means going through every shade in the spectrum. Diving into a rainbow. There's nothing more colourful than our living space, nothing could look more cheerful than our village. Except the people, who have scruffy hair, crooked teeth and worn clothes.

Every time I come back, I get this feeling, just for a moment, that everything's changed – the mentality, the people, the dog bowl by the neighbours' door . . . But it's a short-lived illusion. Nothing ever moves, here in the village. Maybe it's the altitude that prevents any movement, I don't know. The altitude rarefying the air. You'd have to take everyone down into the valley, see if things change. But no one ever goes down there. As if they just have to stay up here, cut off from anyone else, cut off from a life outside these brightly coloured walls with their pictures. You see, our village has another distinctive characteristic: people draw on walls. Frescoes, caricatures, random things, animals, nothing goes unrecorded by the artists' brushes. A sort of vast, ever-present open-air comic book.

It was six o'clock in the morning. The first bus of the day had just dropped me off on the main road through the village. Six o'clock in the morning, a time for stray dogs and travellers newly arrived in the port fifty minutes earlier. There have always been as many stray dogs as people, respectfully sharing out the time: daytime for the humans, night-time for the abandoned mutts. There were a couple I recognized, even though I came to the island less and less. You have to be brave to go back to the place you were born, the place where you grew up, and see it through an adult's eyes. I wasn't brave. Every trip back was painful, making me suffer more and more and giving me less and less pleasure. I lived far away from this little world, in France, without the bright colours of those houses, without pictures on the walls and without stray dogs.

As it happens, one of the dogs came over to me as I stepped off the bus, as if to sniff out whether I had any connection with the place, whether I had the right to set foot there. He accepted me by refraining from chewing off my leg. I know I've said this before, but I'm really not brave. As a protection, I put my small suitcase between myself and the dog, the suitcase that held a part of my existence. A little bit of France in Sardinia. My clothes, of course, and the book I'd been working on for several months: a new translation of Herman Melville's *Moby Dick*. There were also the pages of my work so far, which had been arduous to produce. I minded much more about them than my clothes because I'd never had such a complicated job before.

Melville had reworked the book a few months before he died, and my editor, Carlo, had stumbled across this text that specialists didn't know existed. A text that he'd entrusted to me, a translator with a great career ahead of him . . . a future benchmark in the field . . . it was a great honour. A form of recognition, my friends said. What not many of them knew was that the editor's mother was Sardinian. That was why. The real reason. But I kept this to myself. Sometimes it's good to keep a bit of mystery about ourselves and the things that give us a leg-up in life.

I'd said yes to the editor, without realizing how difficult the work would be. Or how important. It was so easy to sign the contract, so tempting. The problems would come later. I hadn't remembered that Melville's book was so long. Seven hundred and forty-two pages in the existing version. Six hundred and forty-one in the version I was to translate. A hundred fewer pages – I could count myself lucky.

So when the dog drew closer to my suitcase, I was apprehensive about my leg, obviously, but I also felt a perfectly legitimate terror at the thought of watching my work being destroyed by a dog that no one had even noticed except for me at this particular moment. It was a good thing, then, that he spared me and left my suitcase intact. He probably wasn't a big Melville fan, or maybe he was frightened of taking on that whale. Dogs are no braver than people, at the end of the day. Eventually, they all wandered off and left me to make my way over to my parents' house.

There was still no one out in the street when I reached the front door. The ghost village was fast asleep. The lock was tricky, as it had always been, as if the house expected anyone who wanted to come in to make an effort. My parents weren't there, they'd gone away for a holiday on the other side of the island. They always let me have a key so I could come back whenever I felt the need to. And that need was proving increasingly rare. Parents think they know best about what their children want. Sometimes they're wrong. The house was cold. The shutters, which had been closed since they'd left, had stopped the sun from getting inside.

My parents were an odd couple according to our friends, they were an odd couple according to the wider family, an odd couple according to other villagers, an odd couple according to the whole world. Some people are just like that, they spend a lifetime side by side when they were designed to be blissfully unaware of each other. Nothing clicked between them.

My father was the incarnation of calm. In ancient Greece he could have applied to be the god of introspection. Few words found an opportunity to come out of his mouth. And because this had been going on for years, the few remaining words available had forgotten how to get to the exit. Every now and then a word would find it, but apparently failed to pass the information on to the others.

My mother, on the other hand, specialized in micro-scandals

and over-inflated dramas. I've lost count of the times she walked out, leaving my father on his own, sad and dejected, his hands tucked into his pockets until she came back. My mother would move in with my grandma, in the house opposite. These escapes lasted two or three days, never more. My father had to *suffer*, that was her watchword. The worst of it was, these arguments should never have happened. They often evolved from completely inoffensive situations. One time my father helped a pretty tourist who'd got lost in our village and wanted to know how to get to the coast. "*Il mare*," she kept saying, swivelling her head from left to right. It took my father five minutes to explain the directions to her.

I was a teenager. The tourist really was very pretty, with direct eye contact and just the right depth of tan, one of those tourists who's mastered the sun's influence on her skin. She wasn't the sort who come to our island to go home roasted. We eat grilled pork, not foreigners. I would gladly have kissed her sleeveless arms. I even imagined asking for her hand in marriage and taking her away from the village for a wonderful romantic idyll in a shepherd's hut. Not too far from my family home, but just enough so we wouldn't hear my mother's shouting.

I daydreamed while my father tried to help her, in English that he cobbled back together specially for the occasion, a sort of mash-up of Beatles lyrics and the remnants of lessons he'd had forty years earlier. After five minutes, he gave up and tried drawing the route instead. Unlike words, anyone from anywhere can understand a drawing. Papa painted house walls when people asked him to, frescoes or even just colours. Painter-decorator and artist rolled into one. Blue, red, green, shapes, figures and words emerged from his sturdy hands. And they needed to be sturdy, to have all that in them.

The tourist moved in closer to get a better look. The sketch was clear, precise, as perfect as her skin – Clara, was her name, she'd eventually revealed, dazzled as she was by my father's skilled cartography. But at the sight of the reduced distance between them, my mother bristled, complaining that never in twenty years of marriage had my father drawn anything for her.

"So you'll draw for a foreigner, Mario, but not for me, your wife, Maria, your ever-faithful wife." My mother had an unfortunate tendency to see herself as the perfect faithful wife.

Clara, who didn't understand my mother's outburst, most likely thought Mama was giving my father advice to improve his map. She smiled at her and I knew my mother's fury would be unleashed in the house as soon as Clara drove away to the coast. "You disappoint me, Mario, never a single drawing for your wife."

She was right. My father never drew, not for her nor for other women. And certainly not for me. He wasn't the type to draw a particular type of car for me when I was little, nor suns or houses. I had nothing from him, nothing tangible, just his eyes filled with despair before the tornado. *The weather's on the turn*, they seemed to say, already misting over. Once we were alone, Clara having gone – and in my mind she had become Chiara, *alba chiara*, a luminous perfection that had now gone – my mother headed straight for thunderous darkness. Inside the house, doors slammed, as did words. She packed her bag, which was in reality always ready, just in case, and went off to my grandma's house. This departure, if her words were to be believed, was for good. She wouldn't be coming back this time. She came back the next day. "That's the last time, Mario, do you hear me?"

I'd noticed that the name Mario was only brought out for special occasions. It was a mark of solemnity, a sign intended to draw my father's attention to the gravity of the situation. At all other times she called him Papa. Of course he wasn't her papa but her husband. He was my papa. As a child, I seriously questioned their relationship. There's no denying this scrambling of names wasn't easy to understand. Luckily for me, these exceptional situations that brought *Mario* out for an airing weren't actually so exceptional.

★ ★ ★

Stepping into the house thirty years later, it felt as if her insults and disapproval lived on between those walls, now yellowed by these old squabbles. It was half past six and I walked, like a ghost, down the long corridor that led to my bedroom. A gallery of family portraits looked down at me. I didn't remember all these people hung around the house. They must have been glad of a visitor in this God's waiting room of a place. But I wasn't here for them. I didn't show any sign of my indifference as I walked along that chilly corridor, eyeing them with feigned nostalgia, its fakery imperceptible to the dead.

I was here for my grandmother, my nonna, who was breathing her last according to the message that my uncle Gavino had left on my voicemail. She had gone into a deep coma. My parents were due back later in the day. They had gone off on an "expedition" in the south of the island, visiting an old friend of my father's who had recently been widowed. And yes, it was an expedition for them to leave the village. My mother didn't cope well with the upheaval – yes, this qualified as "upheaval" to her – and being away from home. As if the walls might collapse without her, as if she were holding up the whole construction. She agreed to this trip to please my father, to allow him to spend some time with his childhood friend, so the two men could look at old photographs together. Side by side, they would laugh – and cry too – while she snoozed on the sofa. More proof of her love, probably.

"Be quick, Giacomo. The doctors don't think she has long."

I was in Marseille, deep into my translation, grappling with *Moby Dick*, when my phone announced the news to me. Gavino never called me, so I immediately knew he must have something important to tell me. In every family, there is one person who takes on the role of bearer of bad news. Gavino had come through the casting session with flying colours, thanks to his exaggeratedly deep voice, that was so good at implying imminent and inevitable doom. Or in this instance, my grandmother's demise. I caught the first available boat, paying through the nose to spend the crossing lying on a bench seat in the middle of the piano bar. An unfortunate singer (I say unfortunate because no one would feel fortunate in such a place) trudged through Phil Collins' backlist, singing continuously to avoid the silence where the applause should have been. Everything about his performance was pitiful: his suit, his voice, his backing track and his audience. And Phil Collins. How could anyone arrange their set list around Phil Collins? Wasn't there someone in charge of programming who could have talked him out of that, at least? Someone with a degree of common sense to tell him that nobody would clap a Phil Collins tribute act?

Moby Dick would have been doing the world a service if he'd decided to attack the boat during this set. We would have all died as heroes, and people would have wept over our terrible fate.

But the sea monster was safe and warm in my bag, happy to stay put. The show on offer was probably not to his taste. After his performance, the singer came and sat near me. You've probably realized I attract this sort of attention, from stray dogs and singers alike.

Like a forest put to sleep by a witch, my bedroom hadn't changed since my last visit, which was now over a year ago, nearly two. The bed was made. Mama always kept it made. You never knew when I'd be there, she would say. "You're like the postman, we wait and wait for him and he doesn't come. Then the next day, when we've given up hope, he turns up. We're a bit angry because he could have come sooner, but we don't say anything, we just smile stupidly, almost apologize for not greeting him with enough enthusiasm . . ."

On my bed was a copy of *Zeno's Conscience* that I translated into English. It had been a gift to my parents. They were always proud to see my name on books, even if it was just on the inside pages. Mama claimed to recognize something of me in my translations, despite not reading English. I lay down on my cold bed and began to read. One page, then two, then three . . .

The ceiling light was flickering, irritating me. I wanted to ignore it and carry on reading, but it was impossible. The text was visible for a few seconds, then disappeared, and I had to start the same sentence again. After ten minutes of unfruitful reading I switched off the light and opened the shutter, letting daylight discreetly fill the room. I stood on the bed to look at the bulb. I didn't have a replacement for it and knew nothing about electricity, but, hey, don't we often do pointless things to make ourselves look important? I'd noticed this with people whose cars break down. Their knee-jerk reaction is to open the bonnet and look at an engine which they have no idea how to fix. But still they look, as though the problem will leap up and say: "I'm right here! You just need to move this here, and the car will start." Until they eventually slouch back to their seat and defeatedly call a breakdown service.

From where I was standing on the bed, the world looked different. Looking at my room from above gave me a panorama of the years I'd spent here. A life lived on an island, far removed from the crowds and bustle of the mainland. With its loneliness, struggles, cobbled streets and inhabitants stationed outside their houses. If I went to the library, I had to cross the main road and walk right past those wizened eyes, those seated figures that never smiled, never betraying any indication of goodwill.

It turned out that the lightbulb in the bedroom had a little collection of dried-out flies on it. Mama was far too short to reach up here. And to think, she spent days on end cleaning the house, hunting down the tiniest speck of dust . . . I wouldn't mention this macabre find. I swiftly ran a hanky over the flies, giving them a little send-off. Here lies one of the flies, etc.

Just so that I'd covered all bases, I twisted the bulb back in a couple of times. This operation did nothing to settle its rubbish illuminating abilities. Never mind, daylight would do. I went back to my book, glad to be reunited with Zeno, my Zeno with whom I'd spent many a long month in Marseille. We were a well-matched couple: he had his cigarettes and I my fear of failure. A fear I could never shake off, probably part of my innermost being.

The ghosts on the landing wall slept peacefully. They weren't alone anymore.

★ ★ ★

"Are you Sardinian?"

"Um . . . yes. I don't really know. It's complicated."

"How are you feeling? Do you not know that either? You *are* funny."

"I was born on the island but I haven't lived here for a long time. Funny, me? How about you, are you Sardinian?"

"No, I'm from Rome."

"Great."

"If you say so."

"Rome's a wonderful city."

"Do you know it?"

"No, I've never set foot in the place."

"You should. It really is beautiful, you're right. I think your phone's ringing."

"It's nothing, probably a mistake. I'm not expecting any calls. Not too difficult, singing on a boat?"

"You get used to everything, you know. In the early days, my voice would rock with the boat. In other words, the show was pretty mediocre. I've got used to a moving stage now. My voice is steadier. Easier on the ear."

"It certainly is, I found it very easy on the ear."

"Did you really listen? Be honest with me, don't spare my feelings."

"At the beginning, yes. But I'm tired at the moment, I can't concentrate. I ended up falling asleep."

"No one normally listens to me, you know. People have better things to do. Like sleeping. Talking, eating. I'm like a bottle of oil on a restaurant table, people only see me if they feel the need."

"I think you're being hard on yourself."

"It's the truth. I've been singing on this stage for ten years. But Phil Collins is my speciality. He's a major artist. And how about you, what do you do for a living? Don't say music producer or impresario, or I'll jump overboard . . . After what I've just told you . . . You're not likely to offer me a fantastic contract and a world tour . . ."

"No danger of that."

"You really are funny. Humour's a rare quality. It's what keeps me going, you know, when I'm singing to a room full of sleeping passengers, all lying awkwardly on these curved seats, with their shoes off and holes in their socks. They find it hard to get to sleep and then wake up full of aches and pains but they still come back on these boats every year! But let's get back to you – I'm a typical artist, it's always all about me. What do you do?"

"I'm a translator."

"Of books?"

"Yes, I mostly translate English novels into French. I also sometimes translate Italian into French. It all depends."

"Depends on what you're offered?"

"Exactly."

"So you're actually copying out books in another language."

"You could say that."

"You say the same thing as the authors but in the language you've been asked to."

"I say nearly the same thing."

"Nearly?"

"It's all about the nearly. I'm the nearly man. More or less."

"And I'm nearly a star . . . What are you translating at the moment, if you don't mind me asking?"

"I'm working on an unpublished version of *Moby Dick*, have you heard of it?

"The one with the whale?"

"Yes!"

"People who work on boats avoid reading that sort of thing."

"If you want to know a bit more about my work, I did an

interview for *La Nuova Sardegna*, the piece should be coming out any day."

"Oh, that's wonderful. I'll look out for it."

★ ★ ★

Being woken by an idiot must surely be one of life's worst experiences. Along with having to eat offal after a bout of anaemia and listening to your mother saying you're not looking as well as on your last visit. Gavino rapped so hard on the window that it felt like a direct assault on my body. I found it very hard to drag myself out of bed. I hate talking when I've just woken up, something that I've tried – and failed – to pass on to the people unfortunate enough to be around me at that time of day. I have to confess that if you don't count members of my family, there aren't many of them.

Gavino is a name you only hear on this island, a Sardinian passport of sorts. I remembered spending a few nights at his house when I was very young. Completely ignoring my struggle to prise myself from the arms of Morpheus, he hollered around the house as if there'd been a Martian invasion and it was his job to let the world know about it. He would actually be looking for his razor, his watch, or God knows what vital item that he'd mislaid. Gavino's memory was akin to that of a goldfish escaped from its bowl. As a child I could cry for minutes at a time while he carried on with his pointless ranting. At last he would find the missing object, only to start looking for something else again just moments later. A perpetual quest.

"Are you there?"

My eyes were still swollen from my brief snooze when, in a burst of intelligence and insight, Gavino asked me this question. He was out on the street, I inside. How could he doubt that I was here when he was looking right at me? Of course I was here! Tired, bedraggled, knocked out by reading Italo Svevo, but very much there in my parents' house.

"Yes, I arrived this morning."

"Did I wake you?"

"Yes."

"Well, you were going to get up, anyway. Five minutes here or there doesn't change much."

With reasoning like that, my uncle could be taken for a half-wit, which he might well have been, actually. Still, as I listened to him I felt something close to pity for him. He'd never left our island. His world was bookended by the signs indicating the start and finish of the village. He had no idea that, anywhere else, his manner might not give a good impression.

"You're right, I was about to get up. Thanks for knocking on the window."

"You're welcome. How are you?"

"Tired."

"That journey's too long! I never travel, which is why I'm never tired."

Gavino was right there – it took far too long to get to the village. Some said it was worth it. Not me.

"Notice anything different?"

"No."

"I haven't shaved. I've lost that damn razor again. Your aunt's behind this, I'm sure of it."

"She may well be."

"Your phone's ringing, Giacomo."

"Let it ring – they'll leave a message if it's important."

The whole looking-for-razors thing was still topical, then. It felt as if life here, right down at the bottom end of Europe, went more slowly than in the north. As if things evolved at a different rate. There was the first division, the mainland where nothing lasted any time at all and people ran around, then the second division plopped in the middle of the Mediterranean, where events took time to happen. The positives and the negatives.

"Your parents'll be here soon."

"You don't have to talk so loudly, Giacomo."

"Why, have you got someone in there with you?"

"No."

"Well then, I can talk as loudly as I like."

"It's just, I've had a terrible headache since first thing this morning."

"Travelling, I tell you, travelling is bad for you."

"For me?"

"For everyone. You look dead on your feet. Get a bit more rest and then come and join us at the house. We'll go and see Grandma later."

"How is she?"

"Not good. Not good at all. You'll see for yourself, Mr. Translator. I'd forgotten we have to talk quietly to you. Your books don't make noise like we do!"

My uncle had never understood my desire to get away, a need that had manifested itself very early on in my existence. To his mind, I was a rogue branch on the family tree, one which would one day snap off. In my teens, reading gave me the escape I was looking for, other people's words offering themselves to me like a bridge thrown across to Europe.

"Have you bought this morning's *La Nuova Sardegna*?"

"No, why? That paper might as well be a floor mop these days. Nothing but gossip. Nothing about real life. A bit like your books, in fact! Do you read *La Nuova*, then?"

"Not always, but they'll soon be running an interview I did."

"An interview with you? What for? I hope you haven't been bad-mouthing the family."

"Do I usually?"

"I don't trust people who leave the village because it doesn't suit them."

"I talked about my work."

"Is anyone interested in that?"

"Possibly. The woman who interviewed me was, anyway."

"Pretty?"

"We did the interview over the phone."

"You'll always be had, Giacomo. It's written in the stars."

My uncle was not improving with age. He hammered out his every utterance as if passing a final sentence. He very visibly delighted in criticizing me for whatever came into his head. He got onto his bike (a design that hadn't been in production for decades, by the looks of it) and, without another word, he set off down the cobbled street. The road surface was so damaged that if I'd been him, on a contraption like that, I'd have fallen off after the first few metres. He, though, having cycled down it thousands of times and aware of all its pitfalls, looked as if he was gliding along a newly opened bike lane. He took a handsome, unwavering route, remarkably balanced for such a coarse, charmless man. But a few seconds later, I did see something fall from his pocket and break as it hit the ground. His mobile. My uncle stopped as if he'd just knocked over a child, and threw himself to the ground to pick up the pieces, his hands snatching busily to gather the remains of his victim. As he knelt there, he looked over at me. "That was my phone," he wailed, but he seemed so devastated that I heard something else, "that was my son" or "that was my child".

My uncle had a long history with telephones. When mobiles were first commercialized in Asia, he dreamed of having one. Sadly, our island still had a while to wait. So Gavino arranged to be sent a fake mobile phone, a huge one that he kept on him at all times, irreparably distending and distorting his pockets. It was an empty shell. I realized this one day when we were at his house for supper. He'd left his splendid device on the side while he set the world to rights with my parents over an after-dinner drink that was about as powerful as detergent. Naturally, I went over to have a peek. My hand slowly moved closer, ignoring instructions from my brain, and this conflict inevitably resulted in the phone falling to the floor. It was made of two pieces of plastic. In between there was nothing but air. I was no budding inventor or even a child with a gift for elec-tronics, but I had no trouble understanding that Gavino's conversations with unknown callers when we had lunch on the beach were actually just a charade. Ankle-deep in the water he would talk loudly to a friend no one had ever met. Until the revelation, we and passers-by alike admired this ground-breaker who never stopped saying, "Everyone'll have them in ten years' time, you just wait and see!"

* * *

As a child, I thought everyone loved me. Teachers, classmates, neighbours and relatives. Everyone loved me. Even domestic-ated animals. The not-so-domesticated ones too. The lizards that wedged themselves between two rocks in the noonday sun, that didn't resent me when I crushed them. I was loved. The cicadas chirped for me, even if I was surrounded by a huge crowd of people (which, incidentally, didn't happen much in our village, given that the word "crowd" doesn't really sit well with it). It was powerful. An all-encompassing love. Some people feel persecuted; I, on the other hand, felt loved. Of course this feeling was based on illusion, but to a child, illusion and reality are neighbouring countries, and it's easy to travel from one to the other. Until the day when border patrols are established.

I played football for ten years. The village grocer had decided to set up and manage a boys' team to challenge nearby commu-nities. Marco the grocer pitched up at my parents' house one winter evening. Now, winter evenings in Sardinia are the embod-iment of absolute boredom, in the same way as there is absolute zero and absolute cold, a temperature at which life expires. So absolute boredom, then, and enforced proximity to others because my father – convinced that the island's climate spared us from plummeting temperatures – had decided not to install central heating, so we all had to cluster around the only source of heat in the house: the oven. Each on our own chair, shoulder to shoulder, like a foretaste of carbon-neutral living.

So I was there reading, while my mother castigated my father for something or other, when there was a knock at the door. I was too young to be sent to open up, and that was fine by me because the temperature in the corridor was even lower than in the rest of the house. My father, because he was the man of the family and therefore had to protect us (but also very probably to get away from my mother), stood up and, as if undertaking a perilous mission, headed for the door. He returned moments later with Marco. At first I thought the grocer was taking up door-to-door sales but, when I saw he wasn't carrying any merchandise, I realized he must have been there for something else.

"It's not very warm in your house," he said to my father.

"The sun'll be back soon."

We were all waiting longingly for the sun, obviously. It would warm the house back up, in two or three months' time.

"I'm here to see the boy."

"What's he done?" my mother asked.

As I was saying, the way I saw it, the whole world loved me. When I saw the look in Mama's eyes, though, cracks started to appear in this theory. She grabbed hold of the newspaper she'd been reading before Marco arrived and rolled it up the way she did in the summer to drive away flies. But it was the middle of winter, there wasn't a fly to be seen. I, in this instance, was the fly.

"Don't worry, he hasn't done anything. It's just I'm taking over the village football team and I'd like Giacomo to be in it."

"Really?" my mother said with an air of great satisfaction as she unrolled her newspaper.

She thought Marco had come to recruit me because I was talented at football. The truth is, I wasn't hopeless with a ball . . . but to get from there to being recruited by a club (even in our village) was as big a leap as stepping over the Mediterranean. My mother probably saw me well on the way to a glittering career. In the island's most prestigious team, Cagliari. Her son, her little boy, recruited for his sporting prowess. She wore her pride as others might wear a glorious piece of jewellery borrowed for one evening. Her eyes had lit up. The cold had vanished.

"Yes, sport's good for children. Can you play football, Giacomo?"

"Yes," I mumbled, seeing Mama's thwarted expression.

She'd just gathered that the grocer was knocking on every door in the village where he'd find a small boy. He didn't even know whether I could play football. Dreams can evaporate in an instant, and that's just as well because Mama would have happily throttled the one that had just vaporized.

"Will you be running the team on your own?" my father asked. "That's a hell of a responsibility."

"No, Manuella's going to help me, thank goodness."

"It'll be easier if your wife's helping. All these scallywags will give you quite a runaround."

I willingly agreed to join the village team. For my health and for Manuella, the sort of *femme fatale* that we only got to see in programmes on private TV stations. Until then I'd never participated in any competitive sport – just saying the words was a source of great satisfaction – and neither had my friends, because our village didn't have a single sports club.

I thought I'd succeed on the football pitch even though it was bare soil, not grass. The local council didn't have the funds to maintain a lawn all year round and, because the sun turned green to yellow, the powers that be had decided to let nature alter the colour as it saw fit. Soil is every footballer's enemy. The slightest fall is synonymous with injury, grazing and blood. And players spend most of every match on the ground. That's why they're made to play on grass. I was worried about my knees but took comfort from the fact that geniuses emerge from adversity. Schopenhauer and his terrifying father, Kafka with his fragile health. Giacomo and the uneven pitch. An incredible career was beginning. I had dreams of sporting exploits but – more importantly – dreams of escape. Scoring goals was my way out of the village.

Marco had no trouble persuading my friends to join his village team. We very quickly became a myth of sorts across the region. In ten years we didn't win a single match. We couldn't be demoted because we were already playing in the lowest league. Below us there was nothing, oblivion. And anything's better than oblivion. Even last place in the worst division. Ten years of defeats. Our opponents used their confrontations with us to try out new tactics. We were sometimes allowed to have one more player than the other team. But one more player was still not enough. As goalie (I wasn't competent enough to play anywhere other than this thankless position), it was easy for me to keep track of their mounting score. I spent a large proportion of each match with my back to the pitch, picking the ball out of the back of the net. We developed a true philosophy of defeat. At first it hurt, it upset us, and then, with successive wash-outs and thrashings, our skins hardened and defeat eventually became a way of life, and a source of pleasure too because we brought happiness wherever we went. No one watched us come out onto the pitch with fear in their belly. Sure of victory, our opponents were already thinking about the post-match picnic.

As for me, I saw every match as an opportunity to spend time with Marco's wife. She was in charge of our kit, and washed it every week in preparation for the next fixture. Thinking of Manuella scrubbing, drying, folding and ironing my strip afforded me great happiness. Manuella, the *femme fatale*, as my mother scornfully called her. Manuella with the big black hair and the floaty dresses. Manuella to whom I handed my kit gently, particularly if it was covered in mud, because I didn't want it to dirty her hands. Manuella who every week had a kind word for each of us, although I heard only the one addressed to me, wishing all my teammates would melt away so she could concentrate on me alone. Manuella who overrode defeat by handing out biscuits she'd made specially for the players. Manuella whose name I was not allowed to utter (not even the first few letters) because my mother was so jealous of this formidable woman, the grocer's wife, the devil incarnate, the too-beautiful-to-be-trustworthy lady who led her son to understand that the female of the species did not stop at his mother.

Manuella was the sunlight in our village, even when it rained. Especially when it rained. Well, especially in winter, because the rest of the year we had the other one, the real one, the one that tanned our skin and made Manuella's the colour of milk chocolate. Teamed with green eyes.

She ran the grocery and her husband often had to go into town for supplies, so I would go to the shop at every opportunity, helped – quite unwittingly – by Mama, who was always missing some vital ingredient (a clove of garlic or an onion, to name the most important) for the meal she was making. When she asked me to do her a favour, I pretended to refuse then craftily capitulated and ran as fast as I could (far faster than on the football pitch) in order to make the most of Manuella. Well, "make the most of" is a misleading phrase. I watched her. I didn't go into the shop straight away but stayed outside, hiding behind an unstripped cork oak. And the unstripped bit was important. I mustn't be seen. I watched Manuella for many a long minute. She worked away, unaware she was being watched. I liked it. She did nothing to protect herself, happy to show her face with no make-up. Society had no effect on her. Like the cork tree, before men came and stripped it to make hideous souvenirs with its bark.

If someone came near my hiding place, I felt I had to leave and go on into the shop. Manuella greeted me with genuine pleasure. Well, I hoped it was genuine. Walter, the shop's dog, jumped up and put his front paws on my shoulders. A sheepdog that had never set foot in a field and knew nothing about livestock other than the meat that came into the shop. He'd been given his name in homage to the national team's goalie. So this dog and I had something in common. Walter the footballer stopped his opponents' goals. Walter the dog was meant to stop thieves. I meanwhile stopped nothing.

I bought the onion or the garlic that my mother so desperately needed and we chatted about the next match – our next defeat. A defeat that tasted like victory to me because Manuella could so thoroughly reward me with a smile or a wink. Absolute proof that we were close. She certainly didn't grant any such familiarity to other customers. She was always very professional. "The pasta's here, the oil over there . . .", no more than that. I emerged from the shop happy, sure of my seductive charms. And on a grown-up to boot. I went back to my observation point to check whether Manuella was trying to watch me after I'd left. I imagined her pressing herself against the shop window and perhaps even spotting me behind the old tree. "*Giacomo, ti amo,*" she would mouth through the window, knocking over the towering displays of food basking in the sun.

In fact, Mama was wary of anything that had been displayed like this. She was worried about bacteria. It didn't matter how many times I told her dry goods didn't pose any risk, she so hated Manuella that it made no difference. She imagined monsters lurking in the produce. As for the grocer's wife, she neither came out of the shop nor ran to the window. She only did that in my imagination. Or, to be more precise, she did do it once, just one little time, to shout out, "You forgot your change, Giacomo." I retraced my steps, disappointed. I couldn't care less about the thousands of liras I'd left on the counter. The lira wasn't worth anything. But Walter the dog did press his nose to the window. He knew I was hiding and seemed to love it. Being followed by a dog when you're dreaming about a woman can't help but be a disappointment. I consoled myself as best I could.

In fact, apart from that one exception, there were too many customers for Manuella to abandon her post. I burrowed my fingers into the cork when I realized she wasn't watching to see where I'd gone. I had to go home. With the garlic, or the onion, in my pocket.

★　★　★

My parents arrived while I was having a shower. My mother's voice, nagging on about how my father had parked the car, made me want to stay there forever. So long as the water was running I felt safe. But only for a while. Because soon enough Mama suddenly remembered her reserves of water. I say "her" because it really seemed to me that the water belonged to her. She came into the bathroom and drummed on the door of the shower. "Giacomo, leave a bit of water for everyone else!" "Everyone else" meaning her. I turned off the shower but didn't get out of the cubicle. "Hello, Mama, I've nearly finished." Her fits of anger had robbed her of basic social niceties. When you haven't seen your son (or a friend) for several months, you start by saying hello. Only then can you have a go at them for using too much water.

"Nearly finished, nearly finished, you're just like your father. You say things that don't mean anything. I'll give you a dictionary one of these days, my boy."

"Hello, Mama," I said again.

"Yes, hello, love. Let me know which edition you want for the dictionary."

Pleased with her joke, she went off to lay into my father again. I turned the shower back on, as hard as it would go. Mama came back into the bathroom.

"Your phone won't stop ringing."

I often wondered why my father stayed with her. There was a time when divorce was banned on the island, but those days were over. Something made him stay. The world is full of mysteries that have researchers fretting over them. Unexplained theorems, inexplicable phenomena . . . the fact that my mother and father were together interested no one, except me. Once, fed up with the constant barrage of criticism Papa endured, I put the question to him.

"I'd be lost without her. Do you understand?" he replied. It turned out he'd got used to Mama's outbursts, just as you can get used to taking medicine every day. If you don't take it you die. A very simple equation. Mama was the poison and the antidote.

* * *

The problem with Italian mothers is that when you see them again after, let's say, a moderate absence, they make you feel as if you've been to Mars for about a decade. When I went into the living room where my parents were waiting for me (my return was an event on a par with the discovery of a vaccination against some terrifying disease), my mother dropped the brush she was using to clean her shoes, and threw herself at me. I was trapped. Of course she'd already heard my voice through the shower door, but there was nothing like my physical presence right there in front of her. She put her arms around me and hugged me with all her might. Luckily my ribs are sturdy. Is this what she did when I was born? I would think not, because a new-born wouldn't survive a grip like that. "Nine months I've been waiting for you . . ." Surely that deserved a smothering!

Papa threw me the usual "You alright, sonny?" that came with my every appearance at the family home. He did not, strictly speaking, have a gift for reunions. Neither did I, actually. I managed, with some difficulty, to extricate myself from my mother's arms. She shot me an icy look, deeming the hug too brief. Even though I hadn't been entirely consenting, for those few seconds the two of us had become one. She and I, just like during her pregnancy, like when I was tiny and I couldn't get away. When there wasn't an expanse of sea between me and my mother earth.

"Have you bought *La Nuova Sardegna*?"

"No, your father didn't want to stop off at the kiosk. He was in a hurry to get here. I don't know why. Mind you, neither does he. It was just one of those things. He probably wanted to disagree with me, rub me up the wrong way, as usual. Do you read our local paper, then?"

"I have done recently, yes."

"Why?"

"Because I gave an interview and they're going to run it some time soon. Maybe today or tomorrow . . ."

"Good God!"

The Martian had returned, with a priceless gift. A mother's pride.

"Did you hear that, Mario? Our boy in the paper! Are you hearing this?"

My father was hearing it and responded with a "Well done, sonny."

Mama was infuriated by this reaction which she apparently deemed too cold, too offhand – too everything, in fact.

"Your son tells us he's going to be in the paper and it doesn't mean anything to you. If he told you he'd bought the bread for lunch you'd have shown more excitement. What am I doing, still with you? After all these years, I should have left. Giacomo's grown up now, he's standing on his own two feet, he doesn't need Mama and Papa to be together."

Listening to my mother was like winding back the clock. I could see myself with my first travel bag, ready to go off to university which, thank goodness, would get me out of our brightly coloured village.

My father got up and muttered that he had to empty the car. When my parents came home from a trip, he made sure he always left a bag or a suitcase in the car. It gave him an opportunity to escape for a moment. An effective ploy, and a clever one too, I thought. But my mother was aware of it, so she sometimes emptied the car herself without my father realizing. She'd done that this time.

"There's no point," she said, "there's nothing left in the car. Unless you want to take out the seats or the roof."

Papa pretended not to hear her and went out.

"So what is it you're talking about in the paper?"

"My work."

"Wonderful! I hope you mentioned me."

I owed her everything, I owed them everything because nothing is worth more than life. And yet I didn't think of my parents for one split second during that interview. And I didn't feel the least bit guilty. Why would I mention my mother in an article about translation? If the topic had been communication breakdowns between adults, well why not? I'd never succeeded in translating into words the love my parents felt for each other. I wished I could stop the rows and the shouting but it was beyond my scope.

"Of course I did, Mama."

* * *

I'm thirty-five and I'm sitting in the back of my parents' car. Seatbelt well fastened. My mother keeps looking at me in the rear-view mirror like when I was two or three years old. I mean, she practically put a booster seat in before I sat down.

"Not too blowy for you?" she asks affectionately.

She refused to let my father buy an air-conditioned car because she's worried about her health. Air conditioning would give her endless throat infections. To be honest, I couldn't say, because she's never come into contact with air conditioning. At least, not that I remember. So we drive with the windows open.

My father drives so slowly that pedestrians have no trouble overtaking us along the streets. He can say hello to acquaintances and exchange a few words with them. Perhaps he's forgotten that cars were invented to save time. Ten minutes after we left the house he stops at the newspaper kiosk run by my childhood friend Fabrizio.

"How are you doing, Giacomo?"

"Fine, thanks. It's good to see you."

Fabrizio inherited this business. His father and grandfather ran it before him. Some people inherit massive conglomerates, incredible houses and vast sums. On his father's retirement, Fabrizio was the recipient of a sort of cabin measuring two by three metres in which he piled up the entire output of the Italian press. Newspapers, obviously, but mostly magazines full of such beautiful people that you gave yourself nightmares if you caught sight of yourself in a mirror after a bad night. Handsome twits and women with extraordinary body measurements eyed you as you approached the kiosk. I was greeted by a dazzling-toothed smile, in stark contrast with my friend's puny and worn physique. Fabrizio had always been a little sickly. Like me, thirty-five years old, to the day, because our mothers gave birth within hours of each other. In our legendary football team, he played centre-back, the last rampart before the goalie. A rampart full of cracks in front of a goalie who was frightened of the ball. I could feel the smack of leather on my skinny thighs all week after the weekend's defeat. I would have needed giant-sized gloves to avoid those impacts, plus two or three friends alongside me on the goal line. Then we really would have formed a rampart.

Standing facing me, cooped up in his boxful of newspapers, was the worst centre-back in the history of football. Fabrizio looked about sixty. His facial muscles had given up holding his skin in place. They'd all slackened as if they woke up one fine day and decided to stop doing their job. Death is always a downward journey.

"What would you like?" he asked, pointing to a magazine with a brash front cover: "The scandal of the year! She cheated on him!"

Fabrizio knew perfectly well I wouldn't buy it.

"I'd like a copy of *La Nuova*, please. Business going well?"

"It's quiet at the moment. There are fewer and fewer tourists. The roads are dangerous and the council don't do anything about it."

"I hope it'll all be sorted out before the summer."

"Are you still playing football?"

"Sometimes, with friends. Just for fun, nothing serious."

"Why, were you ever serious on a football pitch?"

"A bit, at first."

"We were so terrible."

"Don't rub salt in the wound, Fabrizio. Do you still see any of the others?"

"Not much. Each to his own, that's the village motto. The most useless team in history no longer exists."

I just nodded my head. "I'll come and see you again. Got to go now. We're going to the hospital to see my grandmother."

"Give her my love. Don't forget your paper."

I got back into the car and found my mother sitting next to me. She'd abandoned the front seat. She was staring at the newspaper that I'd almost forgotten. She took it from me and leafed through it feverishly. Two or three minutes spent turning it in every direction and scouring every corner of it for my name.

"You didn't use a pseudonym, did you? I hope you're not ashamed of your name."

"For goodness' sake, Mama! I'm not some singer who goes and uses a pseudonym."

"There's nothing in it."

She closed the paper like a filthy rag fit only for the bin, and put it on the parcel shelf.

"You can read the rest of it if you like."

"I said there's nothing in it."

Nothing! Dozens of articles, photographs, paintings . . . Nothing as far as Mama was concerned, because I wasn't in it. So I was everything. Mothers are sometimes dangerous for their children.

★ ★ ★

At the end of our street there's a curiosity, something that exists only in this part of Europe: a *Domus de Janas*, a fairy house. It's a prehistoric tomb, a stone hut which our ancestors built for their eternal sleep. Those who came after them on this street built their houses without causing any damage to the *Domus de Janas*, so these vestiges now stand happily between the new buildings. As a child, I liked meeting my friends here. We'd spend hours in among these tombs, which had long since been emptied. We talked of the future, while we sat in the past. Tourists would sometimes ask us the way to the *Domus*, but we made sure we never told them. We watched, amused, as they searched in vain for the fairy tomb. Or the witch's tomb. Translating *Janas* is tricky: fairy or witch? Good or evil? It was the first word that tripped me up. It was impossible to choose one or the other of its meanings. To this day people still come to the village for the wall paintings and the *Domus de Janas*. Sometimes they'll buy a bottle of water or a fizzy drink but they don't hang around after nightfall. They head back down the steep road that returns them to civilization, or the version of it that lives by the shores of the Mediterranean. To the tourist complexes selling ice-creams and pizzas. Maybe they're frightened of the age-old legend that claims that if you get too close to a *Domus de Janas* you go mad. We might all actually be bonkers without realizing it, because it's typical of madness to think you're sane. That would make our village just a ragbag of insanity. I have serious doubts about some of the inhabitants, but not all of them.

There's a bit of us in those stones, a bit of time, a bit of history. My parents always taught me to respect the place. There's a sort of awe surrounding these buildings, which are so low that adults can only get inside them on their knees. Our ancestors were tiny. No one had introduced them to the pizzas and ice-creams (made of chemicals but invariably sold as *artigianali*) that would see us grow to a respectable stature. I've stopped going inside the *Domus* but whenever I'm home I always cast an eye in its direction. It's still there! Probably an indication that all is not entirely lost.

On the way to the hospital we stopped off at the grocery to buy some of Grandma's favourite biscuits. I wasn't convinced we needed to buy these *formaggelle*. Nonna was so very ill. So near death. What would she do with them? Was she even capable of doing *anything*? Cheese biscuits for a woman about to die. Cheese biscuits that my mother hadn't had time to make herself. Manuella and Marco's were delicious. They didn't really make them themselves, but ordered them in from the south of the island. There was great rivalry between the north and the south. But we were all descended from the *Domus de Janas*. With no exceptions. Marco, who was there with us for each of our defeats, had grasped that internal rivalries would lead straight to failure. A factory in the south produced cheaper biscuits, which allowed him to make a slight profit. You sometimes had to tuck your pride away under your shopkeeper's apron.

"Get two packets for your grandmother, Giacomo."

My mother handed me a couple of coins, like when I used to go to buy an onion and gaze at Manuella.

"Nothing else?"

"No. Things have really changed since you left, you know. The shop sells disappointing stuff. Things he brings in from other places. When we've got everything we need here."

"Why does it matter that things come from 'other places', then?"

"It's a matter of principle, Giacomo, a matter of principle."

There was still a string curtain across the doorway of the shop to keep out the flies. I loathed the thing, it made me want to turn back because feeling those strips of string on your shoulders – or on your face if you weren't careful enough – was so unpleasant. But I had to buy the biscuits for my grandmother. Two boxes. So one for Grandma and the other for Mama. Even if my mother wasn't fond of the grocer's wife, she did – unofficially, of course – like her *dolci*.

The shop was empty of customers or its owners, but I spotted the old dog lying asleep. He was Walter's son. He could have been called Junior like in American families, but Marco and Manuella had found a name for his father and liked it . . . and so the son was also called Walter. It was a bit unnerving because the son was the spitting image of his father. There was nothing to differentiate them, except that the younger incarnation displayed no delight when I stepped into the shop. He simply opened one eye, and must have registered that I was "known" around here. We probably all had something in common. A maker's mark inherent to the village. A white shirt, trousers worn too high at the waist, all of us exponentially and uncontrollably hairy, masses of gel in our hair . . . But my time on the mainland had altered these codes. So it must be something else, something invisible. Walter's eye closed again. A soft whine alerted the owners that a potential customer had arrived. I heard movement from the back room.

A woman with black hair and grey skin emerged from there. The guardian of the grotto where all the merchandise was stored. It was an ageing Manuella. Her eyes were the last vestige of her beauty. Emerald green, like the colour of our eastern coastline, La Costa Smeralda.

There was still the same smell in the place: meats and cheeses mixed with cool stone. A smell you wouldn't find anywhere else. The shop stirred the appetite. Manuella was wearing a grey dress with red polka dots.

"Giacomo, how lovely to see you. How are you?"

"Hello, Manuella, I'm fine. You look very well."

"That's kind of you to say so."

"How's Marco?"

"Things are very quiet now. It really hit us when they opened the supermarket. Marco got depressed. He thought his customers would stay loyal to us, but they got over there as soon as they could. Even the old ones! Everyone going off in their cars to buy their fruit and meat. People are like that, what can you do . . ."

"I'm so sorry."

"It's not your fault. What can I get you?"

"Some *formaggelle*, please. Two packets. They're for Grandma."

"I've heard she's not well."

"It's nearly over."

"Is that why you're back here?"

"Yes, 'that', as you put it, is the reason."

"So are the biscuits for you, then?"

Manuella smiled as she said this. She knew how to defuse a situation. It reminded me of the old days, with our endless defeats. Marco was lucky to live with her. And he knew, as I remember it. Never once did I see him look at another woman in the street. Never once did his head shift to watch a woman walk by. Whilst I certainly looked at women. I always had, ever since I'd peered from around the cork tree, protected from prying eyes.

When I left the shop I walked past my parents' car – to their astonishment – and headed right for that very tree. With its cork coat, it was incredibly wide. Five hundred years it had reigned over the village. That tree had seen everything and heard everything. It knew every single character buried in the cemetery. It had seen my grandmother as a child. It had seen her run when the rain came pouring down. It had seen her come home from school, worried, when her teacher had been too strict. Maybe she came and sheltered under its branches. Maybe it had seen her kiss my grandfather for the first time. The tree never said a thing. Thankfully so, in my case.

"Still a dreamer, aren't you, Giacomo! No one else would gaze at a tree like that. A real poet, my son is. You did get the change, didn't you?"

★ ★ ★

Until the regional hospital opened, it was better not to be ill in our village. We did have a doctor, Dr. Ignazio, a tall man with a permanent smile, but his reputation had taken a few knocks. He was by far the wealthiest man within several kilometres. His cars, which were always new, came in blazing colours that went very well with the walls of our houses. They were noisy, they had to be, and they were huge in relation to the village streets. He had to make several attempts to get around some of the corners. And this, of course, further endangered the patient waiting for him in bed.

The doctor resented those narrow streets, roaring his anger in his stentorian voice when he finally succeeded in passing an obstacle, but it wouldn't have occurred to him to buy a smaller car so he could get around such a small village. People called him because there was no one else to call. They trusted him because there was no one else to turn to, even though no one really understood his qualifications. He had studied at university and had a plaque on his house to attest to that fact.

Even so, I never saw him prescribe anything but a sort of catch-all medicine: lumpy white granules that he took to every consultation in a jar with a colourful label featuring a young blonde woman with a dazzling smile, a generous bosom and a handful of granules. *Effervescente al limone*. A mysterious name that left room for doubt in his patients' minds. He didn't listen to their hearts or their lungs. "Everything starts in the stomach!" was his motto. Headaches, stomach aches, ear infections, sore throats, flu . . . *Effervescente al limone!* The doctor always paused before adding the "*al limone*" bit. You got the feeling he was going to add a final ingredient to the remedy, something precious without which it wouldn't work. As my father used to say, "With Ignazio, you either recover or you die", which was an acceptable appraisal but a bit of an exaggeration, to be honest. There was an alternative, not a very nice one but it did have the advantage of being on offer. If you didn't get better with this medicine that looked for all the world like sweets, you could also end up being helicoptered to the far side of the island, to the big hospital in the capital.

The day I turned twenty I moved to Marseille. A small, dark, damp apartment on rue Estelle. I fell ill a few days later. Homesick, most likely. *Nostalgia di casa* in Italian. *Le mal du pays* in French. The languages were all mixed up in my head and as they came out of my mouth. *Notalgia di casa*, nostalgia for home. Home was the island and the island was home. Another thing I was missing was medication. I went to see a doctor who examined me and diagnosed a flu-like condition. Nothing serious, he said. Later, when the pharmacist came over to me with two or three boxes of pills, I was amazed not to see Dr. Ignazio's perennial jar of *Effervescente al limone*. The pharmacist grasped that I was really traumatized by this oversight. I spent ten minutes trying to explain what I'd been prescribed since infancy. Confronted with the man's incredulity, I even found myself drawing the jar they usually came in. And the girl on the label, smiling, her symptoms relieved by those granules *al limone*. And her bosom, her generous bosom. In the end the pharmacist recommended I went home swiftly and started taking my prescribed medication. "You have a high fever, your eyes are red. Go home quickly, take some paracetamol and get some sleep." I realized later that he had put my longing for *Effervescente al limone* down to my temperature.

Back at my cheerless apartment, I went to bed, crushed by the fever and my disappointment. I was woken by the ring of the telephone. Mama was worried about me.

"Have you been to the doctor?"

"Yes, Mama, don't worry."

"Did he give you any medicine?"

"Yes, of course, doctors give their patients medicine in France too."

"What did he give you?"

"I can't remember. French remedies."

"*Effervescente al limone*, I hope!"

"Yes, two jars, huge ones."

"What do they call them there?"

"Effervescents."

"*Al limone?*"

"Yes, they're lemon flavoured, Mama, they're lemon flavoured. Lemon's a key part of the remedy. The French know all about that."

"Yes, but it was a Sardinian who came up with the formula."

"Really?"

"Ignazio told me."

"Well, you can trust him."

A few months later I stumbled across Ignazio's famed remedy. It was in a pitiful, unkempt supermarket with squished lettuce leaves on the floor. In the "Italian goods" department. Which actually amounted to about a dozen products on a small shelf with a map of Italy above it. It showed the boot and Sicily but to my total astonishment, the artist had forgotten Sardinia. I would have tolerated this mistake if it had been the other way around. Our island but no boot and no Sicily. But in this particular instance my insularity reared up and drove me to do the unthinkable: I tore up the map. Without Sardinia there couldn't be any Italy.

Alongside the pastas, tomato sauces and desiccated risottos, the jars of *Effervescente* had pride of place. A revelation. What we considered a miracle remedy was seen here – at best – as something to aid digestion. Nothing more. Like sparkling water, basically. Ignazio had bought himself magnificent cars for all those years by prescribing a placebo. Those small jars in exchange for massive cars. Massive and brightly coloured.

When the new hospital opened in the middle of a field that had previously been populated by sheep, Dr. Ignazio saw his work cut back like the bark on an over-thick cork tree. His cars started shrinking too. And they stopped being replaced. The plaque proudly trumpeting his qualification as a *Dottore* yellowed and the letters gradually faded. Then one fine day Ignazio decided not to open his consulting room. It was a wise decision because, as he told my mother, he spent his days in profound solitude. Depression lurked but luckily he still had significant stocks of *Effervescente al limone!* An excellent anti-depressant that my mother was quick to recommend to him. She's always had a way of putting people at their ease.

Rumour has it that Dr. Ignazio applied to work at the newly opened hospital. Sadly, though, no one there wanted his services. Angry that his expertise had been called into question, the doctor told anyone he met in the village that this rejection was down to jealousy. They were nothing but a bunch of incompetents at this new hospital. They were only doctors who'd qualified on the mainland or – worse – abroad. And according to him, everyone would soon realize that these imports dispensed poor care. But of course it would be too late because he, the wise old doctor with the gleaming, oversized cars, would have taken off. He dreamed of leaving, of new sunshine and greener fields than could be found on the island, of starting a new life. But, as was the case with most villagers who occasionally made similar threats to leave, these plans were never more than a few words uttered on a street corner or at the counter of the village bar after several drinks. No one really left, even when people no longer noticed them.

So there was no danger of meeting him down those long corridors with their cracked paintwork. Unless it was as a patient.

We went into a huge room with masses of beds in it, like a military dormitory, filled with weary old pensioners and young people not lucky enough to be in good health. There were curtains to separate the beds but not all of them were drawn. The registrar was doing his rounds and privacy was not always restored after he had passed by. His assistants sometimes drew the curtains, but not always. There were four of them buzzing around him, like flies clinging to his arms, to his every sacred utterance. Just a few words each time, so these scant utterances were indeed precious. The doctors didn't notice us because the room was busy. Some patients groaned, others talked to their bedfellows at the far end of the room. If there were any rules about propriety, they weren't being observed: nobody seemed to be bothered that they might be disturbing someone who was, only a few paces away, quietly leaving this life.

Grandma wasn't asleep when we reached her bedside. Her eyes were open, staring straight ahead. She lay there, unblinking, as we came over to her. Mama looked for a chair so she could sit down and hold Grandma's hand, but the chairs were all taken, next to other patients. We'd arrived too late to have the privilege of sitting in these chairs which, from what I could see, were so worn they must have been all the way round the island before coming to the hospital. Old chairs for old patients. Mama grumbled briefly then asked my father to go back to the car for the folding chairs that came with them on all their outings. This was an unshakeable habit in this part of Europe: people stopped anywhere and sat themselves down wherever they liked. The island belonged to its inhabitants. Papa went off without a word.

He returned five minutes later and my parents both sat facing Grandma. Two people sitting, one lying down. I sat carefully on the bottom right-hand corner of the bed, where I wouldn't risk squashing Nonna's legs. A laughable precaution, really, because Grandma was so small that you could have put two people her size in the bed. She looked lost in it. An almost uninhabited land in the middle of an ocean. Battered by words from other patients and doctors, by their movement and the life around her. By the life she was leaving behind. I didn't want to touch her, I needed a reason to. Mama took Grandma's hand and brought her face right in front of her. Grandma's eyes didn't even blink.

"It's not good."

The doctor's voice interrupted our silence. I jumped to my feet, out of respect for his position but also fear. I had a terrible fear of white coats, and the instruments peeping out of their pockets. All these tools for such a small woman. All those intellects to tell us what any car mechanic seeing Grandma could have told us: "It's not good."

I waited for more specific explanations (not that I would have understood a word of them, naturally), for details of all the afflictions eating away at my mother's mother, preventing her from tasting Manuella's wonderful biscuits ever again. Instead, this declaration hung in the air, bald and bereft of science. His assistants nodded and appeared to jot down information in their notebooks. For the sake of their careers, they had to view the registrar's every word as the pronouncement of some extraordinary entity. They probably all behaved in the same way when he asked them for a coffee.

Angela Irau: it's not good.

How could he know that this woman had listened to my woes, encouraged my dreams of escape, and calmed my mother when tensions were at their peak? How could he know she'd given me an incredible dose of sweetness, that still slowly released itself through my veins, even when I was hundreds of kilometres from her?

He didn't care. She was just a worn-out old lady who would soon make way for another patient.

"Have you made all the arrangements for the next stage?"

"Yes, Doctor, everything's ready."

The funeral was set up. The undertakers handling it were waiting for the call from my parents to set the operation in motion. The doctors moved on to another bed. There was something repulsive about referring to someone's death in front of them. This was probably part of the new guidelines in our healthcare system.

"We've brought you your favourite biscuits, Mama, can you see? I made them this morning."

There are some little girls, now grown up, who can't help lying to their parents. All of a sudden Grandma blinked, as if her brain were firing up again. She vigorously squeezed her daughter's hand. My mother said that these biscuits always had an effect on her. I couldn't tell whether this reaction was to the biscuits or the doctor's words that had just got through to her mind.

"Would you like one?" my mother asked.

Of course, Grandma didn't answer, not making the slightest move towards the *formaggelle*. The doctor's words, I was now sure, were responsible for her moving her eyelids. We left with the biscuits. Mama claimed they would spoil if we left them or – worse, still – some greedy so-and-so would steal them. Grandma couldn't do a thing. In the car I was still thirty-five, sitting in the back and listening to the sound of chomping from the front.

* * *

I didn't know why Herman Melville had written several versions of his novel, nor why he'd decided to hide one in the oldest library in New York. Novelists get some odd ideas into their heads, which might be why they are novelists in the first place. I really liked *Moby Dick* as we knew it, the first version.

The text I was working on was not as good, not as profound; but I'd made a point of not mentioning this to my editor Carlo. He wanted it to be a publishing coup. No one yet knew about his discovery, except for me and the specialist who'd authenticated the manuscript. And as this specialist had just died, there were now only two of us. Two islanders for a big book about a whale. In this last variation, Melville says nearly the same as he did in the version originally published. It was still all about the nearly. My mother was nearly calm about Nonna's impending death. My father was nearly less evasive. Dr. Ignazio was nearly a real doctor. Manuella was nearly as beautiful as she used to be. And I said nearly the same thing as the writers I was asked to translate. Nearly.

My phone rang when we were about to sit down for supper. Mama picked it up to hand it to me and, more importantly, to see who was calling me. An old habit. A bad habit. It wasn't a girlfriend or anything like that. "It's Carlo," she said, passing it to me. I told her he could wait and I'd call him the next day. "Your editor's not very polite, it's late to be disturbing people. That man's forgotten where he came from. He's a Roman now."

I knew exactly why he was calling. Carlo wanted me to finish the work as quickly as possible. He kept calling me. He was obsessed with me. It was odd because before he gave me this job, I'd call him two or three times a week to see if he had any work to offer me. Carlo didn't reply or claimed he had some hugely important meeting before hanging up. Cat and mouse. Interchangeable roles. I remember how self-important he was when he told me about his discovery. Carlo, the little Sardinian who was now an editor in Rome. Carlo, a native of the most forgettable village on the island, in the centre on a map, where no one ever went. In art, the centre is the most crucial part. Take Vermeer's *Woman Reading a Letter*. Right in the centre we see the letter, the one we'd like to read, the one that fuels all speculation. Is it a love letter? A break-up? A denunciation? Etc. Carlo's village was right in the centre of a vacuum. It bothered him because when people asked where he was from, he always said Cagliari, as if he was ashamed of his village. In Rome he was a Cagliarian. I often teased him about this geographical approximation. He claimed it was easier for people to picture if he said Cagliari. So his lie was just a helping hand he gave to whoever asked. Is a lie paved with good intentions still a lie? A tiny little 200-kilometre lie?

My phone rang again. It was Carlo again.

"If you like, I can pick up," Mama said.

"No, let him fret. He'll go to bed eventually."

I imagined her picking up and berating him with the strongest arguments at her disposal: his leaving the island, his late-night calls, how exhausted her son was, her mother's illness . . . Poor Carlo would never recover. I couldn't do that to him. He gave me a living, after all. Mama, the anti-editor umbrella. The protective mother who, more than anything else, hated her food to go cold. A catastrophe as far as she was concerned, on a par with a crack in a hydraulic dam.

"What an oaf! And he won't give up. He reminds me of Manuella, at the shop. When you played football she was always on the phone reminding us what day the match was, where the match was, what time the match was . . . always a good excuse. I'm convinced she had a thing for your father. Mind you, he was a looker in those days."

Papa got up from his chair and went off into the living room. He knew the conversation would keep going and would not be to his advantage. I was in teasing mood that evening so I picked up on it.

"I didn't know Manuella used to make eyes at Papa."

"He was good-looking, like I said. And he never could resist the charms of a beautiful woman."

Mama said this with a degree of pride because she included herself in this sub-group.

"Well, luckily you were aware of all this. You kept an eye out."

"Yes, otherwise our marriage would have blown apart and you'd be an orphan."

"Why an orphan?"

"An orphan because you'd never have seen your father."

"Would you have killed him?"

"No, you must be joking! I'd have stopped him seeing you, that's all."

"Even if I wanted to talk to him?"

"Even if you wanted to talk to him. No one cheats on me. End of story."

"Well, I'd say the word *orphan*'s a bit strong, then."

"Hey, this editor of yours isn't in love with you, is he?"

"No, he just wants me to work faster."

"Don't kill yourself doing it, my darling. Make the most of being young. Work shouldn't come first at your age."

My father came back to sit at the table. He was carrying a box.

"Here," he said, "this is cork-lined. Put your phone in here so we don't hear it ringing and we can eat in peace."

We had tiny snails followed by meat and pasta. And wine too. Red wine, very red. Bottled by my father, with no label. We needed to drink something strong, to forget our reality. To forget that Grandma would never come and sit next to me again, and that Carlo had perfected the use of automatic call-back on his phone, and that Manuella – but a long time ago now – used to call the house regularly. For my father or for me . . .

★ ★ ★

When I turned my phone back on, long after we'd finished eating, I saw that Carlo had called me ten times. He's obsessed, I thought to myself again. Frightened I wasn't doing the work, frightened I'd spill the beans. I decided not to call him till the following day. I set to work and translated for much of the night, compensating for refusing to talk to him. Holed up in my room in that silent house, I put on a Glen Gould album. Music had always gone hand in hand with my work since my teens. There was no coping without it. I'd listen to the same piece dozens of times, on a loop, up to saturation point, until it was drained of its power, like citrus fruit squeezed right down to the peel. Glen Gould occupied my musical space in those days. And I waited until he sang to breathe in time with him, accompanying the music that inhabited him.

As time went by, my rough notes were slowly covered with drawings, which were terrible in comparison with the text. At four in the morning, probably exasperated by the music, Mama came into my room and delicately ripped the stereo's plug from the socket. My head was resting on my desk, on the marine monster. I had – quite deplorably – fallen asleep over the text in an impossible position which would give me a cricked neck for several days. Mama peered suspiciously at the few pages I'd scribbled. She noticed my attempts to illustrate the monster; it looked more like a seahorse than a sperm whale. She turned the page over to be spared the sight. The old lie dished out to children who come home from school with a hideous drawing – "Oh darling, it's wonderful!" – was no longer appropriate.

"Go to bed, Giacomo, you're exhausted."

I listened to her advice and went straight to bed. Mama pulled a rough, heavy blanket right up to my neck. No way could this child escape. Neither could the adult. I definitely didn't want to, anyway. At that precise moment, as Mama turned out the light, I had a deep feeling of contentment. A simple pleasure, no music but just an itchy blanket and my mother's kiss. A kiss with no words. Her lips on my cheek, as tickly as the blanket. After she'd closed the door, I heard her mutter on the landing, "I'll call Carlo tomorrow."

* * *

When I woke the house was empty. My parents were already at the hospital. I didn't feel very motivated to work or talk to Carlo. I decided to go to the newspaper kiosk to see if my interview had been printed. I passed close to the *Domus de Janas* but didn't stop. Fabrizio welcomed me with a big smile that gave away the good news.

"You're in the paper," he said. "I'm proud of you! It's a good thing one of us has made a success of himself."

Success wasn't a word that suited my actual circumstances but, because my friend had chosen it, I didn't try to contradict him.

"How's your grandmother?"

"Not good. It's nearly over, according to the doctor."

"They can be wrong sometimes."

"Not this time, I think. She's very weak."

"You know, the doctors have buried me several times."

"I do know."

"I was ageing faster than everyone else. My skin started sagging when I was only twenty."

"And you're still here."

"Tired but yes, I'm still here. Every day God gives us, I open my kiosk. Even if no one buys anything. Come blazing sun, come rain, I sell my papers. And to hell with the doctors. They once told me I had *cutis laxa*. I didn't understand a word of it."

"Loose skin?"

My years of Latin were finally paying off. Six hours a week with a completely degenerate teacher. Only 1.5 metres tall but packed with spite and Latin declensions. Nominative, Accusative and a thwack on the fingers with a ruler to make you remember the rest. All of which meant that I could now translate my friend's condition – loose skin – without a thwacking ruler. A perfect translation, the mad old git would have said.

"That's right, *cutis laxa* – all that to say that my skin sags all over the place. But I knew that already, I could see it every morning in the mirror. My jowls, my cheeks, my lips, the skin on my neck, it was all heading south. *Cutis laxa*, seriously? I didn't need a fancy name, I needed someone to *cure* me. We're thirty-five, Giacomo. I look older than your father. But work keeps me going. Come on, have a look at this amazing article. As for the picture – look at you! Clean-shaven, dressed up, a real American actor. You look great."

"Don't exaggerate, Fabrizio. I just made myself look decent for the picture."

"You know the one who played Maciste in the peplum films? Gordon Scott, I think he was called."

"But he was stacked, a real bodybuilder."

"Well, if not your body then your face, Giacomo."

"I don't remember his face."

"Wait, I must have it somewhere in an old magazine."

Fabrizio turned around and started rummaging through a pile of magazines. Just then I heard a voice I recognized over my shoulder. A voice that went right through me, from my ears all the way down to my toes.

"I'd like *La Nuova Sardegna* please, Fabrizio."

My friend almost fell over from standing up too quickly.

"Yes, Captain, right away. I'll have a look later, Giacomo."

* * *

The Captain, it was the Captain. You couldn't keep him waiting. I turned around as slowly as an actor in a slow-motion sequence. With a mixture of fear and curiosity. In my mind's eye I pictured the man I hadn't seen for years, a man who'd mattered to us, a man who wore shirts as colourful as our houses. The youngest of us, and I was one of them, had never seen him wear anything else. He looked like a European bee-eater, those multicoloured little birds that like to nest on electricity pylons. People said he'd done the most extraordinary feats in the war, as proved by the great slabs of iron all over his chest. He'd fought the enemy, saved lives, blown up bridges, destroyed planes, strangled an enemy officer with his bare hands, and plenty more besides. But, sadly for him, the war was over now. All good things come to an end, however hard you try to spin them out. The Captain probably wanted a never-ending conflict, a sort of modern Hundred Years War. But mankind had decided otherwise, making him a hero – because heroes only come to light when the fighting is over – with brightly coloured shirts and nostalgia in his eyes.

The slow-motion sequence came to an end, and so did the memories. The Captain was standing in front of me. My God, how time can change a man, how it can turn our childhood heroes into creatures who, if we hadn't known them in better days, would never attract our sympathy now. A few years earlier I'd met an ageing actor, a former French cinema celebrity, at the launch party for his memoir. He'd played alongside all the greats. His life was just a string of anecdotes and outdated intrigues meant to appeal to ageing fans keen on black-and-white films. Superposing his present state on the mental picture I'd had of him (an absurdly attractive man) demolished the latter. He was something else. And no one asked him to make films any more. So one morning he started writing. Carlo had pounced on the opportunity. A star in his publishing company! And on top of that, the ex-husband of an Italian singer whom his mother adored. The book was a failure; its elderly potential readers had probably all died before it was published. Time is cruel to people. Time is cruel with their stories.

The Captain – because he's the one I intended to talk about at the end of the slo-mo – reminded me of Fidel Castro in his twilight years. In a tracksuit. I kept this comparison to myself. Like Ahab in *Moby Dick*, the Captain had emerged from the past to take on the present.

"Good morning, Captain."

"Good morning, sir."

The old boy didn't remember me.

"I'm Giacomo."

"Giacomo?"

"The beach, the bus, do you remember?"

"Giacomo . . . the little boy who was afraid of the Captain?"

"That's me, yes."

Miraculously, his face relaxed.

"What are you doing here? I heard you were a translator, brighter than any other mind in this forgotten little village."

"I've come to see my grandmother. She's very ill."

"So, as well as intelligence you have a good memory and

gratitude. Fabrizio, you should follow your friend's example. In fact, every inhabitant in this godforsaken place should follow your example, Giacomino."

Fabrizio smiled. Because the Captain's words were loaded with criticism of the villagers and because he'd called me by that slightly ridiculous nickname, Giacomino, a name only the Captain ever used when we were children. We were deeply respectful of the old man, even if he was wearing a tracksuit too big for his depleted frame. Fabrizio handed him his paper and the Captain headed off without another word.

"Captain," Fabrizio called after him.

The old man turned around slowly.

"Yes?"

"Giacomo's in the paper."

My heart thudded and the blood surged through my temples. I was worried about how he'd react. The Captain opened and closed his hand a couple of times, perhaps a sign that he was interested by this news. To be honest, that's only supposition because I'd never seen a gesture like it, except in babies learning to wave. He walked away.

"You're mad, Fabrizio."

"Why?"

"You should never have told him about the paper."

If I'd had the courage I would have run after the Captain. But I was just a translator, a one-time little boy frightened by this old soldier's stature and the medals on his jacket.

* * *

One morning when I was at school my father decided to paint a mural on the side of our house. On the mainland a young man had been killed by the police during an anti-G8 demonstration. We lived a long way from all that, but my father wanted to express his disgust at this immoral show of violence. He was making a stand. Until then he'd always refused to use the walls of houses as a soapbox, a principle I'd thought would never change. When I came home he was still working: sweating, determined and silent. Murals should be spontaneous, instinctive, not premeditated. I'd never seen my father in such a state. He didn't stop for a moment. Even my mother didn't dare interrupt him. As for me, I felt very proud seeing him so possessed by his creative impulse and his determination to denounce such an atrocity. My friends couldn't get over it. And to think they'd always been surprised that we had no paintings on our house. It was one of the few in the village to be left undecorated. Murals had been springing up pretty much everywhere since 1969. 1969, the first man on the moon, everyone knew that. 1969, the first mural in our village. Who knew?

We didn't have lessons that afternoon so I spent the rest of the day watching my father. I loved our school timetable. How slow it was. How leisurely. The way it wanted us to be free to discover the world in other ways than sitting on a school chair. I didn't go off to the *Domus* that day. Nor did I go to look out at the sea from the promontory. Art had invited itself into our home. Green was the dominant colour of the mural. The lower half of the painting was grass. I was soon able to make out a young man lying on the ground with his mouth wide open. A colossal policeman loomed over him, furious and weapon in hand. Papa concluded his work with the inscription *Non si uccide i bambini* – We don't kill children. When he'd finished he took me in his arms for a long time. Without a word. He'd completed the greatest creation of his life. That evening, when I was smoking discreetly out of the attic window to avoid annoying Mama who couldn't bear the smell of cigarettes, I saw her walk over to the painting. She scrutinized it in detail, stepping closer then back again to get a better view of her husband's work. My father joined her to bring her the herb tea she had every evening. A soothing tea. That's what it said on the box.

"Be careful, the cup's very hot."

"Thank you. It's fantastic, Mario."

"I don't know about that, but I'm very glad you like it."

"I'm proud of you."

Mama took my father's hand and brought it to her face. He could hardly look at her, embarrassed by this unusually gentle gesture.

"Poor boy."

"He was the same age as Giacomo."

"The poor are always targeted by those better off than them."

My father remembered that his island had lived in terrifying poverty for decades. With no infrastructure, no work, almost no food, and no tourists. The inhabitants had made do with what the land gave them. People sat outside their houses for hours on end. The mainland hardly took any notice of islanders. Rejection by the dominant force was born. And no one forgot it. Even though investors bought up half the island, banishing cattle far away from the beaches, and even though tourists came in their thousands to swim in the clear, warm water.

Papa watched over his mural all through the night. He was wary of jealous neighbours, of course, but also of rain which could prove particularly aggressive in June, and could destroy a painting. It did, in fact, rain: a deluge that was untimely for our family but welcome to those who'd been hoping for some water. The wind also joined in on the fun. We spent the night holding up a big tarpaulin to protect the fresco. It was impossible to make conversation. All we could do was cling to that protection. Two small men against the elements. I knew Turner had been tied to a ship's mast to paint *Snow Storm*. Papa, Turner and I, united for a work of art. It was a pleasing parallel, except that Turner was exhibited worldwide, whilst my father's art would never even reach the end of the street.

By dawn we were in a pathetic state but satisfied that our work was done. Turner – who'd stepped down from the mast long ago and was now looking down from his cloud – must have been proud of us. Now that the sun was back, Mama brought out warm towels and coffee . . . which was only luke-warm but, after the night we'd spent, was the best I'd ever tasted.

The days after my father's creative spree saw the entire population of the village walk past our house. Everyone came to congratulate my father. Some patted his shoulder, others took his arm, others held his hand for a long time. The entire village recognized his commitment. I watched these comings and goings from the window. The mayor, the doctor and his jars of *Effervescente* (he offered my father one to help him sleep), the shopkeeper, Manuella (so beautiful seen from above) and even Walter the dog. At school I was now seen as the son of an important artist. I was seen, and that was enough for me. Gradually, though, the visits grew few and far between. Another painting on another house came along and "erased" my father's from people's memories, despite not being a patch on it. What did people see in these new murals? Novelty, probably. Nothing more. The doctor came back to our house one evening to reclaim his (now empty) jar; he didn't even look at the painting. Manuella took Walter (the first one) for walks and came past our house, but didn't stop.

Glory never lasts. Neither do paintings. As time went by, the paint crumbled away. First the inscription. The negative disappeared: *Si uccide i bambini*. So did the object: *Si uccide*. Then the young man lying on the ground: Carlo, as we eventually discovered he was called. His legs were eaten away, then the rest of his body. Only the policeman stayed firmly on the wall. A monstrous, enraged figure. I felt that there was a powerful symbolism behind this disappearance. The strong had won, as usual.

* * *

Grandma just wouldn't die. I knew I was going to look like the lowest of the low for saying so, but Grandma wouldn't die. We were in an awkward situation. Like a man on a platform waiting for the train taking away his sweetheart to leave. But the train didn't leave. To pass the time, the lovers might wave and smile, blow kisses, even risk pulling funny faces. Then it would get embarrassing. Because the train needs to leave for life on the platform to carry on, but Grandma wouldn't die. I had work to do. I wanted to do it at home in Marseille. I had trouble getting on with it here on the island. The whole family was waiting for the end, but no one dared say so. Gavino came and knocked at the door every day. I always thought he was coming to tell us Grandma had died, but no, he had come to us for news. He also used the opportunity to show off his stupendous yellow shoes with green stripes – they were so bright you couldn't look at them for long without hurting your eyes. "You wait, everyone'll have them soon." He might have been right about mobile phones, but I couldn't see the shoes catching on.

Gavino also came to tell us what was going on in his life. In fact, we all felt like sharing some news. It felt as if we were committed to telling each other our stories, endlessly. Life went on around Grandma, but it continued to make her heart beat as well. For many years our island had been known for its inhabitants' long lives. When I left, I knew I'd be shaving off at least a decade from my own lifespan. But it was worth it: I was suffocating, trapped by the island's four extremities. People lived longer here than elsewhere; they felt good. A colourful village with sea views, frescoes and a ridiculously attractive grocer's wife: a tempting advert.

The temperature inside the hospital was so unbearable that Grandma had to lie beneath a light sheet. You'd almost think they were trying to accelerate things. The doctor had told me that air conditioning was bad for the sickly. It caused chills. It seemed that my mother wasn't the only person complaining – she was part of a national campaign. I, for my part, would have welcomed some fresh air when I got into the boiling family car to visit Grandma that day. The heat was so unpleasant, I jumped right back out of it. Mama, who had been watching me through the window as if I'd only just passed my driving test, came running out.

"What's going on, Giacomo?"

"Nothing, I've forgotten something."

"Is that what made you shoot out of your father's car like that? In such a panic! Were you trying to frighten me? Do you want to kill me, my son? Tell me what you've forgotten and I'll go and get it."

"I didn't mean to frighten you, I'm sorry. Why were you watching me?"

"I wasn't watching you, I was enjoying the sunshine."

I had gone into the house with no purpose other than to deceive my mother. I'd headed for my bedroom, sat on my bed for thirty seconds (which I estimated was long enough to fetch something I'd forgotten) and gone back out to the car.

"That was quick. What did you forget?"

With hindsight, I'd need to double the waiting time in future to be more credible. Especially in the face of such a formidable onlooker.

"A notebook I use for writing down ideas for my translation."

"You're worrying too much about Nonna, it's making you ill, my darling. She's had a good life, you know. We're all sad, but we have to move on. You're young."

"You're right. Everyone's sad and impatient."

"What are you saying?"

"Nothing, just it's true everyone's sad."

Even though I'd lied to my mother about the notebook, I had taken *Moby Dick* and a pencil. We all need reassurance. Taking work along is as good as doing it . . . sort of. I drew the curtains to restore some of Grandma's privacy but also to shut out the garish sunlight that paled the patients' already pasty complexions, and my own. Why is there so much light in hospitals? I'd rather look at a patient like I would look at a painting in a church, where any imperfections are blotted out by the shadows. Grandma wasn't very talkative – "silent as the grave", to use Gavino's very apt expression. Now we were alone, she didn't look so pale.

"It's a long time since I've seen you on my own, Nonna. There's usually always a cousin, an uncle or a doctor. I don't know if you know this, but I'm working on an incredible text at the moment, a new version of *Moby Dick*, which is an extraordinary book. I'll tell you about it another time – you'll like the story, I'm sure.

"You're not going to die, Nonna, you're not done with this life. I've still got so many things to tell you. I live in Marseille, it's a beautiful city. It's big and it's by the sea and there's everything anyone could want. When I lived here I always wanted to go somewhere else, get away from the village, away from the scrubland and those scary festivals. Have I ever told you that people dressed up as *Mamuthones* didn't just ward off evil spirits, they frightened me too? I could never get to sleep when those celebrations were going on. I know that's not very brave for a big boy like me to say, but there it is.

"If you ask me, there are other people in the village who are just as terrified but they don't dare say so. I've never been frightened of saying I'm frightened. That's what sets me apart from a lot of the other people in the village, and a lot of adults. This translation I was just talking about, that frightens me. I'm worried I won't finish it, I won't have the strength to do it. Even though I've done others before. I've come to understand, that there are just some things that can't be explained. I expect you agree.

"I don't know whether I should tell you this, but when Gavino called me he said you were going to die soon. That's a strong word, *die*, it's the kind of word that makes you sit up and listen even when you're thinking about something else. At first I thought I wouldn't see you alive again. It broke my heart. I didn't want you to die without me. Of course all the others are here, but *I* wanted to be here with you. It's selfish, I know.

"I rushed down to the port and caught the first boat to the island. I usually have my little routine and I take a cabin so I see as few people as possible. I don't like seeing people going home. They look happy but I feel like it won't last. They'll have to leave again. It upsets me, so I like to shut myself up in a cabin without a porthole. I don't want to see anything. I hear people making noises along the walkways and that's enough for me. Sailors have the nasty habit of talking too loudly. I can tell from the rush when we're about to dock. I didn't have a cabin this time, I stayed on the deck and in the bar. Like the people I usually try and avoid. There are always idiots on the deck throwing their plastic bags and cigarette butts into the sea. I didn't say anything to them, I just looked away. You can't fight that kind of complete stupidity with words.

"When I couldn't take watching them any more, I went into the bar and chatted to the singer. A nice bloke. We talked a bit about our work. I explained to him that I say nearly the same thing as the authors I translate. Nearly, that bloody nearly. It's all about that! I couldn't get to sleep on the bench seats in the bar. They're too hard, they make them too hard on purpose. And Gavino gave me such a fright. Gavino . . ."

"*Che stronzo!*"

"You're right, he's a real arsehole . . . Hey, hang on, you just spoke, Nonna!"

Carried away with my pathetic monologue, it took me a few seconds to notice that my grandmother had spoken, which she hadn't done for weeks. I got up to tell the doctors. The curtains were closed, and I had to find the way out, which was difficult when I felt so stressed. I eventually managed to get out but tripped on the excess fabric trailing on the floor that no one had bothered to trim. I fell helplessly in the middle of the room. Worse still, I couldn't see a thing, blinded by the bright light that burned my eyes. Sprawled on the floor, I became aware of a human presence in front of me. Feet. Sandals – a well-known German brand used by most of the medical profession across Europe. A real success story. I felt them with my hand to check that my eyes weren't deceiving me.

"Are you alright there?"

"Yes, absolutely fine. I know that's hard to believe, in my present position. I wanted to tell a doctor that my grandmother's woken up from her coma, she's just spoken."

"I'll have a look right away. But do please get up."

The sandals belonged to a young woman, who helped me to my feet.

"I tripped on the curtain."

"It must have been the shock."

The young doctor – *Dottoressa Alessandra Cau*, it said on her tunic – took Grandma's pulse. She was absolutely lovely, a fact which reconciled me with the island's entire health system. Dr. Ignazio but without the extra years, the beard, the belly, the wrinkled hands, the jar of *Effervescente* and the oversized cars. Dr. Ignazio but with a smile, a gentle manner, beauty, German sandals (he only wore deck shoes, summer and winter alike, protected from the cold by his miracle pills) and competence.

"What did she say?"

"*Che stronzo . . .*"

"That's strange."

"I was talking about my uncle, he's a real idiot, a waste of space . . . If you knew him you'd probably say the same. A man who could do terrible things, except—"

"No, I meant it's strange because her pulse is still very weak. Did she say anything else?"

"I don't know. I came running out straight away and tripped, and you picked me up."

Of course the expression "picked me up" was a blunder. A sign of the shocks I'd just experienced. Grandma nearly waking. It's all about the nearly. And Alessandra appearing. The girl with the incredible eyes. From her sandals to her face. The revelation. For a few seconds Nonna had evaporated. It was like a beautiful scene from a film, an improbable meeting in a hostile place. Next to an old woman who just wouldn't stop living. And dying. And living. I wished I was better looking. What our meeting needed was some music. Something like Rachel's song from *Blade Runner*. If that had been playing, if Vangelis had been there with his full orchestra, but in the corridor so they didn't disturb us, then Alessandra Cau might have found something touching and utterly irresistible in me. Because music helps love. And vice versa. But there, in that hospital, there was no music to be heard, neither there nor in any other hospital. You had to cope without music, just with yourself and life.

* * *

The best way to be in love is by hardly ever seeing each other. Cohabitation wears couples down. Couples wear each other out with their little foibles. My parents were worn out. They could no longer surprise each other because they saw each other all the time. They each knew what the other was thinking and what he or she was about to do or say. It was probably comforting for them. But it terrified me. I could easily see myself keeping up a long-distance relationship with *Dottoressa* Alessandra. My work was conducive to the situation. Anything was possible from Marseille. The boat was just a stone's throw away. I could come over two or three times a month. No problem. There were loyalty cards and special rates for frequent travellers . . .

I was lost in these lovestruck thoughts when the horde – the family – pitched up at the hospital. They all gathered around the bed and strained their ears. But not a sound came from Grandma's mouth. She'd always had her limits. She was the kind to bear a grudge if you played a trick on her. I was convinced she was having a good laugh at us all now, as we leant over her, listening out for the least word, like the faithful on the piazza outside Saint Peter's waiting for the white smoke announcing a new pope. But we were a long way from Rome. And the pope was as robust as the statue of Saint Paul. With less worn shoes, too.

Everyone came up with their own theory to explain the silence. My mother – our very own Sardinian Cassandra – imagined the worst. My father said that if he were in Grandma's situation (in other words, lying down with all of us clustering around), he wouldn't say a thing either. It was a question of pride. And a need to stay in control. I backed his reasoning. Gavino – wound up because he'd spent all morning looking for his keys – kept pacing around the bed. He obviously wanted to say something. He was waiting for the right moment, when it was quiet. Everybody needed to hear clearly what he had to say, as if he didn't dare raise his voice somewhere like this. He waited for a window until one came.

"If the painter and the translator are in agreement, then they must be right. As usual."

The rest of the family didn't react, other than looking away disconsolately. Papa sighed to indicate how absurd this suggestion was. I tried to come up with a snappy retort, a whiplash response that would leave a deep mark in Gavino's mind. Ideas jostled in my head. A few moments later, I'd made up my mind. I would say THE words, proof of my unique and legendary repartee (or at least, the legend that was to emerge as a result of this riposte).

"Gavino," I said with pompous assurance.

"Yes, I'm listening, my boy."

"You see, Gavino . . ."

I said his name again to delay my announcement. Melville did that sometimes, and I found it a very elegant trick.

"Yes, tell me."

Just then a croaky voice piped up. A voice that froze everyone's blood.

"Idiot. Is there anyone stupider than you, Gavino?"

It was Grandma. She'd shut my rude uncle's mouth at a speed I couldn't match. She didn't die, but went straight back to sleep after she'd said her line, like Sarah Bernhardt at the end of her career. The ringing of my phone, coupled with the vibrations that I couldn't seem to deactivate, produced no reaction from her. Carlo again, *Moby Dick* again. I found somewhere quiet at the end of a hospital corridor.

* * *

"Are you making progress with the translation?"

"Yes, Carlo, don't worry."

"Of course I'm worried, what with you vanishing overnight like that and not answering my calls."

"Well, I'm answering them now."

"Don't mess me around. You know this translation's going to be big, it'll put the publishing company in the spotlight. I'm counting on you, Giacomo, don't let me down. When do you think you'll have it finished?"

"I don't know. I'm in Sardinia."

"What the hell are you doing in Sardinia?"

"I've got stuff going on."

"Everyone always has 'stuff going on' over there. It's too colourful over there, it's bad for the eyes and the head. Drives people mad. I never go back. Will you have finished in two weeks' time?"

"My grandmother's about to die."

"I'm very sorry. Would three weeks work better?"

"I don't know."

"How old's your grandmother, Giacomo?"

"Somewhere between eighty and ninety . . ."

"You don't even know how old she is and you want me to believe you're so upset you can't finish my translation. That's rich!"

"It doesn't matter how old she is, Carlo. She means a lot to me. More than *Moby Dick*."

"Nothing matters more than *Moby Dick*! Pull yourself together! I'll leave you alone for a few days, then I'll call back. Don't forget, nothing matters more than *Moby Dick*. Think of old Captain Ahab, he needs you . . ."

Captain Ahab didn't need anyone. In the last version of the text, the one I was translating, he survived the whale and came back a hero. Madness didn't drive him to his death but to the comfort of his own home. I was more preoccupied with another captain.

"Are you coming home with us, Giacomo?"

"Yes, I've finished."

* * *

On the dining-room table at my parents' house – a table usually clear of clutter to avoid damaging it – sat a pile of about thirty copies of *La Nuova Sardegna*. They had all had one page cut out, the one featuring my interview and a picture of me standing with an evasive expression and bad hair. The editorial board had thought it was a good photo, but I was slightly ashamed of it. It didn't look like me, and didn't capture anything about me other than my excessive embarrassment in front of the lens. The cuttings were piled very neatly, one on top of the other. My mother wanted to keep a memento of this glorious day when her son had a leading role (even if it was really more a walk-on part) in the paper and on the table. The quantity of copies was because she was afraid of losing this vital proof of her son's importance. She was dreaming big: next to the cuttings was a ring-bound file on which she'd written GIACOMO in gigantic letters. She probably thought this interview would lead to others. It was a wonderful proof of her love.

Besides, I understood the significance of this gesture because the dining room was usually a sort of sacred space, somewhere we only rarely went and never lingered. It was like the Sistine Chapel, you got a visiting slot. And there was no negotiating with the curator woman. Everything in there had been the same since I was a child, set out in the same unchanging way. The (empty) green vase in the middle of the table. The photographs on the huge long sideboard that was never opened. The curtains stayed closed too. Sunlight encouraged dust and yellowed the photos. This darkness was mostly an efficient way of discouraging potential visitors – and the child I once was.

Each item had ended up taking root and leaving a mark on the place where it belonged, which meant that nothing could be moved by so much as a centimetre. A crucifix hung opposite the Virgin Mary. Every excursion into the room took place under their divine gaze. Jesus, Mary, all that was missing was Joseph to complete the family. A bit of straw, too, and a few animals. Fake straw, though, to keep things clean. And plastic animals that wouldn't smell bad.

I'd always wondered why they'd created a dining room like this, robbing it of its primary function. I picked up one of the press cuttings and wedged it into my wallet. A memento for a poor man who might, in difficult times, need reminding that once upon a time someone had been interested in his opinion.

"What are you doing, Giacomo? Don't hang around in there, come and have a coffee with your old mother."

My visiting slot in the Sistine Chapel was over, the curator was keeping things in line: it was time to leave.

* * *

The Captain's house was a little way away from the others in the village. It was so tiny that I couldn't understand how such an imposing man could move around in such a cramped space. He must have got used to it, I suppose, since coming home to the village, as I'd grown accustomed to defeat as a young football player. After the war, the injured Captain spent many years in various hospitals on the mainland. He had to learn to live with what he had done, with what he had seen and heard. Having been thrown into darkness, he came back to our colourful world one fine morning, just like me. The boat, the bus, the dogs, nothing ever changed. Everyone had their rightful place.

"What are you doing here, Giacomo?"

I was startled by the Captain's voice coming from a half-open window.

"I . . . I . . . was out for a walk."

"You mustn't lie to the elderly."

The Captain's face had appeared at the window. "I read your interview in the paper," he continued, perfectly relaxed and sure of himself. "A nice piece. You're a very talented boy. Your parents should be proud of you."

"They are. My mother bought about thirty copies of *La Nuova Sardegna*."

"You're the pride of the village right now. Makes a change from painters and sheep."

"Don't forget yourself in that list."

"Ha ha ha! You're talking about a long time ago. I'm no

longer a source of pride to anyone. But if you've come to flatter me, I won't put up a fight! Happens very rarely nowadays."

"I mean it, you're one of the people who mattered to me. More than some members of my family."

The Captain was moved by this, I could see it in his eyes. And I certainly wasn't lying. When I thought about what he'd done for me in comparison to my uncle Gavino, it seemed only natural to tell him so.

"Listen to me, my boy, you've made me very happy. I've got people coming over soon, friends from here and there, people you don't know, from this village and from others too, old soldiers, civilians – well, you know what I mean, you're intelligent, I'm expecting guests. I need to get the house ready. I need to get myself ready too, spruce myself up because you don't welcome guests unshaven, unkempt and underdressed. I need to ready myself, do you see what I mean, Giacomo? I do have a body attached to this head!"

"I see exactly what you mean, Captain. I'll leave you to it."

"Come back whenever you want to and we can chat, if you'd like."

"I'd be delighted."

The Captain stepped back and closed the window. He'd seemed so uncomfortable, so embarrassed by his excuses, that I doubted they were true. He'd said he was expecting "people" and I wanted to know if it was true. In my early childhood, I'd often hidden behind a cork tree and spied on Manuella. I decided to do the same with the Captain. I took up my position behind some type of tree I couldn't name. I didn't really know about trees or anything else that came out of the ground. All I knew was cork oaks, maritime pines and the scrubland that covered our island. The tree screening me was wide, that was the only thing that mattered.

The first thirty minutes went on forever. No one came to this part of the village. Not even a cat or a dog. No-life-land. After that half hour, time became suspended. No sound nor movement disturbed me in my hideaway. I thought about my translation, the passages I'd already worked on, the alterations and improvements I could make; about Ahab standing on the whale roaring; about Alessandra, the doctor, and how I could show her the press cutting so I wasn't reduced in her mind to some clumsy oaf with his hands on her sandals. It would have been nice, the two of us here, hidden, spying on the Captain. Her with her back against the tree and me with my hands around her waist. "Don't worry, I'll let you know if anything happens." And I'd have prayed for nothing to happen and for her to stay leant against the tree. My hands still there, around her waist. You were allowed to think about whatever you liked, on your own, waiting for *people*. I thought about Grandma too. If she'd seen me there, skulking behind a tree, she'd have had a good laugh or she'd have dealt me the same thing she'd said to Gavino. I preferred to think it would be the former. Time had disappeared and one idea followed another. No one came. No one would come, that was screamingly obvious now. When the sun started to set, I resolved to leave. The Captain had lied to me.

At the end of the street I looked at my watch. Seven o'clock. I hadn't moved so much as a toe for three hours. I had obeyed the first law of this part of the village: immobility. I'd never held out so long for Manuella. Twenty minutes, at most, I'd waited for her. I was fascinated by the Captain. I'd known him when I was a child, I'd looked up to him, put him on a pedestal, on top of the shelves where I lined up my books. That was how important he was. Now, as an adult, I could see his eyes and not just his neck and his chin. I was on a level with him. And right now, I could feel them on me, telling me to come back. Once the people had left, of course.

* * *

"Giacomo, there's a letter for you."

"Thank you, Mama."

I was amazed to have mail because I hadn't lived in the

village for years and the last letter I'd received at my parents' house was probably a school report.

"It must be an admirer, she'll have read the interview in the paper."

"Or he."

"Don't joke about that!"

There were some subjects on which the mentality didn't change much in this part of the Mediterranean. My mother crossed herself and went back to her chores. That particular morning she'd decided to tidy the attic, which was as good an idea as any. My father was supposed to help her in this gargantuan task, bound to fail since the place was so cluttered with all our lives. Three lives piled up and spread out through books, records, discarded objects and Papa's painting materials. Mama's grumbling went on and on, cutting through the house and reaching me. Like this letter. Which had no stamp. So it had been delivered straight to my parents' letterbox. My name was spelled out in beautiful, diligent, serious writing. We show a lot of ourselves in our handwriting. We reveal ourselves. I thought this must be a woman's handwriting. In my mind women had tidy, considered writing. I'd noticed at school, college and university that boys (including myself) wrote scruffily and carelessly. Exactly the opposite to girls and women.

One time when I'd gone to the grocer for some *bottarga* and a couple of other things, Manuella had written a note to my mother on a scrap of paper, to explain that they didn't have exactly what she needed. She had *nearly* the same thing. It's all about the nearly. This was when I discovered her perfect handwriting. Her letters were rounded and generous. Just like her. I kept that precious note afterwards and I'd still have it today if Walter the dog hadn't eaten it on another of my trips to the shop. While I was waiting patiently for Manuella to serve me, because there were lots of customers, the dog came to play with me and in the tussle the little note fell to the floor. Walter ate everything he could lay his chops on. I did try to save the piece of paper but all I managed to salvage from his fangs was a slobbery, incomplete relic. My attempts to dry it on my bedroom windowsill were in vain.

This time, though, there was no danger of Walter the younger chewing up my letter. A letter from his mistress? But why would Manuella be writing to me? To apologize for her dog's behaviour? It was water under the bridge and poor Walter senior had been laid to rest in the family garden where he was probably greeted enthusiastically by the pigs that they reared. The revenge of those who sleep outside. No, I wouldn't really have been interested in a letter from Manuella. It was selfish of me, I agree, but the grocer's wife had had her time. And she definitely didn't have a chance with me now.

Then I thought of *Dottoressa* Alessandra. It was from her, it had to be! Our near-miraculous meeting had had a cataclysmic effect on her life. A thunderbolt. I personally couldn't be so decisive, I needed a bit of time to think properly about my feelings. We're not always aware of the full impact we've had on other people. It's chemical, really, physical . . . Alessandra must have found out who I was by looking at Grandma's files. It's a small island, everyone knows everyone else, someone would have given her my parents' address. And her shyness had stopped her saying anything in person. A real letter, like in the old days, before we started sending each other messages online. I was thrilled.

I opened the envelope carefully, and my hopes took a nosedive when I caught sight of the signature at the bottom of the page.

Capitano Vincenzo Frau

I was wrong. This wasn't from Alessandra but from the Captain. I would never have dreamt he'd write to me. Now I had to explore the content of the letter. My eyes scanned upwards and found nothing. Well, almost nothing. There were just a few words, written as neatly as my name on the envelope.

It was nice to see you.

It couldn't get more concise. One word on the envelope, three for the signature and six for the message. The Captain certainly cut to the chase. All the same, this letter was a pleasure for me, an honour even. For years I'd lived near this strange, terrifying and very mysterious man who'd led me to believe, only the day before, that a number of guests were about to turn up at his house. He'd wanted me to go away and I didn't understand why.

I had to cope with my mother's comments about the author of the letter throughout the rest of the day. She wanted to know everything. I didn't want to tell her anything. I went back to see Grandma who still wouldn't die. And had stopped talking.

* * *

The Captain had come home from war wreathed in glory. The welcome he was given by the inhabitants was legendary. The women had dressed themselves up in their prettiest dresses, the ones they only wore on big occasions (the happy ones, of course – festivals, processions, weddings and baptisms). The ones that set the rhythm for village life. The ones that brought people together. Mama had not escaped this striving for love-liness. The only time I remembered her looking so beautiful was for Gavino's wedding. Mama looking so gorgeous for such a chaotic wedding: my uncle flushed scarlet with happiness, his bride terrified (by him, I think) and half the guests drunk, gamely fighting the wind that was swishing the limbs on the trees. A ravishing white bride who answered to the name Gavina. Gavino and Gavina. No one had those names, except them! As if the two families had decided to mate a male and female of the same breed. The Gavin breed . . .

I'd been chosen to help the parish priest in his duties. In the front row, I could see Gavino winking lewdly at all the girls attending the ceremony, except his mother and sister. From the front row, I could hear the priest whispering to me because I wasn't doing things right. I mustn't get anything wrong, like drop a Bible or an incense burner. Anyone would have thought it was a member of the English royal family getting married.

There were nothing but drunks. In every colour. Red cheeks. Pink shirts. Grey trousers. Orange trousers. Blue shoes. All the colours of a life lived far from the outside world.

For the Captain's homecoming, people had decorated the walls of the school, made banners and little flags, and rehearsed two or three songs. The schoolmaster had taken out all his maps and his most beautiful history books. He kept telling us how well he knew the illustrious Captain. The village wanted to demonstrate how happy and proud it was to see its valorous soldier home. It has to be said no other village on the island could count a captain in the national army among its inhabitants.

The *sindaco*, the mayor, had gone to collect him from his home, the same place where everything was now so quiet and still. The Captain had settled himself in the handsome mayoral car, and the *sindaco* had treated him to a triumphant procession worthy of the most illustrious Roman emperor. This war hero was loved. He was loved all the more because he had needed years of recuperation before he could come home to his brightly painted village. He was asked to sign bits of paper, to stroke children's faces and pose for photographs, but did anyone know why? The Captain was so happy that he refused no requests. How wonderful it was to be loved by everyone! What a pleasure to be putting the smile on every face he saw! For this man who'd fought the Germans, the Americans and then the Germans again. Because enemies had been allies and vice versa. It was hard to make any sense of the situation. In January the Captain asked his men to attack the Americans, by February things had changed so much that they now had to open fire on the Germans. If you added to this the soldiers' insularity and loathing of mainland Italians, they needed to keep a pretty tidy balance sheet to avoid getting the wrong adversary. Italian-style schizophrenia for a country that no longer knew how to be unified. To those who asked for war stories, the Captain said that he took a couple of minutes first thing in the morning to "take stock of the situation", to avoid descending into madness.

Mama listened to him, and so did I. Papa thought his stories were a little exaggerated. A load of poppycock! Who'd seen him in combat? Who could testify? And as for his medals . . . you see, in Rome – because my father knew Rome well, he'd been there once – in Rome you could buy medals, completely meaningless medals. Medals for singers, medals for swimmers, medals . . . for dogs! Yes, you could even get medals for the most beautiful dogs, so the abundance of trinkets on the Captain's jacket didn't convince my father. Mama meanwhile was under the spell of this soldier with the weather-beaten skin. The allure of uniform, most likely. She gazed at him happily. To think, she'd nearly stopped noticing my father! It's all about the nearly. I have to say, I understand how she felt because the Captain did cut a fine figure. He frightened me with his official suit and his big hands, with which I imagined he had brought about the deaths of dozens, hundreds – what am I thinking? – *thousands* of enemy soldiers. He could have wiped us all out with a single sweep of his hand. Perhaps that's another reason the villagers welcomed him with smiles. They were frightened. We always smile at the dentist because we hope he won't hurt us.

When all the celebrations were over, I would sometimes come across the Captain on the main road through the village. People offered him a coffee or a strong drink (because soldiers only drink potent alcohols). The Captain would accept. He was given the best seat, where everyone could see him, on the café's terrace. He beamed, talked loudly, held people's hands for a long time when he shook them, and stood very close to anyone he met. The Captain wanted to compensate for his past absence with this hyper-presence now. He blocked the view but no one seemed to mind. Quite the opposite. The Captain was like those big clouds that hide the sun for a few minutes during a heatwave. He gave the villagers an opportunity to catch their breath for a moment while they thought about something other than their petty squabbles.

★   ★   ★

Before his illness ravaged his skin, Fabrizio and I used to like looking up at the sky through maritime pine trees. Someone who does that can't be bad. The sea was a long way from the village but it brought us a taste of itself by giving these trees as messengers. They did look a bit lost this far from the coast, I have to admit. Hours spent gazing at the sky in silence. With the branches piercing the blue. Sometimes a bird would come and disturb the picture. What picture? The sky belongs to everyone. So the bird would appear and we'd hope to see it disappear – an error of judgement that, luckily, time has corrected. We sometimes feel as if one small element of something bothers us when it's actually there to make us aware of how beautiful the thing is. The bird wanted to show us that it could touch the thing we looked at longingly. It didn't want to belittle us, just show us the way. Fabrizio would pick up a stone and throw it. The bird flew away. Flew out of the picture. What picture? The sky through the maritime pines. Throwing stones, beauty coming to an end.

The pine trees around the village had been decimated by a terrible disease that made them die from the inside. You couldn't see the problem and then one day the tree would literally collapse. There was nothing left inside it. An empty shell, like the *Domus de Janas*. No hope of salvaging its branches or trunk. The top specialists in the country came to the island to try to solve the problem, but they failed. The trees died one after another and no one really knew why. The scientists stayed with locals because there was no hotel in the village. We had one at our house, Professor Ventrano, a man from Milan, a cold northern city. He was a very serious, very polite little man, rather frightened by our eating habits: raw vegetables, olive oil and pasta. It has to be said, Papa and Mama were pretty strapped for cash. There wasn't much call for house painters because no one was building anything. But we were glad to host the professor. He told me about the Duomo in Milan, which I'd only seen on TV (when it was working), and Leonardo's *Last Supper* which is in a small church in that big

city. I used to ask him a thousand questions every day. Mama
tried to protect the scientist from my constant assaults. "Leave
the professor alone, you can see he's tired." But I persisted and
Ventrano always answered calmly and patiently. "You'll end up
working with trees, Giacomo," he often said. Trees, but what
trees? I only know two, cork oaks and maritime pines. What I
was interested in was the city, cathedrals, museums and monuments. *They* didn't collapse. And if they did eventually fall,
someone always found an explanation.

Ventrano stayed with us for a month. A month of relative
calm because my mother had declared that she wouldn't be
aggressive towards my father so long as the scientist was staying
with us. A domestic truce. They played their parts of the perfect
spouses and I liked it. There was no more shouting at mealtimes
when he wasn't completely fascinated by what she was telling
him. She didn't criticize him for being an unworthy husband,
a bad father, an incorrigible womanizer and everything in
between. They listened to each other and the house could
breathe. All thanks to a Mediterranean tree specialist from
Milan. He may not have been healing the trees but he was
healing a marriage. Which suited me fine.

And as far as the trees were concerned, I could lend him
a hand because, deep down, I knew the answer. The trees
were dying of sadness and loneliness. No one was interested
in them except for Fabrizio and me. And they were such a
long way from the rest of their kind. How sad to see your
family all those kilometres away and never be able to touch
them or hug them. Or talk to them. Because trees talk to each
other. I heard on TV that when there was a long drought in
South Africa and the acacia trees had become the only food
for antelopes, they'd magically raised the tannin levels in their
leaves. The starving antelopes ate the leaves and died. The
trees had talked to each other to survive. Back on the island,
then, the depressed pines had opted for collective suicide.
They knew they'd never join their family. All that was left of
them were battered trunks. It upset me but I told myself the

trees had made a courageous decision. We mustn't stay around when life's too difficult.

My explanation didn't convince Professor Ventrano. I set it out for him the day he left to return to Milan. He listened attentively and responded to my analysis by saying, "You could well be right, Giacomo. Trees do talk to each other. Sadly, we don't understand their language at all. It will take us a long time to learn it, but I need to go home. The university have called me back. There's no money left to work on why the pines are dying. I promise I'll come back, and we'll talk about this again . . . with the trees." He put his hand on my cheek and patted it. He knew he'd never be back. Everyone who came to see us said the same thing.

The next day, once the goodbyes were over – with lots of tears and hugs and promises – my mother summoned my father to the kitchen. The time had come for *il conto*, the bill. With the truce over, she wanted to let him know everything she'd found unacceptable during Ventrano's stay. It was to be a very long list, and my father now owed my mother an unimaginable sum. *Il conto* – Papa had to pay the price. I slipped away to my room and dreamed of the statues in Milan cathedral. Ninety-six statues, all separate, standing on their own plinths. No one ever bothered them.

"What you're describing there's really lovely, Giacomo."

It no longer surprised me when I heard my grandmother's voice coming from her weary body. I didn't jump to my feet, didn't shout, but just sat there calmly. It was the only way I could make the most of being with her.

"I'm so happy you talk to me, Nonna."

"I've been listening to everything, you know, from the start. I don't say a word, except to you."

"But why don't you want to talk to the others?"

"Because they do nothing but bother me with their problems and their theories about my condition. So I sleep. The only thing I mind about it is not being able to eat the biscuits your mother brings every day. I couldn't care less about anything else. Everyone treats my body as if it were already dead. I couldn't care less."

"It's our secret!"

"Yes, like when you were a little boy and you came to tell me what was going on in your life. I never told anyone. I'm trusting you to do the same now."

Grandma was play-acting. The monologue I'd addressed to her was morphing into a dialogue. There was theatre everywhere on our island. In fact, people often criticized us for this. On the mainland we were seen as bad actors. Every year one of the national dailies would reveal an exceptional case of *pensione* fraud, benefit fraud: a "blind man" on state benefits would take part in a car race and win. All the glory made him forget his disability. Then the money had to be paid back! And what about all the islanders who were out of work, who refused job offers on the continent because they were ill . . . imaginary invalids! I thought this unfair. We didn't deserve to be treated like that. The sun beat down on our heads but not enough to make us all thieves, liars or madmen. Nonna had always been honest and I thought she was a pretty good actress.

"Do you remember the day you hid in the *Domus* on the hillside?"

"Yes."

"The whole family looked everywhere for you. Your mother shrieked and your father searched and searched in silence. People thought you'd run away or, worse, been kidnapped."

"I'd had enough of Mama's dramas. And Papa's silence too. I needed somewhere to get away. The *Domus* on the hill was perfect. The only conversation to be had was with sheep. And you, when you found me in the middle of the night."

"I was pretty sure no one would kidnap you, with a mother like that . . . Your abductors would have too much trouble getting rid of her!"

A nurse came over to Grandma to take her pulse and her blood pressure. Grandma closed her eyes like someone closing the metal shutter on a shop at the end of the day. Late customers could knock all they liked, no one would answer. The nurse looked at me admiringly.

"It's so nice to see a grandson at his grandmother's bedside every morning."

"I think it's only natural."

"It's rare, I can tell you. No one's really interested in the elderly any more. Except for their inheritance . . . when there is any."

"There's always an inheritance."

"If you say so."

With these words she left to see another patient. Grandma had no money to leave us, just a gloomy old house no one would want; three hens who now only laid very occasionally; a cockerel tired of crowing; and an obese cat, Mila, who spent her life curled up on a cushion. (She looked as if she'd set her sights on the title of fattest cat in the world.) But Grandma had something else: memories, emotions and gentleness. The way she toyed with the world too, and made fun of it occasionally. And I was up for that.

"She's gone, you can wake up now."

"That nurse takes good care of me. She talks to me sometimes and I find that touching. She talks about her life. Her husband's a brute and her son's a lazy waste of space. Poor woman. She swears under her breath so no one hears her. Everyone has problems on this wretched earth. God's hard on us. I'm old, I accept my suffering, but younger people shouldn't have to suffer."

I didn't know what to say. I thought of Fabrizio and his drooping skin making an old man of him before his time. The last few times he played in our wonderful football team, the opponents refused to let him onto the pitch. *Il Vecchio*, they called him, "the old man", and they said he had no right to play in schoolboy matches. They yelled at him to go back to his nursing home. Sometimes they jeered at him. Fabrizio never cried, he kept his composure and pretended not to hear. Spite came from other people's mouths, not his. Still, I thought that once he got home he must have railed against the whole world. One afternoon when we were sitting in the *Domus* he showed me how he tried to pull up the skin on his face to see what he would have looked like without the disorder. "Look, Giacomo, I'm not all that bad. Look, I'm nearly attractive."

It was all about the nearly. Fabrizio had a girlfriend, in the early days. But his skin ended up getting the better of her. The girl, Lucia, very soon fell for a healthier boy. Fabrizio knew his skin would cause problems in his relationships with women. He was no fool, even when his parents tried awkwardly to reassure him. To reassure themselves. "You'll find someone in the end." But you don't *find* someone, you *meet* them. And after his failed relationship with Lucia, Fabrizio didn't feel like meeting lots of people. Except me, he liked seeing me. I sometimes had girlfriends, but I never abandoned him, except when he said I could. In return, Fabrizio let me use him as an excuse with Mama. "I'm going over to Fabrizio's," I'd say and my mother would always say the same, fatalistic words: "Fabrizio, that poor boy." My friend had become an illness, he no longer existed other than through the increasingly visible symptoms modifying his appearance. He was no longer Fabrizio, the son of the newsagent. No, he was that poor boy, the sick boy. As a result, he took refuge within the walls of his kiosk, where no girl would ever meet him.

"What are you thinking about, darling?"

"Nothing. I need to go, Nonna. I must get on with some work. Are you going to carry on playing dead?"

"Yes. I'll stop when everyone stops coming to see me. I've put up with my family for all these years. I've helped your mother and your uncle, coped with their problems, their anger, their rows. I have a right to get my revenge now."

"One last question, Grandma."

"Yes?"

"Why didn't you speak to me straight away? Why did you wait a while?"

"I wanted to know if you'd come like they all do. As soon as I knew the answer, I talked to you."

* * *

Knocking on someone's door and knowing that they're in but don't want to see you is a particularly uncomfortable feeling. The Captain was playing dead, like Grandma. I knew he was there because the curtains had moved – the old soldier had lost some of his gift for camouflage. Being spotted by a translator . . . could there be a worse failure? A sedentary lifestyle is a curse. I went back to my spot behind the tree. Yes, *my* spot because no one else in the village ever took it. I didn't want to stay there too long. I chose it automatically. As a child, I'd developed the habit of getting a bit of distance to see more clearly. Without being seen. At thirty-five this skulking could damage my image. I took out my notebook, wrote a few words addressed to the Captain and tore the page out untidily, planning to slip it under the door. There was such a big gap between the bottom of the door and the ground that I could push it right inside. The house had no letterbox, so I was forgiven. Then I went back to my hideout, and two minutes later the door opened and the Captain emerged from his lair. He looked from right to left. He was looking for me. I showed myself. Two appearances in two minutes.

"Hello, Captain."

"Hello, Giacomo."

"So you *are* there."

The stupidity of my words matched my embarrassment. Yes, he was there, right in front of me, otherwise how could he have talked to me? And yes, he'd reacted to my note because my knocking on the door had had no effect at all. The pen is mightier than the fist, I'd always known that.

"I was having my siesta."

"I'm so sorry."

"No, don't worry, I was about to get up."

"Oh, good."

"I've thought about all those years, the hours we spent together."

"So have I. I'll never forget them."

"I'm happy to hear you say that. I didn't know you remembered. You're now a great translator, an important figure. You must meet famous people, so the fact that you remember an old man like me . . ."

"Actually, I'm working on a book about a captain at the moment."

"Really?"

"Yes, Captain Ahab, in *Moby Dick*."

"So you can't get away from captains! I hope he's nice, at least."

"Not really! He's more over the top, a bit mad, even."

"Like me!"

"Let's say all captains are a little alike."

"That's it! There's a breed of captains. Strong men who talk loudly, are self-assured . . ."

"But you're generous, you're selfless, and this Captain Ahab of mine isn't really."

"Come in and have a drink, we've got things to talk about."

His invitation was like a knife driven into the middle of our conversation. I couldn't imagine contradicting him, so I followed him into his house. I'd built the house in my head a thousand times since I'd found out where he lived. It had become an almost magical place in my childhood world. Such a major figure must have an extraordinary home, he'd never settle for a house like my parents'. In fact the Captain's house smelt musty, and the hero's whole life was shut away within those four walls. Military uniforms in dusty display cases, medals all over the place, and photographs of animals taken in the dead of night.

"Did you see this one?"

"Yes."

"It's an owl about to grab a rat. I waited three weeks for that shot. Three weeks hiding in the barn every evening. I couldn't make any noise, like waiting to go into combat. Staying absolutely silent so as not to disturb the bird. And waiting for the prey to come out. A rat the size of my fist."

"I'd never have the patience to wait so long."

"Because you've got friends and family. I don't have anyone. I could hole myself up somewhere for a month waiting for a wild boar to pass, and no one would wonder what had happened to me. Animals pay more attention to me than the other villagers do."

"Why?"

"Because glory comes to an end eventually. Because I was important for a while. Because people are frightened of my hands. Because they attracted the women in the village. Because there are a thousand reasons, and because the people on this island are about as warm as the bottom of a well."

I spent the rest of the day with the Captain but didn't talk a great deal because he had so much to say. He said it was ten years since anyone had sat down next to him to chat. I was the rat in the trap. I didn't dare get up and say how happy I was to have talked to him but also how glad I'd be to get out of his house and back into the sunshine and the clean air. I was suffocating in that dust. I sneezed a lot. My old allergies were resurfacing. I could feel my eyes swelling, and my throat constricting and tickling. The Captain eventually noticed the desperate state I was in and led me back to the door.

"You wouldn't have lasted long in battle."

"That's why I didn't go for a career in the army."

"Go for? You make it sound so casual. Let me tell you, there's nothing casual about war."

"I'm sure there isn't."

"You'll come to see me again."

"And to talk to you."

"Of course. I'll open the windows before you come, get some air into the old place."

"I won't sneeze so much!"

"Here, have this back before you go."

The Captain handed me the piece of paper I'd slipped under

the door. As I walked home along the street, I unfolded it and read the words that had brought the soldier out of his lair:

Thank you for the sea.

Five words that had decided the shape of my day and, probably, the rest of my life.

★   ★   ★

I thought all night about what the Captain had said. Impossible to get to sleep and impossible to work. The soldier had filled my whole head with his old stories. He explained something no one knew: once the celebrations were over, he'd ended up with nothing to do, but he wasn't the sort of person to do nothing, so he'd tirelessly walked the streets of the village.

And with all that walking he came to realize that his official uniform was over the top, too serious, too strict. He didn't want to frighten the villagers, so day after day, parts of his outfit would disappear, replaced by more colourful items. No one noticed anything because no one was really paying any attention to him. Lack of gratitude shown by the liberated towards their liberator. "They're bound to notice eventually," he thought. "I'm the only soldier in the village, I'll soon be the only inhabitant covered in different colours." A man who looked like the local houses.

By the end of the week there was nothing left of his uniform. Red. Blue. Yellow. Green. From head to foot. The Captain wanted to show everyone that he'd finally turned the page on his years at the front. But one page wasn't enough. He hadn't grasped the fact that his old classmates had closed the book that he was trapped in. Like the rat confronted with the owl.

The village mayor was well aware of his most highly decorated citizen's distress and decided to call a meeting with him to suggest a way out for him.

"My dear Captain," he said, "this situation can't go on. You're underutilized in our little village. As mayor, I feel duty bound to honour you."

Another medal! the Captain thought. My chest isn't wide enough to accommodate another one. And a medal for what? I've got them all: a medal for merit, military glory, courage, for family (even though I'm single and my parents have been dead so long I hardly remember them), the country, the town, the village, my street. A medal for my house! Awarded by myself: "We are gathered here today in this home to hail the culinary skills of my own person." No, it must be something else.

"I'm going to offer you a position worthy of your magnificent career," the mayor went on, and as he spoke his great red neck seemed to palpitate with the pounding of ten hearts. "Every Thursday in the school holidays you will escort the children of the village to the beach. The trip will be made in the municipal bus. The children will be utterly and completely your responsibility. It's your vocation to mould our youngest citizens, to shape them like men, seeing as you're such a fine example in their eyes." This formal speech was made all in one go with no pause for breath. The mayor was a little afraid of the old soldier.

The Captain had never heard anything so ridiculous. Even when he was at the front and someone asked him to fetch water for a soldier completely mutilated by a bomb and who everyone knew would die very soon (before he was back with his drinking bottle), he'd do as he was asked and come back with the water. It was ridiculous, he knew it was. But for the mayor to suggest he played schoolmaster . . . he might as well award him a medal for stupidity!

But was there any way he could refuse? In the morning he was alone, lunchtime was the same and the evening too. No one ever knocked at his door, except by mistake. No one ever rapped on his window to get him to come as quickly as possible. In his house there wasn't a single movement, a single shifting of the air caused by anyone other than himself. How nice it would have been to feel the air moved by a woman's leg while he sat quietly in his armchair reading the newspaper. Proof of his own existence.

And look after children? He knew nothing about children. Children don't go to war, that was all he knew about them. But anything was better than this vacuum.

"Mr Mayor, you do me a great honour. I'd be delighted to accept this task." Like every inhabitant in the village, the Captain was a finely crafted liar.

That's how I came to spend many, many summer days by his side as a child. It was inconceivable to get to the beach on foot from the village, so for the youngest of us, the sea was unreachable. Always visible, always there, right under our eyes, its smell wafting up to our noses, but still unreachable. We met at two in the afternoon under the scorching bus shelter, and the colourful Captain won us over: the strong handshake he granted each of us transformed us momentarily into adults. I was frightened of no longer being a child but instantly reverted to being one if he raised his voice. Fear and appeal. Colour and darkness. When I watched him walk slowly towards us, his great muscular frame on the horizon, his dark skin, his white teeth, I'd glance left and right to map potential escape routes. "Don't worry," Fabrizio used to say, "if he's decided to kill you, no bolt-hole will ever be safe enough to keep you from him." Oh, the pleasure of knowing you're lost, surrendered up to a more powerful being. I smiled.

The first time he introduced himself to us, my friends and I weren't sure what to call him. Papa had told me to call him plain Mister. "He's a civilian now, Giacomo. We're in peacetime and there are no soldiers in the village now." Obviously, Mama was opposed to this and wanted me to call him Captain. "Your son's not in the army, why should he call a swimming supervisor Captain?" Papa asked, grabbing this opportunity to fire a few poisoned arrows. He wanted to discredit the soldier, because he loathed anyone who carried or had carried arms. Only paintbrushes found favour in his eyes.

In the end it was the soldier who resolved the question, as if he'd anticipated our embarrassment: "Call me Captain," he announced to the whole group. A categorical imperative that no one dared contradict, and certainly not me. "Call me Captain," a phrase I came across, nearly exactly the same, a few years later in Melville's novel: "Call me Ishmael." The first words of the book. Of course, it was all about the nearly, but when I'd read that opening, the Captain, my one, the one who took us down to the sea, came right back centre stage. I was in Marseille, a student sitting in a freezing university library. For a moment I was back under a scorching bus shelter, quaking with fear as the soldier drew closer. In my pocket was the coin my parents had given me for the bus fare. In my bag, an unsuitable snack of bread and cheese. And a book, it doesn't really matter which. Reading on the beach, the sound of the wind in my ears, the sand clinging to my skin. All that was worth a bit of fear.

When we reached the beach, the Captain would stay on the promontory and watch us. He didn't take his eyes off us for a moment: I could feel them on me as I undressed, on me and everywhere else. Captain, I used to think, the enemies have gone, no one's interested in our terrible land, relax, come and swim with us. He never did. A real Drogo, counting water droplets, focused on his pathetic mission. The truth was, as he admitted to me during our conversation, he couldn't swim. "A captain must always give the impression he can do everything!" he explained. "In actual fact I was terrified of the water. I knew that if any of you got into difficulties, I wouldn't have been able to save you. I didn't dare tell the mayor. I was supposed to set an example. Can you imagine an example with a rubber ring and armbands, like a little child? No, I couldn't. I had to keep up the illusion. The heroic soldier watching over his troops while they took a dip. Luckily you were careful."

* * *

"I'm very happy that you're meeting up with your childhood hero, but where've you got to with the translation?"

"I'm making progress, making progress. I get the feeling you're a bit cynical about the Captain. He means a lot to me."

"Why don't you bring him back to Marseille? You told me he was single . . . That reminds me of an Edith Piaf song, *Mon legionnaire*, do you remember it? . . . 'He was slim, he was beautiful, he smelt of lovely warm sand . . .'"

"Carlo, that's enough of your nasty comments."

"Your life's full of captains at the moment!"

"You're absolutely right."

"Concentrate on Ahab, he'll do you more good than this chap who took you down to the sea."

"What about you, though? Did you go down to the sea much?"

"Hardly ever. It was too far and my parents hated it."

"You needed a Captain!"

"I'm frightened of the water, and besides, sand's full of germs. To be honest, I've never felt the need for the sea. Did you know I had a friend who drowned?"

"No."

"In the sea. He was bowled over by a wave and then he sank like a stone. He was found three days later with a starfish in his mouth."

"That's horrible!"

"Yes. Anyway, none of this tells me when you'll get this translation back to me. My publicity strategy is ready: we've got presentation stands, posters, a press campaign . . . All that's missing is the text!"

"The most important part . . ."

"Yes."

I had a teacher at high school who pronounced the word "text" as if he were possessed. Every lesson he'd tell us that the text was everything, the text was always right . . . the text, the text, a calabash of water for a man lost in the desert. The life-saving text. Carlo had got to that point. He was waiting for his text and his whole life spiralled around the anticipation. His family must have been bored of hearing about this text. His barber (he did have a bit of hair left), his butcher (he saw him once a week, just to reassure him), they were all overrun by the text . . . the one I *wasn't* writing.

"Giacomo, you need to hurry up."

There were practically tears in his voice, but the man in despair wasn't the one you would have thought.

"I want to deliver serious, sound, flawless work. Then everyone will be in awe of your publishing company."

To calm Carlo, to soothe him, you had to appeal to his emotions and get him to believe that time was synonymous with quality, and that this quality would bring him glory and recognition. To be honest, I wasn't making much progress. My mind was too full of life on the island, my grandmother, the Captain, my family and everything I'd wanted to do for many years. Here the monastic work of translation went onto the backburner. There was too much noise. That was why I'd left!

Carlo seemed to be appeased by my argument, but I then had a moment of madness . . . we sometimes say things that wipe out everything we've tried so hard to achieve. I should have ended the conversation, stopped right there, taken my leave on the grounds that the text was sitting there waiting for me. As if a text could ever wait for someone. I took another direction, a catastrophic one. For no reason.

"I've almost finished, Carlo."

For many years, the signal on the island was appalling, and when communicating with the mainland, you caught only every other word of what the person on the other end was saying. It used to give me an excuse to cut short my mother's daily phone calls asking about every single detail of my life, a bit like those journalists who slavishly cover the Giro d'Italia cycle race blow by blow. "Lemond broke away from the pack today, Hainault had a puncture . . ." I didn't want to tell her anything. Besides, my life was a lot less eventful than a cycling stage around the Alps. It was flatter, not such a bumpy ride. Unfortunately for me, our voices eventually took to crossing the Mediterranean unimpeded. Clearly audible.

"Have you really? I'm so glad. If you were here, I'd hug you."

"Sadly, I'm too far away for that."

"I'll call you back soon. By the way, you should read *Translator's Monthly*, there's a piece about you."

"Oh, I didn't know. Speak soon, Carlo."

★ ★ ★

There's a bookshop in our village. That's an astonishing sentence: a bookshop in such a hostile place (hostile because the roads are difficult and the people not very inclined to conversation). I went there to buy *Translator's Monthly*. If it said something about me, it was bound to make for good reading. Maurizio, the bookseller, had returned to the island after living in France for many years and had decided to open his establishment on the main street, a choice spot for a shop, and I'd waited impatiently for it to open. I no longer had to beg my father to drive me into town to buy books. Maurizio's plan was wonderful: bringing books out to the countryside, bringing culture to a place where it was usually cruelly lacking. Even the Ministry of Cultural Affairs thought that we little villagers lost in the mountains weren't interested in anything but sheep and pigs. It was a radical and dangerous vision. In fact, if you never nourish a population culturally, their brains are bound to rot. The government wanted to keep us stupid, because the stupid never complain. I have to say, we'd got so used to not having a bookshop that no one in the village felt deprived. We coped without.

When Maurizio came back from France with his idea to set one up, he had to meet the mayor and other bigwigs who were deciding how the former cheesemonger should be used. Because yes, the bookshop would be taking over from a cheesemonger. The mayor wasn't a great one for literature. He'd read one book in his life, *Romeo and Juliet*. We all knew this because he never stopped quoting from it. Whatever the situation, he found a way to drop in an extract, a sentence, a scene, and this eventually became insufferable. A balcony, a goblet – Shakespeare was everywhere. In the end the mayor gave Maurizio permission, on condition that the bookshop was called Capulet. Why not Montague, I hear you ask? Well, he felt that sounded too French and, as Maurizio had suffered a broken heart over a French woman, the mayor preferred not to give him too many reminders of the country he'd lived in for many years.

To my considerable surprise, the alterations to convert from one business to another didn't take very long . . . which meant that on the day of the opening, a strong smell of cheese still lingered in the air, very strong in fact. If you closed your eyes, you had no trouble picturing ewes being milked rather than books waiting to be sold. Maurizio had waited a long time for some premises to be free but, as I've already said, people in our village aren't keen on dying too young. Before ninety is even considered a sin! Giovanni, the cheesemonger, had gone west after ninety-three springs, and that was only the official number. The springs are very long on our island, so he must actually have been more than a hundred.

Maurizio had trawled from one end of the island to the other to tell people about the bookshop opening. He was very driven. Fabrizio and I were there an hour before the event – we didn't want to miss it! No shops ever opened, so a *bookshop* . . . I was beside myself. I talked about it a lot at home. Mama predicted a sorry fate for the Frenchman, because – oh yes – given that he'd chosen to leave our island for France, that was what people called him. With a note of resentment. As if no one had any right to go and check out anywhere else, as if we were prisoners in this village and on this island. As if those who tried to get away would forever be cursed.

When I went into the bookshop I realized Maurizio would never get rid of the smell of pecorino. He was lining books up on a shelf, busying away in a sleeveless woollen cardigan and trousers that were far too small for him. From behind he looked like a stooped old man.

"Hello, Maurizio, I'm hoping you might have a particular magazine."

"Giacomo! How nice to see you! Have you been back in the village long?"

"A couple of weeks, I think. I lose track of time here."

"It's because the air's pure, that's all there is to it. When you say a 'particular' magazine, do you mean something a bit naughty?"

"No! Definitely not!"

"But you'd have every right to, Giacomo, you're a grown man now. Your mama can't scold you. And don't forget, most great authors are absolutely filthy. Think of Sade and Apollinaire . . . very naughty, the lot of them. And without photos, too. Just with their words."

"You may well be right, my friend, but I'm looking for something completely boring, the *Translator's Monthly*. Do you have it?"

"For goodness' sake, it's all I do have! I've been ordering it ever since I knew you were a great translator."

"Not all that great."

"Wait there, I'll go and get it for you."

Maurizio climbed a small set of steps and reached for a copy of the magazine. He wasn't lying, he had the whole collection.

"There you are, the latest issue, hot off the press."

"Thank you, Maurizio."

"Do you need anything else?"

"Not for now, no. I'll be back, though."

"I've lost count of the customers who are meant to be coming back . . . If they really did come back, I'd need a shop ten times the size of this one!"

At the end of the day, I was like all the others, I never did go back. There was indeed something about me in *Translator's Monthly*: I was mentioned as one of the most promising translators working today. There were words in there to make my mother weep. And me too, if I'm honest, mostly because this arbitrary ranking wouldn't help me conquer the translation of *Moby Dick*.

* * *

I was still in Sardinia on my birthday. Originally, I was only meant to stay a few days but because nothing was happening as anticipated – Grandma wasn't dying – I'd made up my mind to hang around a bit in the land of my birth. Thirty-six. The night before, I'd set my alarm for five o'clock because my parents were morning people, and I slipped out without a sound. I knew Mama would throw her arms around my neck the minute she saw me . . . so I made sure she wouldn't see me. I left a copy of *Translator's Monthly* in the sacred dining room, open on the page where my name was mentioned. It was cruel, I knew that. I didn't want to hurt my mother (my father attached no importance to commemorations), but if she'd arranged a family meal, I knew how it would end up: shouting and arguing and a lot of noise about nothing. I'd decided to spend the day quietly by the sea. Firstly, to fish and then to enjoy the beach for a while before the tourists showed up. I came across the usual dogs in the village, but I was in a car so they couldn't do me any harm. I turned into the Captain's street and he was waiting for me, dressed in every colour under the sun.

"Call me Captain," he said with a smile. We'd agreed to go down to the sea together. The Captain hadn't been there for years. Of course, he didn't know it was my birthday. We wouldn't be marking the day. On the way there we came across a family of wild boar who didn't seemed bothered by us driving past. Not one of them ran away. The Captain asked me to turn back and he took pictures of them. I've never thought of wild boar as particularly photogenic but my passenger thought they were.

"Look at that, they see so many people, they're no longer frightened. They'll be like dogs soon."

"Well, then we'll abandon them like dogs."

"No, you're wrong there, we'll keep them till the very end, to eat them. Have you ever eaten dog meat? It's indigestible. That's why we don't eat them. Dogs think we love them but they're wrong. We'd eat them if they were good enough."

"Whereas wild boar . . ."

"Is delicious, yes! You can drive on, I've got my pictures. Without going to any trouble, without hiding for two days and nights. Today must be blessed. You bring me luck, Giacomo."

My past as a sporting disaster hadn't prepared me for this. Not me, the king of failure, the worst goalie in the worst football team in history.

"I seem to remember you played football back in the day."

"That's right."

"You never thought of going into that rather than translation?"

"Never."

"Why not?"

"Football was just a hobby, translation is my passion."

"I see. What I mean is, football could have brought you fame."

"I'm not looking for fame."

"That's why you were buying the newspaper the other day . . ."

"It was for my mother."

"Fabrizio told me she bought the whole stock."

"It wasn't for the fame, Captain, it was for recognition of my work."

"And without recognition would you not be able to do anything?"

"Without recognition I'd do less. Less well, less quickly. What about you, have you experienced fame?"

"For a few weeks, yes. It was extraordinary."

We reached the creek where we were going to fish. It didn't appear in any tourist guides, which meant we'd be left in peace. How many places like this were there left on the whole island? No more than a dozen and I was lucky enough to know one of them. There was a man there, a fisherman who never stopped reeling in catches. He was helping himself as if plucking them from a stall at a fishmonger. Easy as you please. The water was clear. And still. Every now and then a ripple would disturb it. But not for long. The occasional bird would alight on it to cool off and then fly away again. The smell of the scrubland hung in the air. This is what I missed when I was away. A sense of solitude and infinite pleasure. There was no need to talk. We just had to look. Everything was on offer for those who knew how.

We could see the fish. They looked as if they'd be easy to catch. But they actually made fools of us. They knew who they were dealing with. I was as bad at fishing as I was at football. Luckily, the Captain proved more talented. At lunchtime he lit a fire and grilled the two sea breams he'd caught. I hadn't caught anything except for a couple of defenceless hermit crabs. The fish was delicious, much better than wild boar. Lighter. I released the hermit crabs before setting off towards the beach. An arbitrary decision, because I could. The fisherman waved goodbye, slightly taunting.

The word *lido* originally comes from the barrier of sand that encloses the Venice lagoon, and the rest of Italy has adopted the term for large commercialized beaches that crawl with people in summer. The Captain used to take us to the *lido* every Thursday. Today the roles were reversed. Dotted about the beach were the parasols left by regulars while they had their lunch. No one would move them, even though there was no official document to assign them that patch of sand. It was a gentle appropriation, ratified by the passage of time. We found a spot where we were sure we wouldn't disturb anyone. It was two o'clock and anyone who dared lie out on the sand risked being instantly grilled. Like our lunchtime bream. The locals had gone home to take shelter and eat. It was just us and a few tourists who longed to be by the sea. People who'd only just arrived (they were betrayed by their diaphanous skin). They threw themselves into the water with obvious delight, oblivious to the fact that, come evening, they'd be tending to burns all over their bodies. And they'd come back the next day covered from head to foot, usually wearing long white T-shirts to ward off the heat. Their holidays would be ruined by those first minutes when everything seemed so wonderful and welcoming, even the sun.

"If you're too hot we could go into the pine woods."

"Are you worrying about me? I fought in Africa. I know everything there is to know about the sun."

"I wouldn't want anything to happen to you."

"Don't you worry. It went up to fifty degrees in Ethiopia, so this little bit of sun's not going to do me any harm."

We sweated copiously. The sand was baking hot and the horizon quivered slowly.

"Tell me, Giacomo, are you married?"

"I was."

"Is your wife dead?"

"No, I left her. Well, we left each other. It was better that way. Jessica and I went through some difficult stuff and, as is often the case, our relationship blew apart mid-flight. But don't worry, she's still alive, which is a good thing, actually. I bump into her every now and then. She's a translator. We work for the same publisher. How about you, Captain?"

"Never married – impossible! Love's always been impossible for me. If love wasn't impossible we wouldn't try so hard to catch it, it would be easy. I always fell in love with impossible women. A general's wife, for example, Carmella, a Venetian woman I met at an official reception. A stunning woman, no one could take their eyes off her, everyone wanted her."

"Did you have an affair with her?"

"Because it was impossible, yes! Me, the little captain, in the general's bed. Not when he was there, though, don't worry! In Carmella's arms. Her name reminded me of the delicious *caramelle* sweets I used to love as a child. We always met in secret, it was an adventure for both of us. It suited me better than a conventional, official relationship. Furtive rendezvous at night, listening out for every noise, being careful not to get caught."

"A bit like the owl that wanted to catch the rat."

"A bit like that, yes. It took patience and precautions but . . ."

"But?"

"But one day the general caught us. He'd hidden on the balcony. I was the rat and he was the owl."

"What happened?"

"What always happens when two military men find themselves in that sort of situation. A frank discussion and then Africa for me."

"And what about Carmella?"

"She claimed I was just a fling, a symptom of a loss of interest on her husband's part. It brought him to his senses and their life went on as before. But I have no regrets, love should be impossible, believe me. The more impossible it is, the more beautiful it is."

I decided to have a swim because the heat was unbearable. The Captain was happier going into the shade among the pine trees.

"I still can't swim," he said with a note of disappointment.

"No, but you can fish."

I'd dived into that water dozens of times – always a little carefully because I'm no swimming virtuoso – so I knew the place and all its quirks, every stone on the ground, every change in level, every current. There were no surprises, but I wouldn't have swapped it for anywhere else in the world. I came back to it again and again, as if endlessly translating the same book, with the same enjoyment. It was as though there was a part of me inscribed into the landscape, a bit of my parents, a bit of my family and all the island's inhabitants. Each of us had left a trace and we immediately recognized ourselves here. As for people just passing through, they didn't stay long enough to notice us, we were just shadows talking a strange language. We'd have to keep them here longer, make them spend more than the week or fortnight they managed to afford once a year, so they could discover us in a different way and finally see us.

A bus stopped above the beach, very nearby. Thirty or so holidaymakers alighted with their tour guide, who gave the place a one-sentence introduction and suggested they had a nice swim. "We'll leave in an hour," he said loudly so they would all be sure to hear him. One hour to discover part of my universe. The group separated: the more enthusiastic members threw themselves into the water while others bought themselves a drink or an ice-cream from the little van that had been coming here for as long as I could remember, an ageless vehicle that only appeared in fine weather. How did it get here? You turned up one morning and there it was, as if by magic. The salesmen changed but not the van. I was sitting on my towel drying off when a tourist came over to me. People in swimwear form a community apart; we find it easier talking to someone in the same state of undress as ourselves.

"Excuse me, do you live around here?"

"Yes, you could say."

"Do you know any nice spots in the area?"

"Are you staying long?"

"We're flying home in two days. We've travelled all round the island. It's glorious."

"Thank you. If you have a chance, have a look at the *Domus de Janas*."

"What are they?"

"Tombs."

"Oh really? I'm not sure my friends'll want to visit tombs. Are they near the sea?"

"No, inland. In practically every village. In mine, for example, Arza—"

"We never go inland."

"You should."

"*Domus de Janas*, is that what you said?"

"That's right. Fairy houses."

"Fairy houses, fairy tombs. Thanks for the advice."

★   ★   ★

The water droplets didn't take long to dry and left salty white marks on my skin. I headed into the pine forest to find the

Captain. I imagined he'd watched me intently, keeping an eye on me as he had when I was a child. There were people everywhere, keeping out of the sun; I came across more of them with every tree. Groups that had virtually set up house with tables, chairs and the full complement of equipment needed for survival out of doors. The trees must have loathed them, probably talking amongst themselves about these vulgar invasive nuisances. I couldn't see the Captain . . . perhaps he'd joined one of these groups, but I doubted that. I scoured through the trees for a long time, walking over litter wantonly abandoned there, and the odd towel left out to dry. I was reprimanded. "You could be more careful!" said a man about as hairy as Chewbacca. I looked away, thinking, So it's okay to have a go at someone about where they choose to walk, but you give yourself permission to pollute the pine forests with your cigarette butts . . .

I reached a clearing where a group of children were playing football. I stopped to watch them as they shouted to each other, hurled abuse for illegal moves and ran about all over the place.

"Would you like to play, mister?"

"No, thanks."

"Don't you know how to?"

"Yes, very well, actually."

"Let's see!"

"I'm recovering from an injury, I can't."

"What injury?"

"Cruciate ligaments."

"Cruciate, that's bad!"

The children clustered round and looked at my knees.

"Look, you can see the scar."

I did have an old scar on my right knee, a memento from the umpteenth defeat: when an opponent had taken a powerful shot at the goal, I'd thrown myself on my side in the hope of stopping it, and the ball had come into the net just as a piece of glass on the goal line made its way into my knee. It went in easily, not having to force my thin, tender skin. Manuella pulled it out with one swift flick. I had to pinch my left thigh hard to take my mind off the pain. I held back my tears so I wouldn't look soft in front of her. I still had the mark on my right knee, the mark that these children were taking as evidence of an operation on my cruciate ligaments.

"Will you never be able to play football again?"

To a child this question felt fundamentally important because football was vital. There was compassion in the boy's voice. If I'd told him I'd never walk again he wouldn't have been so moved. I personally would have been very happy if I'd "never played football again".

"Yes, I will soon, but I need to wait a bit longer."

"Will you come back?"

"Of course."

Some people alter crime scenes, and I'd done that with the truth. We should never lie to children; never let them believe they're good at something when we can tell they're incurably bad at it; never make them think they're exceptionally intelligent when they're obviously intellectually challenged; never play on their gullibility. We should have been told that our football team was useless and that the Captain couldn't swim. I'll have to come back one day and tell the truth about everything.

The Captain's hand came to rest firmly on my shoulder. I hadn't seen him come over.

"Have you been looking for me?"

"Yes, all over the place."

"I was sleeping. The heat got the better of me in the end. Do you want to play football with these children?"

"I'll be fine, thanks. They're much too good for me . . ."

* * *

The wind sometimes blows here all the way from Africa. It flushed us out of the pine forest and started whipping up baking-hot sand that blurred our vision. Tiny grains filled our eyes, so we headed back to the car with our heads down. The tourists ran off the beach: they'd been promised sunshine, not sand. Towels went flying, beach balls made their getaway and people darted about, trying to keep hold of their belongings. When all these people were snuggled up at home in the middle of winter, only venturing outside to get more wood for the fire, they'd remember this day when they had to run away from what the summer offered them. What was initially a hostile event would evolve over time into a good memory; they would even look back on it with longing. At the end of the day, everything is just a question of perception.

I dropped the Captain at his house and went home. Mama was sitting in the living room, still as a statue.

"You're ashamed of us."

"What makes you say that?"

"You're ashamed of us. Doing this to me on your birthday – you, my only child. Going off without a word, without letting me hug you."

"I didn't know my birthday meant so much to you."

"I'd got everything ready, a wonderful meal, the table nicely laid . . . the three of us were meant to celebrate it together."

"I'm really sorry."

"Too late. There were presents too. Listen, Giacomo, being ignored by neighbours or former colleagues and the like is one thing, but being ignored by your own son is the worst humiliation."

"Mama, I didn't mean to. I just wanted to be on my own for a bit, somewhere quiet. I don't like commemorations. Of any sort. We can eat together this evening. I'm going to see Nonna, and I'll be back. Forgive me."

"You should spend more time with the living than the dead, Giacomo."

★　★　★

When I got to the hospital I found the spot for Grandma's bed empty. I knew she wasn't dead . . . maybe her ploy had been found out. I went to the nurses' station where I was told the doctor would come to talk to me. And that was all. I wasn't familiar with the medical world, it frightened me, as it does anyone who acknowledges they'll have to get to know it someday. I stood there waiting, facing the nurses who chatted away, perfectly relaxed. I strained my ears to hear whether they mentioned the deception that had been discovered. Unfortunately, I only caught snatches of their conversation. Every now and then one of them would turn to me and smile. Grandma had definitely pulled the wool over their eyes. Then I started pacing up and down the corridor, making the most of its length so I wasn't just staring at the nurses. An "I'm here" rang out eventually, releasing me from this mind-numbingly repetitive exercise. It was Alessandra. In my imagination we were so close that I allowed myself this familiarity. In the real world, things were a little different.

"Good afternoon. There's something I need to tell you."

"I know."

"Have the nurses told you?"

"Yes. They're doing an incredible job, I really admire the medical staff here."

"Thank you."

"So how did . . . ?"

"Very well."

"How do you mean?"

"The tests showed no abnormalities."

"Is she coming out of hospital?"

"Is that a joke?"

"No."

"She's unconscious!"

"I forgot."

"Well, I didn't."

Grandma's deception was still up and running. I'd had my hand on my wallet from the start of our conversation, ready to whip out my article, but I didn't think this was the right moment. I'd just made myself look like an idiot to Alessandra.

"Have you worked here long?"

"A few weeks. Why?"

"Because I'd never seen you before we met the other day."

"Do you come to the hospital a lot?"

"Never, before my grandmother was here."

"Do you live locally?"

"Marseille."

"Well then, it's only natural you haven't seen me. I don't know Marseille."

"It's a beautiful city."

"I'm sure it is."

"Are you from Rome?"

"Yes, how did you guess?"

"Everyone here's from Rome. They say, 'All roads lead to Rome' but they could also say, 'All doctors come from Rome'!"

"Nice one!"

I wasn't proud of my pathetic and falsely intellectual wordplay, but it had helped me go back up in the doctor's opinion.

"I'm a translator."

"Perfect."

Alessandra's answer didn't make any sense. It was about on a level with my statement. Why did I tell her that? Why tell this stranger about my job? To impress her? Fighter pilot, yes. Secret agent, yes. Quantum physics researcher, yes. But translator . . . Who could be impressed by a translator? Particularly as I hadn't had the chance to expand on my speciality: novels. The doctor (who I didn't feel quite so close to now) might have thought I translated instructions for flat-pack furniture, or lawnmower manuals. It didn't say "I'm translating *Moby Dick*" on my T-shirt.

The ensuing silence was rather awkward.

"I translate novels. Mostly. The noble side of translation. But please don't think I have anything against people who translate instruction leaflets and manu—"

"It must be a very interesting job."

"Yes."

"To get back to your grandmother, we'll be bringing her back to the ward soon. You'll be able to see her."

"She means a lot to me."

"That's only natural, Mister . . ."

"Call me Giacomo."

"Okay, Giacomo."

"Thank you, Doctor."

There, of course, I was waiting for a "Call me Alessandra". And anyone would have expected the same. Naturally. I saw her at the hospital every day, I'd still be seeing her for some time to come, and I found her very attractive (for a Roman), so it was logical to envisage becoming more familiar. To me, the Romans had a reputation for being distant, aloof, a bit cold. Not very friendly either. Nice to look at, like the monuments in their city. My ex-wife was Roman.

"My pleasure. Goodbye."

Try as I might to see these words from every angle, I couldn't discern any form of familiarity in them. They were collectively distant. And beautiful, too, if beauty was based on courtesy. The Coliseum seen from a speeding taxi.

Grandma was wheeled back to her space by a hospital porter who looked like a bodybuilder, and who pushed her bed with the same ease as he would an empty shopping trolley. Grandma soon noticed I wasn't on my best form . . . and that it wasn't down to the injury I'd sustained to my knee twenty-five years earlier. I told her about the doctor, and Grandma said she'd noticed I acted differently when she was around. I didn't ask how she'd noticed because she always had her eyes closed when Alessandra came over. I didn't feel like having an argument. The elderly often think they know things, by a sort of premonition. Nonna knew everything because I'd told her everything. I was thirty-six but, sitting there next to her, I was like a little boy again, a little boy dreaming of kissing a girl.

* * *

The meal was about as dismal as the rain splattering on the windows. Mama had warmed up the food she'd prepared for lunchtime and it was inevitably not so tasty. Papa commented on this and, astonishingly, my mother didn't fly into a rage. All her rage was focused on me and my absence. My parents claimed they hadn't even eaten lunch when they realized I'd slipped away. They'd waited for me for a long time before declaring me an ungrateful son. I'd dulled their appetites (even though there was some leftover lasagne in the fridge). I didn't believe them for a moment.

"I really am sorry."

"It doesn't matter."

Only the sound of chewing interrupted the contagiously stiff atmosphere in the room. It was a rubbish birthday. Like all the others. Until I'd left for the mainland, I'd had a succession of sad birthdays with no surprises. The same meal, the same presents. If I was hoping for an item of clothing, I'd be given a magician's set; if I wanted playing cards, I was given a mask and snorkel. My parents always got it wrong. To be honest, none of us were very good at birthdays in my family. I knew they didn't like the presents I gave them either. And the presents they gave each other were only ever a disappointment. It was a fact, an unchanging constant. When my friends talked about perfect celebrations with fireworks, trips to Cagliari (no one ever went further than that) and famous restaurants, I envied them this perfected art of pleasing another person. I wasn't familiar with it at all.

Once the meal was over my father got up and went to fetch my present from the garage. It was a tradition for Christmas and birthday presents to be kept in the garage, but never cars because they made the garage too dirty. Along with the dining room where we didn't eat, we had a garage where we didn't park any cars. My father was the one who dealt with the presents and the only one who could reach them because they were kept on such a high shelf. He handed me two parcels in a sombre silence. Mama pretended not to be interested in watching me open them. And yet, as is often the case and even if they didn't like it to be obvious, the givers were more impatient than the receiver.

"I honestly don't deserve this."

"Go on, open them, you can stay at home for your birthday next year."

"This year's a bit of an exception, Papa. I should be at my place in Marseille."

"So it's your grandmother's fault, is it?"

"I didn't mean that. It's just that I live in France. There's nothing to stop you coming to see me."

Since I'd been in Marseille they'd come to visit only once because, apparently, that was how it was. The journey only went one way. The island's coast was their boundary, the edge of their world.

"That's the plan."

"Fantastic! When?"

"Soon. Go on, don't change the subject, open your presents. They're going to cheer you up, seeing as you spent your birthday all alone on a beach. How sad!"

"But I wasn't alone."

"What?"

"I was with the Captain."

I saw the disappointment on Papa's face. This revelation was a real affront to him. The man of the house had had his child seized from under his nose by an old soldier, a man whose moment of glory was long past. His little Giacomo would rather spend his day with that old tramp than with him. I could read all this on Papa's face because I knew the book by heart. I'd seen it snap shut so often when a storm approached.

"Is he all that interesting? Is he really better than me?"

"But I'm not comparing you. You're my father, he's something different, and I'm fond of him."

At that point, I should have told Papa that I loved him and that this made all the difference. Except, it was unimaginable on the island for a son to say, "I love you" to his father. That was just the way of things. It was so stupid. There were ancient traditions that flowed in my veins. And in my father's too. Papa left the room. Doors slammed. I knew everything he'd done for me. The tough work with the reek of paint in the pounding sun. The never-ending days. Worrying that he couldn't give me what other children had. Worrying when I had a temperature and they had to take turns at my bedside all through the night, laying cool flannels on my forehead. And then going to work the next morning with dead eyes, but not saying a word to his employer. And the university fees he'd had to pay. I'd blown his whole life.

"You've upset your father, Giacomo."

"I didn't mean to."

"That's what you always say, you never mean to. But you still hurt us. You're intelligent, so be careful next time. Look after your parents."

Mama left to join my father. I heard the front door close. I was alone with my presents. There were no indulgent eyes watching me now, just the photos on the wall. I felt as if all the family ancestors were staring at me with loathing. Even the baby in one of the pictures seemed to be saying I'd gone too far and had succeeded in hurting my parents. And this was no minor footballer's scrape but a deeper wound. Like the prow of a boat carving through the water and settling deep into it. The baby in the picture was me.

I didn't try to persuade those eyes loaded with resentment. The defeat was ratified. And so was my mistake.

Inside the parcels I found an illustrated copy of *Moby Dick* and a painting by my father of Captain Ahab standing on the whale in the middle of a storm. A crazed, desperate man, full of rage. The painting was influenced by Turner, with a fiery sky and light everywhere. Painters in the village were talented copycats. One worked in the style of Picasso, another Chagall. Papa idolized Turner because, he claimed, Turner managed to make the English sky the most beautiful in the world. More beautiful than the Sardinian sky, in other words.

I was still convinced Papa could do better than painting

buildings and the odd fresco in the village. All he needed was the nerve, because he had plenty of vision. With everything he'd accepted and kept quiet over the years, he could have painted incredible pictures. Luminous, noisy and turbulent. A Sardinian Turner. It was a funny idea, a Sardinian Turner. The South and the North, the heat and the cold. Sadly for him, he'd only ever be a little exterior decorator, disappointed in his own son. Because I would probably never tell him everything I was thinking. My parents had genuinely touched me this time, but they didn't know it.

*   *   *

My parents spent the night at my grandmother's house, hoping the cat would give them more affection than their son had. The common denominator in our family was escape. The minute something bothered us, we ran away, not to sort out the problem but to avoid having it right there in front of us. We did need a reconciliation, though. In the meantime, I was buckling down to work on *Moby Dick*, when voices out in the street interrupted my work. My commitment and concentration were so flimsy that a fly buzzing past slightly more noisily than usual would have been enough to give me pause. It's a feeling every student knows. Your exams are looming, you should be working, but the weather's so nice outside. The warmth of spring, those forgotten colours, the newfound laughter. Work is torture. Work, travail, *tripalium*. Although I was long past being a student, that part of my life still haunted me and my memories. I did need to move on to something else some time.

I left Ahab hunting for his whale and went over to the window. A tourist bus was trying to turn down the street; it was so wide that the driver had to manoeuvre with tremendous precision. The engine roared and the brakes produced a smell of burning. Several villagers – elderly people nearing their century – suddenly had an impromptu job as runway personnel, though without the hi-vis gear. They all gave their considered advice to the driver, whose face streamed with sweat. They argued about the best solution and shouted and cursed at their rival guides. If they'd been on an aircraft carrier, all the planes would have ended up in the sea. The poor driver was getting frantic, peering left and right while everyone gestured at him.

The best thing to do in a stressful situation is to stop and think, that's what school is meant to teach us. During his training the driver must have been confronted with simulated fires, accidents and blow-outs. But no one had anticipated that he would one day find himself stuck in a narrow street surrounded by an army of competitively bad-tempered nonagenarians. A critical situation, then, but not a desperate one. Ahab did get the better of the whale; the bus would eventually be extricated. The passengers inside pressed their faces up to the windows. Anxious faces. I watched this chaotic scene and didn't miss any of it. I was still too young to intervene, I was a good fifty years short on experience.

The bus was registered in France. In the end the driver decided to turn off the ignition. The tourists alighted slowly and with some difficulty because, when they emerged from the vehicle, they ran straight into the wall of a house – one way of getting a feel for how locals really live, a far cry from their hotel where there was so much space and no one was old. I recognized the man who'd come to talk to me on the beach, and whistled to attract his attention. He turned round and came over to the house.

"We're meant to be seeing the *Domus de Janas*. Is it far from here?"

"It's at the end of the street. So you managed to persuade your friends after all."

"The hotel arranged a visit in a flash. But the driver should never have tried to come down this tiny street."

"The last time this happened, the bus had to be completely dismantled and put back together in a garage."

"Really?"

"The locals here are liars."

"You're a local, if I remember rightly."

"Yes. Shall I take you to the *Domus*? It's sort of my fault you're stuck here . . ."

"Of course it isn't! But we'd be delighted if you showed us the way. Let's leave the driver to sort this out."

"He won't be alone, just look how keen the 'younger' inhabitants are to help him."

"Is it always like this?"

"Yes, Sardinian hospitality is a tradition, a bit like in Greece. Everyone helps everyone else. In theory. The truth is, the elderly get a bit bored. Some have been retired for nearly fifty years. That's a long time! So they watch what's going on under their noses. A car exhaust making a slightly whiny noise, someone tripping, an argument . . ."

I led the group to the *Domus*, and they were a little disappointed. Very disappointed, in fact. Maybe they were expecting to find huge monuments right in the middle of the street. Pyramids in a Sardinian village lost up in the mountains. A spectacular site. There was none of that. Just an unpretentious, tumbledown little building, spoiled somewhat by the odd nutcase heading home after a heavy night out. I didn't want to leave them feeling cheated so I started talking, explaining the role of these *Domus*, their strong symbolism and the magical times I'd spent in them: the discussions with friends, the fits of laughter when we pretended to be prehistoric men, and the floods of tears when Fabrizio told me he could no longer play football because of his condition. Our small lives in a small edifice built by small but very, very old men – far older than the ones giving bad advice to the bus driver.

"You really love this island, it's obvious from the way you talk about it."

"I love it as much as I hate it. When I'm far away I miss the place, deep inside. When I'm here everything about it irritates me, everything happens too slowly and nothing changes. But I wouldn't want you to have a bad impression of our country. You have to forgive it its strange ways."

The bus eventually managed to manoeuvre its way out of the street. The driver emerged looking as red as my uncle Gavino's tomatoes and was offered refreshment at the bar on the corner: a bottle of water, "the purest in the world", which flowed from the mountains in the centre of the island. The label featured several paragraphs about its virtues and the prizes it had been awarded. Along with the names of the scientists who evaluated it. There must be *some* people interested in that sort of information. People who aren't really thirsty.

To the dehydrated driver it probably really did seem like the purest, sweetest water in the world after everything he'd suffered in the heat of that vehicle. A bottle of ice-cold *frizzante* water that was sure to cause him digestive problems at the end of the day. The very pinnacle of coldness and bubbliness – the greatest risk for tourists. The other visitors sat down at tables and reassured him. They were worried they wouldn't get back to the hotel, they had to keep him sweet. Everyone ordered water and laughed good-naturedly. They'd had a narrow escape! The waiter replaced their empty bottles more or less instantly. A choreography of bubbles and coldness. The tourists didn't know what they were in for. I meanwhile ordered an espresso: two millilitres of coffee lost in the bottom of a cup. Hot and devoid of bubbles.

In the end they decided to cast an eye over the murals before leaving, and took photographs of each other in front of frescoes. I pointed out one that I particularly liked: an image of three old men sitting on their chairs out in the street, with shotguns in hand. It was a good summary of life here.

In our village – this was what the tourists would remember – people painted on the walls. You didn't visit the monuments because they were too small, and centenarians gave advice to drivers but, thank goodness, the water was delicious.

★ ★ ★

Since our expedition to the beach the Captain had taken to picking me up every day. He knocked at the door and it was often my mother who opened it for him with a smile. Never my father, who still resented him, all these years later, for fighting and – especially – for coming home alive, a heroic figure in the village. He also resented him for stealing women's hearts with a few trinkets on his chest. In my father's view, it was better to paint than make war. So when he heard a knock at the door, he mumbled, "It's for you, Giacomo, it's the hero." I didn't react to this provocation, it was too funny, too witty.

My parents had already forgotten the hurt I'd caused on my birthday and had forgiven me. Parents always forgive their children because there's a part of them inside, like two planets that were one before a colossal explosion. I hadn't forgotten, though, and I thought myself lucky to have them back, even though I'd known they wouldn't stay exiled at my grand-mother's house for very long. Papa loathed Grandma's cat, he found her too invasive, in every sense of the word. Too fat, too in your face. The runaway parents ended up coming home, for their own comfort.

The Captain and I went fishing every morning. I actually hated fishing but it meant I could spend time with the old soldier. We didn't talk a great deal because we'd already told each other pretty much everything. When two old friends meet up, a great tide of apparently inexhaustible words springs up, until eventually there are only scraps of conversation left. Very soon they stop seeing each other to avoid admitting they have nothing left to say. In the creek where we'd become regulars, we always met the same expert fisherman, who just couldn't stop filling his creel. One morning, he came over to chat to us, and we had so much to talk about.

"So you were a captain in the army, then."

"Absolutely. My younger years were a succession of conflicts. Europe, Africa . . . war certainly improved my geography."

"I did military service and I have very good memories of it."

I was redundant in this conversation between two former soldiers. They discussed the names of their rifles, the gauge of the ammunition, how powerful the things were . . . A real festival of armaments. I only went to literature festivals.

"Have you ever killed someone?"

"Poor boy, if you only knew, I've killed hundreds! I was a shark. Not the old man you see now. I never gave up. You need sharp teeth to be a good soldier."

The fisherman was impressed by the Captain's words, especially when he described several of his exploits in detail. The Captain even showed us a few photographs of himself in uniform. Battered old pictures with ragged edges showing him posing proudly, carrying his rifle and wearing a serious, determined expression.

"And don't you miss the fighting?"

"Of course I do! I dream I'm at war every night, some conflict at the ends of the earth, in the middle of the desert. War is a hard drug."

Every time the Captain paused the fisherman tirelessly repeated the words, "a shark, a shark . . ." to demonstrate his full admiration. The two men were carried away with their anecdotes and had completely forgotten about me. I was about as interesting as a hermit crab. Shortly before our divorce was made official, I read some texts on my wife's phone. In one of them, addressed to her best friend Catherine, a children's author, she said I reminded her of a hermit crab because I changed my appearance so often: "Happy one day, sad another, running away the next, then coming home to hide . . ." I hadn't viewed the comparison as a compliment. Still, I didn't hold anything against the crustacean. Confronted with these two testosterone-fuelled men, my mind alighted on hermit crabs, first as a memory and then more literally because I started collecting them on the damp sand. I didn't want to kill them, just chat to them for a bit. I told my three prisoners about my wife's comment. Three, the perfect number. Three crustaceans, three men.

"And is your son a soldier?"

Given that the crabs weren't answering and I was only

whispering, I had no trouble hearing the fisherman's question. Images of my father painting and the Captain with his rifle in his hand telescoped in my mind. I didn't want to confuse them, each man should stay in his rightful place.

"He's not my son, but he might as well be. I often looked after him when he was a little boy. But he can speak for himself. Giacomo, come here."

I stopped talking to the hermit crabs and went over to the two military men, who now seemed to remember my existence. On an evolutionary scale, I was above crustaceans. The man asked his question again because he didn't know I'd heard it. He simply removed the father–son idea.

"Are you a soldier too?"

"Absolutely not. I'm a translator."

"A translator, marvellous. What do you translate?"

"Fiction."

"Would I find these books you translate in a bookshop?"

"Of course."

He took a notebook from his pocket. There was a pen inside it and the pages were smothered with a series of tiny numbers.

"I make a note of all my catches in here. Write down the name of a book you've translated. I'll go and buy it."

I wrote *Zeno's Conscience, Italo Svevo* in my finest handwriting under a long list of fish: grouper, sea bream, sea bass, sea perch, sardine . . . quite an aquarium.

"And what's this book of yours about?"

"A man who wants to stop smoking."

"Interesting! Is that all?"

"Very interesting, yes. There are other things, you'll see."

I'd spent several months with Zeno but I couldn't talk about it. I slept with him, ate with him and even spoke to him when I was talking to someone else . . . Translation gives you a taste of obsession . . . with the characters and with the author. Not wanting to betray him, trying to follow his aims without adulterating them. I felt translation was more complex than writing. Svevo was no longer around to contradict me. I remembered the scene of the marriage proposal, but didn't dare mention it. Four women, four wishes, three refusals and a marriage. The art of bouncing back in Trieste. It's always risky talking about books we've loved.

The fisherman started gathering his things and said goodbye, turning to me first.

"See you soon, Mr. Translator."

"See you soon, Mr. Fisherman."

"My name's Alessio."

"Will you tell me what you think of the book?"

"Certainly."

Then he turned to the Captain and, with great respect, shook his hand firmly. The handshake lasted some time, the two men pumping their forearms up and down, staring at each other intently. It must have been some military sign, completely beyond me. If you asked me, a handshake should last no more than two seconds. More than that, and there was something disturbing about it and, if it ever happened to me, I tried to withdraw my hand. But I wasn't a soldier. I never had been.

"Honoured to have talked to you, Alessio."

"The pleasure's all mine, Captain."

The fisherman reclaimed ownership of his hand and almost whispered the words, "A shark." He had spoken to a "shark" and this was a source of great pride to him. A shark with no shred of pity for his adversaries, a shark toughened by hardship, with impenetrable skin. A shark covered head to foot in medals. A shark that couldn't swim.

The Captain was back to the man I'd known as a child. He seemed younger, as if the conversation had allowed him to return to a previous self. Our chats didn't transform him in this way. With me he seemed to miss his past; with the fisherman he'd relived it. I felt slightly disappointed not to have the same effect, the same impact on him. Like Dr. Ignazio's granules of *Effervescente*, my active ingredient wasn't one. I had no effect.

The Captain didn't talk on the way home and sat very upright in his seat. He was no longer carrying the weight of his existence and all the woes that went with it. Every now and then he murmured the word "shark", brimming over with satisfaction at the sound of that one syllable. The disappointment had passed, and I felt comfortable in my role as chauffeur to a seasoned soldier. And never mind if there were better people than me to talk to. It was a nice open road along the coast which seemed to go on for ever. From time to time we passed a fruit-and-vegetable stall by the roadside, the watermelons were enormous. When we ate them at home, my father opened them with a knife the size of a sabre. I always shuddered to see him so easily slicing up what nature had taken weeks to build. Everyone held their breath but when we bit into that blood-red flesh we forgot our fear. Still, that knife could have chopped us in two, no problem.

"Would you like to buy anything, Captain?"

"No, thank you. I haven't brought any money, anyway."

"I can lend you some."

"You already offered that a long time ago . . . when you were a boy."

"I remember that."

"And I refused."

"Yes. Much to my disappointment."

"Well, I refuse again. A shark . . ."

Driving along the precipice, the car hovering weightless over the sea, I turned on the radio – music could only add to the perfection of the moment. One of the stations was playing a Phil Collins song. I switched it off straight away. Music is a double-edged sword, as dangerous as my father's knife.

We still weren't talking so I thought some more about my ex-wife's friend, Catherine, who was always trying to think of the next idea for a children's picture book. Well, I had a title for her, a title and the story to go with it: *The Shark that Couldn't Swim*.

★　★　★

I told Grandma all about it. Like a little boy. She didn't answer this time because there was a lot going on in the room. Some patients were leaving hospital, others were just arriving, a toing and froing worthy of a seaside hotel. Except that the destination for one of them on this particular day was the morgue. The staff didn't have time to be emotional; they busied themselves, talked softly, each perfectly fulfilling his or her duties in this chore-ography of whites. Alessandra walked back and forth several times, to my total delight. She had been assigned the care of the most elderly patients a few days ago, which meant she was responsible for my grandmother, so it was nothing to do with me.

I made the most of the opportunity to talk to her every day. I asked her endless questions about Nonna's condition, endless boring questions which she answered willingly, either because she thought I was nice (an idea that thrilled me) or because she didn't dare give short shrift to a rather tiresome visitor (an idea that thrilled me a great deal less). I was generally nice, I'd often been told that at school, so my first guess was most likely. Some of my questions were the product of my own research into my grandmother's health. I jotted down the names of conditions and repeated them, not without difficulty, to the doctor. This gave me a certain status. But as soon as Alessandra went into complicated explanations, I let go as quickly as a man with olive oil on his hands hanging from a cliff. I didn't understand a thing. Sometimes, when I hadn't had time to prepare for my visit, I would ask Alessandra about my grand-mother's hair, her nails, anything that came into my head. When I resorted to this, Alessandra adapted seamlessly to her audience, said, "It's completely unrelated" and carried on with her visits.

I kept up this little performance until Alessandra knocked it on the head after I'd asked a question about Nonna's facial hair.

"You're an intelligent man, Giacomo. I don't believe you're in the least bit interested in how hairy your grandmother is."

"But you must be aware it's been growing very quickly since—"

"Giacomo, a member of the nursing staff will deal with it."

"Good, but I was saying—"

"Giacomo."

I knew the hairiness issue wasn't a brilliant idea. I'd chosen it because I was reaching the limits of my ability to produce medical interrogations. I didn't want to aggravate my case by trying to fall back on a failed argument, but I liked it when Alessandra said my name.

"So I—"

"Giacomo."

"We could talk about all this, and other things of course, if you'd agree to meet me outside the hospital."

I was as brave as Captain Ahab on the whale's back, harpoon in hand. From Grandma's hairiness I'd segued straight to a potential date. With no harpoon for self-defence. Alessandra could have swept me aside with a single word. Ahab wasn't just brave, he was mad.

"Are you suggesting a date?"

"Yes."

A whale's back can't help but be slippery, I mustn't fall. I mustn't fall. I mustn't fall . . .

"Are you there, Giacomo?"

"Yes, um . . . sorry, yes, I'm here. I sometimes lose . . ."

"It's a yes."

"I'm planning to spend the day on the island of Caprera on Sunday. Would you like to come with me?"

"Very much so. I don't know it."

Alessandra broke into a smile at the name Caprera. But more about that later. Right now, even though I was desperate to, I knew I mustn't go running through the corridors hollering my happiness to the whole world. *Urbi et orbi.* I had to exude composure and maturity, devoid of self-satisfaction, I had to stay natural. It was impossible. I was thirty-six years old and I had tears in my eyes. I left the hospital straight after our conversation because I couldn't breathe. I hadn't slipped and fallen. I was standing on top of the whale, guiding it into the harbour.

★ ★ ★

Summer was in full bloom and the island was invaded with tourists. I had nothing against these visitors who gave our parcel of land a livelihood. Besides, they sometimes showed it more respect than the locals did. On my way to the Captain's house I walked past an empty plot between two buildings that served as an open-air dump where anyone who chose to could get rid of a fridge or a tired old mattress. There was a proper rubbish tip but something – exhaustion due to the sun, most likely – stopped people going there to offload their detritus. To the right there were views over the emerald bay. To the left, rubbish. It was all there, all in one place, beauty and ugliness. And all perfectly normal because it had always been like this.

I knocked on the Captain's living-room window but he didn't answer and the door didn't produce any better success. This was unlike him because he usually came bounding out of the house at the first rap on the window. Sometimes even just before it. I knew he waited for me and watched me.

"Don't break the glass, Giacomo, I'm here," he'd say.

"Alert as a shark . . ."

Perhaps the shark was ill today. I went back to the door but it was locked. I had to get inside, whatever it took. I knew that it was easy to get the better of a lock with a bank card. I tried for five minutes, but didn't get anywhere. My card can't have been the right kind for this sort of break-in. I didn't force it because I didn't want to damage the card. In the end I broke a pane of glass, pushed the window open and climbed into the Captain's house. Nothing moved but I noticed a general state of untidiness. I could hear voices, lots of them, laughing and clapping. I went to his bedroom because he'd told me that was where he spent most of his time, in his armchair by the window, overlooking the street. He wasn't there but I had a strange feeling I could see his reflection in the window. He spent so much time in this room that his reflection was still there after he'd left. I quickly inspected the other rooms in the house, but the Captain wasn't there. The television was on: the laughter was from the programme that

Michaël Uras

was airing, a game in which contestants were dancing half naked. For no reason. I turned it off, then I headed for the hospital, thinking the Captain must have had a funny turn and the emergency services had taken him there. The mess, the TV talking to itself, the sound on pretty much maximum volume – there couldn't be another explanation.

I arrived at the hospital, as panic-stricken as if I was escorting my wife on the point of giving birth. I'd experienced this first-hand a few years earlier. I didn't really want to remember it but sadly, we can't always choose our memories. Some things come back just like that, with no warning.

At the reception desk they suggested I went to A & E because there was no record of the Captain. If he'd recently arrived his registration wouldn't have been processed yet.

"Have you received a patient – either this morning or during the night – by the name of . . . ?"

"We've had no new admissions since yesterday after-noon."

"Are you sure?"

"So listen, I spend my life here, do you really think if a Captain what's-his-name had turned up, I wouldn't remember? . . . I never forget a patient."

"Do you have written records of everything?"

"I don't have written records of anything. Paper's for people with bad memories."

"I meant on computer."

"It's turned off, look."

I leant over and the computer facing the receptionist was indeed turned off.

"Is it a real one, at least?"

"More real than real! Anyway, nothing lasts, so I prepare myself for possible crashes by not using it. My brain works perfectly well."

"So no Captain, then?"

"No Captain, but go and have a look in General Medicine, you never know. He may have slipped through the net. Patients sometimes go to that department and we don't know anything about it. A bit like items at a lost-and-found desk. You don't know they're there until a family comes looking for them."

"That's horrible."

"Well, life's horrible, I'm afraid! Were you in any doubt about that?"

"I don't know . . . I'll go and have a look in General Medicine."

This was the department my grandmother was in. I knew it by heart, so it didn't take me long to realize the Captain wasn't there. While I was there, I went to give Nonna a kiss. Someone had removed the excess hair from her chin and cheeks, which made it much nicer to put my lips to them.

"Thank you for coming, my little one. And thank you for kissing me. People don't usually kiss the dying. They're too frightened."

I made no comment about the newly restored softness of her skin. The body is a complex and absolutely incredible machine that copes with physical and psychological shocks . . . and one fine day some microscopic element decides to stop working, to disappear or to multiply exponentially. And then this beautiful machine becomes a burden. We'd like to have another one but that's impossible. We live with it, in spite of everything, still remembering its original perfection. We should have made better use of that. Basked in the sun while we still could, run along the beach despite the wind, eaten those huge cakes that made our mouths water, and dived into cold water in the early days of spring. But time passed and we were sensible, too sensible. And then it was too late. Grandma's facial hair was proof of that. We had to be unreasonable if we wanted to have no regrets. Living on an island, leaving it, coming back to it. Playing football even if you were the worst goalie in history, hiding to spy on a beautiful grocer's wife or translating an umpteenth version of *Moby Dick*.

In the end I bumped into Alessandra who walked back to the exit with me.

"There's no Captain here," she said with a mischievous smile.

"Still up for Sunday?"

"Still up for it."

The door, which was as heavy as the stone rolled over Christ's tomb, closed before I had time to say another word. Which was just as well. I didn't have a chance to get bogged down in ludicrous pronouncements.

★ ★ ★

Everyone benefits from the work of translators, but we rarely get any recognition. Would Joyce bask in the same glow of recognition if translators hadn't broken all their teeth over his impenetrable sentences? And Kafka, and Borges? Writers don't exist without translators. There should be a memorial built to every translator. Well, perhaps I'm exaggerating a little. There should be memorials in varying sizes depending on the translator's work. The biggest of them would be for literary translators, then slightly smaller ones for film translators; further down the scale would come translators who work in television. I'm bound to be missing some out but in any event, the smallest memorials, smaller even than the *Domus de Janas*, would be for translators of instructions for flat-pack furniture. Let's be honest, their work is thankless, but they don't even try.

When I was married I spent hours trying to put together furniture by following the leaflets. I was too sensible, clinging to the written instructions and the illustrations when none of it worked. The translator's fault. I've always followed instructions, unswervingly. At school, on the football pitch, when I tried my hand at wall painting . . . In this case, I should have deviated from the guiding principle. When the time came to put together a cot and changing table, I was out of my depth. The bolts wouldn't go in and the nuts didn't secure them. Was a bed without a base even a thing? No body, however light, could sleep in that. In the end I had to ask for help from a more able friend, who threw away the instructions and put the furniture together. Something I would never have dared to do. The finished cot was gorgeous and when my wife came home, she was really proud of me. Actually, I'd never seen her so proud. The nursery was beautiful, serene, ready to welcome a new arrival.

I parked next to a stony path to get down to the creek where I'd decided to spend some time. Because the Captain wasn't with me, I could walk at my own pace and enjoy wandering through the scrubland. Lizards scuttled away at the sound of my footsteps. They might have been descended from the ones I enjoyed dissecting as a child. I wouldn't do them any harm this time. The sea was down a slope and I made my way through the vegetation to reach it. In the distance I could see luxury yachts that came and dropped anchor in our calm waters. Their passengers never came ashore – they weren't interested in the land, just the water.

I heard voices from down in the creek, and noticed some movement too – someone had found my hideout. And there I was, planning to relax and leaf through the illustrated copy of *Moby Dick* that my parents had given me. I hadn't even brought my fishing rod. Manuella sold perfect paninis and I was looking forward to eating one when I got hungry. A book and a sandwich, what more could I hope for? The poor Captain had disappeared. I walked towards the place where I liked to sit and saw two men sitting with their backs to me, so close they were almost touching. I recognized the Captain's colourful shirt and the fisherman's adventurer accoutrements, a bushwhacker outfit for catching suicidal bream.

I had raced to the hospital and all over the village looking for a man who was having a nice time by the sea with a friend. He'd abandoned me for someone more interesting. They turned round and saw me but can't have been the least bit bothered because they turned straight back to their original position. I was part of the scenery, like a tree or a lizard.

"Hello, Captain," I said, moving closer.

"Hello, Giacomo."

They carried on with their conversation. They wouldn't have behaved any differently if I'd been a waiter bringing them a drink.

"A colonel's wife, I tell you. A real beauty! An impossible woman!"

"Extraordinary!"

I knew the story and hated hearing it being trotted out again. Except for one detail: the general had become a colonel, a demotion in the military hierarchy. But the woman was still impossible. A translator colleague of mine had an annoying habit of repeating stories word for word several times a week. Like a goldfish, he forgot everything. I wasn't unkind so I'd listen to him. I should have told him that repetition drives you mad, that production-line workers acted out the movements they did at work even when they were asleep, which was definitely worrying. The Captain was altering his story, lying was a division of the truth. I should have pointed this out to him but I didn't want to embarrass him. Besides, I didn't have the courage, which is a difficult thing to admit. Alive but invisible, like a hermit crab.

"I went to your house to pick you up this morning, Captain."

"But my friend had said he'd come and pick me up. I completely forgot to tell you. I hope you're not annoyed with me?"

"Of course not. I was just a bit worried about you."

"You're like a mother to me, boy!"

The Captain was absolutely right, I was treating him the way my mother treated me . . . except that I was far too young to take on the part.

"You said he was like a son to you the other day," the fisherman said, "and today he's your mother! Things change quickly on this island."

The two men laughed heartily and I joined in with more restraint, then I left them to enjoy the beautiful day, and headed back to the village. The Captain had a friend, at last. As for me, I'd learned that nothing was ever in the bag, even with a despairing old man. The old had resources to draw on, they were buried deep but there all the same. Grandma and the Captain were brimming with energy, an energy that meant they could hold out through hardship, old age and abandonment. Perhaps that was why the island's inhabitants didn't die. I was delighted to think I had this energy deep inside me. Even though I left the island as soon as I felt the need, I was fundamentally a part of this place. It was a ball and chain around my foot and an oxygen tank. The latter had served me well, and still did.

On the way home I gathered some herbs and small branches. They could go in my bedroom, bringing the outside in. I'd always tried – and failed – to bring the smell of the scrubland with me. It only had that distinctive smell because it was whole. In snatches, the magic disappeared so I knew the branches and herbs would dry out without releasing their lovely smells.

* * *

"You know there are soon going to be uber-accurate translation apps?"

"I've heard about them. They'll translate basic texts, sappy romances, but they'll never be able to translate Joyce or . . ."

"Melville! I'm not so sure about that. Artificial intelligence is coming on in leaps and bounds."

"You're only saying that to make me work faster, Carlo. I'm not a complete idiot."

"I'm going to tell you something. If there was a programme that could translate this bloody text, I'd buy it in a flash."

"Are you joking?"

"Absolutely not! What are you doing, still in Sardinia? You're getting nowhere. You were meant to be sending me material regularly. It must be getting lost in the Mediterranean."

"I'll send you the text when it's completely done."

"I don't believe you."

"You should."

"Go home to your apartment. Your parents spoil you too much, you can't work properly. No one works on that island of yours. The air just doesn't lend itself to concentration or excellence. When you spend two hours over a meal and three having a siesta, how could you possibly achieve anything? Besides, you do too much brooding when you're there."

"There are some things I can't forget. It doesn't matter where I am. Carlo, there's something I should tell you before I hang up and get back to work. I've been offered a big contract."

"Really?"

"Yes, Neptune Editions have offered me part of Simenon's complete works to translate."

"That's a handsome *oeuvre*."

"And a handsome offer."

"Did you accept?"

"I haven't replied yet. I'm waiting a while."

"Would you leave me?"

"Would you replace me with an app?"

I wasn't lying to Carlo, I really had been offered work translating Simenon. On the other hand, I had exaggerated a little with the notion of a "handsome offer". We hadn't actually discussed money yet. It was a significant factor but I didn't know what they were going to offer me. I didn't mean any harm to Carlo but, because I'd been at sea with that whale for a while, the whole job was starting to make me feel sick. I felt nauseous just seeing the book on my desk and did my best to avoid it, to pretend it wasn't there, so forbidding with its hundreds of pages staring at me, reminding me I should be taking an interest in them, devoting most of my time to them. Anyone who hasn't translated such a gargantuan novel wouldn't understand my agitation. It haunted me so terribly that I hid it in my wardrobe at night. And the minute Carlo's name came up on my phone, I was reminded of the whale and even though, little exiled islander that he was, he weighed no more than sixty kilos, he became *Moby Dick*. Our phone conversations only made the situation worse.

"Take your time."

"To think about it?"

"To translate."

"Come and spend a few days here, it'll do you good."

"I don't have time."

"Your parents would love it."

"Don't talk to me about my parents. I have my mother on the phone twice a day."

"You'd talk to her less if you were here. I'll be finished in a couple of weeks."

"You're like a brother to me."

* * *

After I'd renovated the floor in my little boy's bedroom, painted the walls and arranged the furniture, I'd morphed into an interior decorator. Devoid of talent, perhaps, but determined to do a good job. The baby had to be pleased with what his father had done. And so did Jessica, my ex-wife. Pleased she was, and I was very happy about this because I'd never really been good at DIY before. I'd had help of course, but no one knew that. Officially, I was the great creator of the new room. I'd put the books I'd translated on a small set of shelves. It would be a while before the baby realized they had any connection with me, but the thought thrilled me in anticipation. What father wouldn't want his child to look up to him? I felt my work would allow me to earn this credit. My boy could tell people at school that his father translated world-renowned books. It brought tears to my eyes. My ex-wife, however, wasn't entirely happy to see my books on the shelves. Partly because hers weren't there, but mostly she just felt that books like that didn't belong in a child's room. It has to be said that at that time I'd only translated *Lady Chatterley's Lover* and Marguerite Duras's

L'Amant. People teased me because I specialized in lovers . . .
an unfortunate coincidence. Scandalous books with pride of
place in this partly aqua-blue bedroom. Partly because you
can't have a bedroom which is just aqua blue, so it was aqua
blue and wild flax.

Jessica and I had gone to an interior designer who told us
what colours to use in the room. Coming as I did from a village
where the houses were all painted in clashing tones, I'd inherited a gift for combining colours that should never have met
in the same room. Or anywhere else, for that matter. Clashes
were my go-to, but the interior designer unceremoniously put
paid to this tendency. She had a perfect grasp of every colour,
even those with the weirdest names. "Peacock blue" for example,
and "Legendary teal". Jessica and the designer eventually
convinced me and we left laden with pots of paint. A little
poorer too, because the teal may have been legendary, but not
as much as the woman's prices.

The walls were waiting for our little boy. The furniture was
waiting for our little boy. The whole apartment was, down to
the grout between the floor tiles. There was nothing particularly
original about it, except for the colours.

*   *   *

Grandma had asked me to bring some of her favourite biscuits.
I bought them from Manuella who was starting to wonder how
anyone could eat so many *dolci* without being ill. Grandma
savoured them slowly, which made the whole operation perilous.
A member of staff or, worse, a member of the family might
come in at any moment.

"You should have brought an extra box."

"Don't overdo it, Nonna. You're meant to be fed by this little
tube, not a concentrate of sugar."

"At my age, I can do whatever I like. I don't want to count
anything anymore. When you're old, you spend your whole life
counting. The days and months you have left. The hours that

need filling before someone might drop by. Give us another biscuit!"

"You'll end up falling ill."

"Well, I'm in the right place to be ill, aren't I? And I'm lying down, so how do you expect me to fall?"

"Your mind's still just as sharp, Grandma."

"Thanks to the biscuits!"

"Could well be."

"Have you heard from Jessica at all?"

"Not for a while."

"Do you still talk?"

"We haven't fallen out. We still need time."

"Life is a hard thing, merciless. If I could have carried your burden . . ."

"You're very kind."

"I would have taken it on my back to give you some relief."

"You're so tiny, you would have disappeared."

"Your mind's pretty sharp too, Giacomo."

"Thanks to you."

Grandma was the only person in the family who still asked me about Jessica. As far as the others were concerned, she no longer existed. She had come with me on several trips to the island, but not anymore. Mama avoided broaching the subject, and that was just as well. In fact, if I happened to see Jessica at our publishing house in Rome, we acted as if our life together had never actually happened. The years methodically erased themselves with an invisible rubber. There must be no trace left behind. But that was impossible, there would always be something there.

"I knew it!"

Gavino started shouting down the whole hospital.

"I knew it! You've been playing us along for weeks! Come on, Mama, what got into you? I thought you were going to die. You're just pretending! And with the worst of accomplices . . ."

My uncle had rumbled us. He'd been hiding behind the curtain I'd drawn, spying on us. We should never make presumptions about other people's naivety. With our secret outed, there was no possibility of suggesting an agreement, a non-aggressive pact with Gavino. He would have his revenge.

"If my phone wasn't being repaired, I'd have called all the others already."

"They'll know anyway if you keep yelling like that."

"A bit of respect, Giacomo, you owe me some respect. I'm your uncle!"

"Respect isn't to do with family ranking, you're not the best example on the subject."

"We'll talk about that later. I'm going to call an emergency family meeting."

An emergency family meeting – the word was out. Gavino had just opened the door to a gathering that happened only in exceptional circumstances, and he relished the expression as he would a succulent cut of meat.

The last time the family had met like this had been on the death of a great-great-uncle who'd signed a 103-year tenancy agreement on this earth. We'd all assembled at Grandma's house and everyone sat round her huge wooden table – a table which, had it been able to talk, could have told a large proportion of our family history, because objects hold our lives within them, hiding them, protecting them, like Russian dolls that hold within them a series of slightly different copies of themselves. Sometimes we need only touch these objects, move them or feel them, for a little bit of memory to escape before settling back where it came from.

Mama had rested her hands on this table to eat, do her homework, draw (badly), write about her first love, announce my birth, and announce deaths too. Every component of our lineage had at some time or other sat at this expanse of wood.

My great-uncle had died the summer before and we'd had to discuss the distribution of his assets, around this very table. Oddly, no one was interested in his furniture, crockery or linen. Everyone wanted his land – fields close to the sea where cows grazed slowly. Animals weren't in the least bit interested in a view over an emerald gulf. Men were. Several members of the family had made the journey to our village from the south of the island: everyone suddenly feeling close to the deceased, even if they hadn't seen him for half a century. Death revives family ties, particularly when gain rears its ugly head. Everyone suddenly recalled some anecdote, a story, a special episode with my great-uncle; everyone had to prove to the others that they deserved their place around the table. In the space of a few hours, a life was dismantled, pulled apart. The body would take far longer to disintegrate.

Voices were raised to stake their claim on the assets. Not the linen. Not the crockery. I would have no trouble picking them up. My parents had no gift for being combative, and easily surrendered the parcels of land. They were promised a little money in return, enough to buy a few tubes of paint and some delicious biscuits. I would take the sheets back with me to France, beautifully cut sheets, full of Sardinia and enriched with several lives and deaths. As well as some rather ridiculous little glasses with badly drawn animals etched onto them. My great-uncle had used them for his daily tot of lemon liqueur which he made with lemons from his own garden. Surely having a lemon tree in your garden is the definition of absolute happiness? The colour, shape, density and flesh of the fruit within reach. After many hours of discussion, with the spoils shared out (inevitably unfairly), everyone went back to their respective homes, more or less pleased with their inheritance. There was no need to contact a notary. No stranger needed to intervene in a family matter handled simply, with love and goodwill.

So Gavino had promised to convene the family council to decide Grandma's fate, given that she just wouldn't stop living.

★ ★ ★

We used to have favourite seats on the bus that took us to the beach every Thursday. The Captain sat at the front, to the right of the driver, where he could chat away to him. Meanwhile, I would sit next to Fabrizio, behind the Captain, and every week we listened discreetly while the two men talked. I watched the Captain's muscular jaw open and close to let the words out. Words he seemed to set free. I also took advantage of this opportunity to study his pockmarked skin, imagining the imperfections to have been carved by desert winds and the whistle of passing bullets in combat. The Captain's skin was an adventure in itself.

On the way to the beach, the driver always stopped to buy cheese from a friend of his, whose shop consisted of a tiny van mounted on a scooter engine. The driver would pull over onto a layby overlooking the sea, where we weren't allowed to get out because it was too dangerous for children. The question that plagued me every week was: Why would someone wanting to sell cheese position himself on the edge of a precipice? I couldn't find any rational explanation so I eventually decided to ask the Captain, whose reply was: "Pecorino has to be earned." So that was it – you had to take risks to earn a right to this cheese. People who weren't born here couldn't understand this. There was something highly symbolic and perfectly inaccessible about it for the locals. The inhabitants of this island were obsessed with cheese, it was a sort of Nantucket of the south, but focused on ewes rather than whales.

The Captain reiterated the fact that we were not allowed off the bus by standing in front of the open door. Anyone who wanted to get out would have to go over him. It happened only once when Fabrizio felt a need to answer a call of nature.

"Why do you want to get out?"

"Let me through, Captain, please."

"Why do you want to get out?"

"I'll tell you afterwards."

"You'll tell me now or you won't set a foot outside."

At this point the Captain was behaving like an officer in a military operation. He defended his position and showed no indulgence towards Fabrizio. Perhaps he saw him as a soldier armed to the teeth and not a youngster in shorts and beach shoes.

"It's urgent."

"What's urgent? Your need for cheese?"

"No!"

"Well, you don't have a valid reason, then."

"I hate sheep's cheese."

"So why do you want to get off this bus?"

"Because I need a wee."

The Captain hadn't thought of this possibility – he really knew nothing about children. In the end he took my friend outside and escorted him to the edge of the precipice where he could release the excess lemonade he'd drunk just before we set off.

"Listen up," the Captain said when we were all back on the bus. "There won't be any more exceptions. You'll need to take precautions because next time you'll have only one option: wetting yourselves. A rule is a rule. I'm here to escort you down to the sea, not to the toilet. Understood?"

We were terrified but also fascinated by the man's power. Someone who so respected the rules and was so determined to execute his duties conscientiously. Like Ahab in *Moby Dick*, nothing could divert him from his purpose.

★ ★ ★

Of course, Gavino went and told Alessandra about Grandma's lie. He couldn't miss an opportunity to feel important. My efforts to dissuade him achieved nothing: a man without his mobile was inconsolable and therefore, inevitably, single-minded. My uncle wrote an official statement in which he asserted that Grandma's hospitalization was the result of deceit. Every member of the family received a copy (he'd made these copies at the village post office at the expense of a three-hour wait – it was pension day – which demonstrated his iron-clad determination). Naturally, he cited me as an accomplice to the fake patient, which compromised my standing with Alessandra.

Back at the hospital, Grandma had been talking in a clear, uninhibited voice since she'd been found out. She no longer tried to hide the reasons for her silence from anyone. She said she was feeling really rather well, and the medical team didn't feel betrayed by this foolish old lady. One of the nurses even told me that the incident brought a bit of excitement to the department. "The ones who seem to be dead very often are, so when someone in rather good health plays dead to get their revenge on their family, we find it pretty funny. And your grandmother didn't give us any trouble. We prefer a silent patient in good health than an aggressive one who's really ill." I personally felt every single person, every single object in the hospital was watching me. In reality, very few people knew what had happened, but my tendency to paranoia overrode common sense. If I came across a patient at reception, he knew. If I met a nurse from another department, she knew. If I walked past a trolley full of medicine bottles, it knew. Even the light switches knew. I wasn't proud, but I wouldn't have given my grandmother's game away for anything in the world. She had every right to her revenge.

"Can I have a word, Giacomo?"

"Of course."

"Follow me."

Alessandra led me purposefully to her office. We made the trip in silence. There was just the sound of our shoes on the plastic flooring. For the first time in my life, I'd have been very happy to hear a Phil Collins song. Anything's better than a deadly silence.

"This whole business is unbelievable."

"Are you angry with me?"

"Why?"

"For not telling you my grandmother was putting it on."

"I don't know."

"It's just, she gave me so much support when I needed her. I would have been an ogre if I'd told anyone about her lie."

"You were a prisoner to her little act."

"Exactly. I didn't know how to get out."

"Let's drop it then, and move on to something else."

"Are you still on for Caprera?"

"Caprera's definitely another subject. But, Giacomo, I want you to know I hate liars."

"So you hate me, then?"

"We'll talk about that another time. I've got work to do."

It was decided that Nonna would return home as soon as possible. Fake sufferers were not kept in. Walking along a corridor – where I still felt spied on – I was stopped by a man in pyjamas and I didn't immediately recognize him. It was Dr. Ignazio.

"Are you ill?"

"It does happen to doctors!"

"I'm so sorry."

"It's nothing. I started swelling yesterday. It's quite impressive, look!"

Ignazio had known me all my life and, although I was now a grown man, he still treated me as he used to when I was a little boy and he came to our house to tend to me. Sure of himself. Full of charm. But this time, he was in pyjamas. He lifted his top to reveal a protruding stomach. It looked as if it had been filled with helium.

"And my calves, look at this!"

His calves had undergone a similar expansion. Ignazio seemed proud. In fact he proceeded with the same self-satisfaction as when showing off the exceptional alloy wheels on his car to passers-by. I couldn't disguise my amazement.

"It's nothing, like I said, too much bicarbonate of soda. In a couple of days I'll have my perfect figure back."

"Well, that's reassuring."

"What about your grandmother, though! I heard the incredible story. It's all anyone can talk about in the village."

"I'd rather not talk about it."

"You sly little fox, you! Say hello to your mama from me."

All this nonsense was giving me a headache, a migraine strong enough to knock a whale for six. Once home, I'd barely made it through the door when I ran to the medicine cabinet in search of a box of paracetamol. That was the most important word in the world for me at that particular moment: the great god paracetamol – he was all that mattered. Unfortunately, the door to the cabinet wouldn't open. The lock seemed to have rusted. I trickled some olive oil into the lock to ease it, but that didn't change anything, except for the smell. The ancient cupboard with its unyielding orangey lock now smelt quite pleasant. It would take more than olives to get what I was looking for, so I started forcing it by pressing on the other door with my left hand and bracing my feet like a boxer about to throw an uppercut. Surely, the cabinet couldn't stand up to that. It didn't. The door flew off and I reeled backwards. A waterfall of medicines spilled out. All sorts of colours, capsules, pills, phials, compresses, bandages and a jar of *Effervescente*, which shattered when it hit the floor. I watched this crashing wave, powerless. A spectator who would now have to pick up all the debris to avoid his mother's wrath.

I started by collecting up the pieces of glass. Luckily, they were quite big. The jar probably wanted to stay in one piece. It thought it had a chance of being put back together because it had avoided shattering into hundreds of tiny pieces. But it was wrong. The whole thing needed throwing away. I put the remains into a bin bag. The last piece had the *Effervescente* label on it. Coloured paper featuring a clear blue sky and a rounded lemon ready to drip its juice into the glass waiting beneath it. A promise of well-being and refreshment. Under the photo was a list of ingredients: "Sucrose, bicarbonate of soda, malic acid, glucose syrup, lemon flavouring (0.14%), lemon juice (0.1%), colourant: E132."

I'd never taken an interest in these ingredients that, often against my own better judgement, I'd been ingesting for years. Apart from sugar and the notion of lemon (0.24% could be considered as a vague notion of the fruit), I noticed the presence of bicarbonate of soda.

Dr. Ignazio had bloated as a result of an overdose of bicarbonate of soda. So he had never moved on to another medication, he'd stayed with his lemony granules. Sadly, ongoing training isn't compulsory for doctors. His body had consumed the stuff for years without reacting but was now exacting its revenge by swelling up. Deceptions are always unmasked in the long run. I finished clearing everything up and went to put the plastic sack into the bin outside the house. When I opened it, two emaciated cats jumped out, furious at having been disturbed. They went straight back to whatever they were doing. Animals recognize injustice, just as humans do. Mila, Grandma's cat, slept peacefully on her cushion while her two fellow cats spent most of their time scavenging in dustbins.

Meanwhile, the migraine that had blinded me had now completely subsided. Probably from coming into contact with the *Effervescente*.

* * *

Family reunions are terrible things, they display every human vice: arrogance, pride and slander are guaranteed an appearance. We were sitting around Grandma's table and she, by chance, was still in hospital. She wouldn't have to witness this accumulation of petty lives. None of them took any notice of me. Well, they were angry with me but I couldn't have cared less. I often played the role of the baddie in this rather miserable performance: the one who left the island, the one who thinks he's better than everyone else, the one who should stop coming back. Gavino ran the discussion like a good master of ceremonies (a status conferred on him because he discovered the lie). It was his job to resolve the problem as quickly as possible: what to do with Grandma. The doctors strongly advised against leaving her alone in her house. They understood that she was faking but couldn't be sure she wasn't concealing a more deep-seated problem – madness. Grandma, mad? That's what everyone in the family was saying.

I wished I could turn the question on them. Weren't they all mad, coming together in this way to carve up other people's assets? I let them do their talking, because I knew my parents would inherit Grandma herself. Nobody else wanted her, and we were on her doorstep, our houses nearly touched. It's all about the nearly. Making her move to another street or, worse, another village wouldn't be fair, at her age. Even before the question was asked, it had already been answered, despite everyone pretending otherwise. They scratched their heads, they sighed, they feigned thought on the matter, and, as usual, everyone's memories of Nonna resurfaced. It was always the same: they had to prove they loved her, and how attached they were to her, describing in turn a particularly telling event, a funny or perhaps serious anecdote, before announcing that this wonderful Grandma couldn't, in all decency, be taken from her own home.

After two hours of false deliberation, we proceeded to a vote. I noticed that my raised hand did not appear to be taken into account by Gavino. It was decided that Nonna would come to live with us. And of course everyone committed to visiting her regularly. Here, rather like anywhere else, promises weren't worth a great deal. I kept promising Carlo his manuscript, Gavino kept promising he'd stop shouting to anyone who'd listen. As for my father, he was meant to be painting something other than houses before he could no longer hold a paintbrush. Everyone made promises without really believing what they said. The day ended with a copious meal which did nothing to console me for raising my hand to no effect.

At midnight, exhausted and despairing about the human race, I went off to bed. Gavino didn't miss this opportunity to have a dig at how feeble I was, whereas he could go three whole days without sleep. But what was the point of such a feat for a man who did absolutely nothing with his life but cycle idly round the village or look frantically for his mobile or his razor? I let him have his rant and wished everyone a good night, feeling fairly sure none of them would sleep. It was traditional not to abandon the gathering for as long as there was still plenty of wine and food. I didn't like this awkward phase when we stayed together because there was still something to eat and drink. We had nothing left to say to each other.

Mama knew I would do some work before going to bed, and came up to my bedroom to see me. My parents were ignoring me a little less than other members of the family. In fact they admired my loyalty to Grandma. It didn't make the lie disappear but it did soften it.

"The others are angry with you, you know."

"I know, it's only natural."

"I'm pretty annoyed with you, too."

"Yes."

"But not as much as they are. Don't worry. You're my boy. All children lie."

"A thirty-six-year-old boy. You know, Mama, I don't regret helping Grandma."

"You must never have any regrets. You chose that solution for your grandmother. It was an act of love."

"And hate! Hate for all the others!"

"Come on, that's enough. Everyone here loves you."

"Well, they have to, after everything that's happened . . ."

"Don't say that. We need to pick Grandma up from hospital tomorrow. I'd like you to take care of that."

Given that I'd been her accomplice, my punishment was to go and pick up the impostor from hospital. There was nothing earth-shattering about that: picking up a healthy person when they're discharged from hospital is a good thing. I'd done it before, when Jessica came out of hospital. It wasn't in the same place, or the same person, but setting out alone to come home as a twosome left me with a bitter taste in my mouth. A taste of difficult times.

"I'll go and pick her up, don't worry."

"I knew you'd say yes. Thank you. Tell me, Giacomo, how are you?"

"How am I? I've been here a while, you've had plenty of time to see for yourself."

"Some sadness can't be seen."

"I'm not sad."

"I don't believe you. You can talk to me, you know."

"Everything's fine."

"How about your work, is it coming on?"

"Yes, I've nearly finished. Then it'll be high time I had a rest, did something different, took a bit of a breather."

"You can get some rest at home, with us. We won't bother you."

It didn't matter much what I actually said, Mama thought the family home was the best place to rest, to work, to sleep, to laugh, to scream, to play sport (in the yard), to travel (you could see the sea from the window), to do a bit of DIY . . . to live, basically. And that was as it should be. My parents didn't have much, and they weren't perfect, but they were there.

The next morning I went to see Fabrizio to ask whether he'd come to the hospital with me. He agreed, and his father came to take over from him while he was out. Even since we'd last seen each other, his illness had worsened. His skin hung down so badly that he looked even older than before. His voice, however, was still the same, unchanged since it broke in his teens. His voice and body were in striking contrast with each other, which never failed to attract attention. The nurse who dealt with us in the General Medicine department couldn't hide her amazement when Fabrizio spoke to her. His voice belonged to the past, his body to the future.

"Your grandmother's ready, she's waiting in her room. But you'll need to have her discharge papers signed by a doctor."

We went to find Alessandra, who made us wait in the corridor for half an hour before she saw us. I remembered these words from Roland Barthes: "The inevitable identity of a man in love is none other than: I am the one who waits."

We waited. Fabrizio was waiting for a doctor. I was waiting for Alessandra. For a signature, of course, but also for what I wanted. Was Alessandra familiar with Roland Barthes? Had she read his *A Lover's Discourse: Fragments*? I should ask her because

I'd need to find out later whether she'd wilfully made us wait so long.

While I theorized about Barthes, Alessandra emerged from her office with Dr. Ignazio.

"My dear colleague, I trust you won't have any more bicarbonate of soda for the next ten days or so. Your body needs a chance to forget about the stuff."

"You can count on me. I don't want to look like an airship. They always come to a sticky end. Do you know what happened to the *Lindbergh*?"

"Yes, of course, I've seen images. You're right, don't end up like the *Lindbergh*."

Ignazio then saw us, leaning unobtrusively against the wall.

"Giacomo! Have you come to pick up your grandmother?"

"Yes. She's getting out this morning."

"Well, that's more good news. I'm coming out this morning too. My calves hurt a bit, but I'm going down, I'm going down . . ."

With these words he left, whistling to himself. Something told me he'd throw himself at the *Effervescente* the moment he was home.

During the meeting with Alessandra, she couldn't stop looking at Fabrizio. I hadn't told my friend how attracted I was to the doctor, nor had I told Alessandra anything about Fabrizio. When all the formalities were over, Fabrizio walked out of her office first.

"Is that your grandfather?" she asked.

"No, he's a childhood friend."

"My God . . ."

Nonna was waiting for us, sitting in a chair far too big for her small body. She gave me a long hug and thanked Fabrizio for coming. "Two young men going out of their way for such an old lady, that doesn't happen often," she said. No one stared at me in the corridors anymore, not patients, not staff, not even the light switches, and Fabrizio had little more success than me: people only had eyes for the compulsive-liar grand-

Michaël Uras

mother. Grandma was having her fifteen minutes of fame. At eighty-six. People whispered and smiled as we passed. One patient even went so far as to clap the impromptu star. "Well done! You really got them. And they think they know it all!"

* * *

We put Grandma in the small bedroom next to mine. I liked knowing she was so near by, in the room my father had redecorated a few years earlier, painting the walls blue, or rather painting them blues, because he'd wanted different shades of the same colour. It was during his blue phase. Mama hadn't objected. Grandma was now enjoying the colours and seemed happy with her move. "I couldn't see myself going home on my own after all that time in hospital. There was always someone dropping in to see me there. I got used to it."

Life was easy with Grandma. She spoke slowly and chose her words carefully to express what she meant. It made a change from Mama's lyrical flights of fancy which, to be honest, were becoming increasingly rare. Grandma made the tiniest thing seem very important: laying the table, folding napkins, putting away cleaning products . . . she liked making herself useful and we were grateful for her contributions to running the household. It was touching, seeing her go about these humdrum activities so earnestly.

Mila and the cushion she lived on had also come to join us, to her absolute delight. Papa ignored her magnificently even though the cat, like any animal that feels rejected, came and rubbed herself against his legs whenever she saw him. The relationship needed building gradually, Mila was well aware of that. Grandma, who'd seen my father's reticence, asked him to feed the cat every morning. Papa couldn't refuse the old lady anything now that she was so polite and considerate, so he would open a tin of tuna and mix it with a little rice. It was an unpleasant smell early in the morning but Papa bore it graciously and served Mila her meal. By way of thanks (I can't think of another explanation) the cat then tried to join him when he was in his armchair reading his paper. She jumped heavily onto his lap, having lost all her grace when she tipped over the fifteen-kilo mark. It was an affectionate gesture, but my father couldn't bear any physical contact with the animal. He'd rather silently leave the room than sit with the cat on his lap. Grandma would then put the cat's cushion in the armchair, and Mila – never far behind – would curl up on it peacefully to sleep.

Meanwhile Mama was full of little considerations for her mother. She had probably understood that the old lady had played dead because of our family's unacceptable behaviour towards her. Mama stopped sending me to Manuella to buy biscuits and had gone back to making them instead – with varying degrees of success, as it turned out. And when they found no takers because they were a tad too dense (we risked suffocation with every mouthful), Mila made sure they didn't hang around. She'd soon need a second cushion to stretch out comfortably.

Grandma spent the hottest part of the day in front of the television watching her favourite American soap, *The Bold and the Beautiful*, which had been contributing to the golden days of pay TV for decades. She hadn't been able to watch it during her weeks in hospital so she spent her days avidly watching the reruns. This American family's life really was an inexhaustible succession of confusions. It made our small community seem quite insipid in comparison. Over the years, Grandma had seen all the characters develop, she'd seen the children grow into adults, the adults become elderly, and the elderly die one after the other for on-screen reasons that struggled to disguise the fact that the actors had died off-screen. It was the great show of life.

After a few days, Nonna had overdosed on *The Bold and the Beautiful*, and understood that terrestrial channels broadcast only one episode a day so that spectators would survive the series. The show had too many stories, too many problems, too much make-up and too many cosmetic-surgery operations for anyone to cope with a whole afternoon of watching it. So she came to find me in my room.

"Are you working?"

"Yes, I need to deliver this translation very soon. Why?"

"No reason, sorry for disturbing you."

"You're not disturbing me. What's the matter?"

"I'm a bit bored."

"Have you stopped watching TV?"

"All those muddles are exhausting. Did you know Ridge was no longer with Brooke? And Brooke's going out with her daughter's fiancé?"

"I watched a few episodes a long time ago now, but I never got hooked."

"Thank goodness! It's a drug! But I can't take any more of Brooke, the man-eater. Let's hope she dies soon! She's aged a lot recently. I don't think she's as pretty as she used to be. I need a bit of a break . . ."

"Fair enough."

"But, tell me, Giacomo. You've got lots of books on your shelves. Which would you recommend for me?"

I'd never seen Grandma read, so I was thrown by this question.

"I'd recommend all of them!"

"You'll put me off, saying things like that."

"It would be best for you to choose one yourself."

Grandma went over to the bookcase and started scrutinizing the books. She would take one out, open it, close it again, read the blurb.

"Oh, it's so difficult to choose."

In the end she plumped for a book and brought it to me as if I were the local librarian in charge of loans.

"That's an exceptional book. It's a classic, it's been translated all over the world."

"So has *The Bold and the Beautiful*."

"Yes, but there's no chance of coming across Brooke Forrester in that book."

"Do you mean Brooke Logan? I told you she's separated from Ridge Forrester."

"That's right, Brooke Logan! You'll see, this book's also all about family and never-ending meals . . ."

"Could you read it to me, Giacomo. My eyes are so tired . . ."

"It would be my pleasure, Grandma. It genuinely would be."

Nonna settled into my armchair and I started reading the first pages of the book she'd chosen: *Mrs Dalloway*.

Mila soon nudged the door open and joined us. She sat on her mistress's lap, almost completely hiding Grandma's legs under her copious stomach. Five minutes later Grandma was sound asleep. But not Mila, who peered at me intently. She probably enjoyed Virginia Woolf's writing.

★ ★ ★

Why do we always have to leave? When I was lucky enough to go on holiday, I always wanted to stay where I was, never leave this wonderful new place that was just right for the kind of life I wanted to live. Anything was better than my village. As I grew older I still thought the same way. Bellagio, for example, on the shores of Lake Como, where Jessica and I went one May – that struck me as the perfect place. At the time I was translating *The Charterhouse of Parma*, a novel partly set in that region. There was something in the air there that was conducive to dreaming, to work and to love. Jessica and I weren't thinking about divorce yet because life was being good to us. The sky was clear before the storm.

We took a room in a hotel with a view over the lake, and I worked on the terrace while Jessica snoozed beside me. She'd stopped working a month earlier, and Marseille was too noisy, too fast and too frenetic for her to rest. Like in my village, there were lots of colours in Bellagio: pink, red, yellow and orange houses, but they had no pictures or political messages. A pause from the clamouring offered by the village of my birth. No one rebelled in Bellagio, even the water hardly moved. It wouldn't dare wake the wealthy holidaymakers. My parents couldn't understand why we didn't want to go and stay with them. Jessica would have been so happy in the Sardinian mountains. Everything was ready. Except us!

I would have liked to live the rest of my days on the shores of that lake with Jessica on the chaise longue and perfect sunlight on the terrace. I watched boats draw up close to the hotel. One afternoon we decided to visit Villa Melzi's gardens. The boat dropped us near this site which had been recommended by all the guidebooks we'd brought with us. About ten of them in all. We'd broken the region down into subsections, and left nothing to chance: all our excursions were planned a month before we arrived. But there was a world of difference between the planning and its execution. Idleness had eaten away at our ambitions, and the guidebooks stopped coming out of our suitcases. Jessica still remembered the Villa Melzi because of its exceptional plant life and impressive architecture. She'd studied botany before becoming a translator. This excursion didn't appeal much to me but she wanted to do it. We had to take a pretty steep road to get up to the villa and although the sun was beating down hard on our backs, Jessica felt strong enough to walk. We eventually reached the villa after a climb worthy of the Tour de France, albeit with no spectators or cheering. Or pit stops. And we'd forgotten to bring water. I was exhausted but didn't want Jessica to know. A southerner couldn't be affected by the heat at Lake Como.

The gardens overflowed with everything on earth that grows in the Mediterranean climate. We stood still for several minutes, gazing out over the lake. I remember different sensations: the feel of my wife's skin under my fingers, orange and lemon trees laden with fruit next to white statues. There were signs everywhere saying, "Touching the fruit is strictly forbidden". The grass was cut to perfection. A group of gardeners were throwing ice-cold water over themselves to keep cool. They pretended to spray us and I said I was happy to be doused too. My happiness had made a rebel of me – I normally loathe having wet clothes. Jessica brought me back in line with a "Stop it Giacomo, you'll catch cold." She was right, I didn't tolerate quick changes in temperature. I'd just suddenly had an urge to be a bit of a risk-taker, and I was suffocating in the heat. But we belong to a type right from the start: the naughty boy, the delicate boy, the kind boy, the rebel . . . I was, and always would be, the delicate boy. The gardeners teased me but held off. It has to be said they'd just been joined by their boss, so they didn't dare spray me.

We had to leave. I remember what Stendhal's hero said: "I will often return to this sublime lake; there is no more beautiful sight in the world, at least not for my heart . . ." He never went back. It was while walking back down that Jessica started to feel unwell. Stendhal was never ill on the shores of Lake Como. She sat down on a lumpy stone in the shade of a tree.

"Rest for a bit."

"I'll be fine."

One of the gardeners was going the same way as us and stopped to offer her some water, to drink this time. He was wonderfully thoughtful towards Jessica and escorted us down to the jetty. There was no question of waiting for the next shuttle now, we needed to get back quickly, so I called a water-taxi which cost me the equivalent of several dozen pages of translation. And translating Stendhal wasn't easy.

Back at the hotel, a doctor came to examine Jessica. A tall, serious northerner with no eccentricities and no *Effervescente*; he prescribed rest and sedatives. We felt reassured and I hoped we could stay by the lake a little longer, but we left for Marseille the next day; Jessica didn't want to stay on till the end of our break. Happiness had fled the region.

★ ★ ★

When Fabrizio knocked at the door I still had about twenty pages left of my translation. It was nine o'clock in the morning. As usual, what had first seemed like an unfinishable task was about to end. Every time I started a job, it felt impossible. Except once. There was only one text which I didn't manage to finish.

Julien Green's *Le Voyageur sur la terre*. The text looked easy to me but all my ambitions died as I tackled it. Julien Green and his secrets . . . They still left a bad taste in my mouth.

My friend hadn't come to talk about Julien Green however, he just wanted us to have a coffee together. I could have told him I needed to finish my work, but sending away a friend was something I couldn't contemplate. Besides, what nicer thing is there on earth than having a coffee in a small Mediterranean village? All around us the elderly talked about their last supper, not as in Leonardo's painting, just what they'd had for dinner the night before. Everyone had all sorts of advice for each other, ideas for recipes and recollections of wonderful dishes eaten. When Italians sit around a table, all they can talk about is food. It doesn't matter what sort of table it is. On the beach, too. So we were surrounded by food. It had us in its clutches and we felt as if we were permanently eating. Or living inside someone's fridge. Fabrizio and I listened to them attentively.

"How's your grandma?"

"Very well."

"Is she getting used to her new home?"

"She doesn't have any choice. Seriously, she couldn't go back to her old life. We were happy for her to move in with us. Not that we had much choice, mind . . ."

"You can't help joking about it, can you? You'll never change."

"It's a flaw."

"No, I've always admired the way you can laugh at everything. Even the worst. I know you used to make me laugh to put me in a better head space when we were young. You didn't like leaving me to cry about my situation. Even when there was plenty to cry about. Thank you, my friend. I hope when we're old we'll be able to come back and have coffee here. We can smugly look at all the youngsters, because we'll know everything and they'll know nothing. And we'll talk loudly!"

"Of course we'll come back here!"

"You once told me people are always saying 'I'll come back' but they never do."

"Don't listen to me, I'm an ass."

"*Asinu!* There are so many asses on this island of ours. And sheep and goats and wild boar, a real bargain-basement menagerie. No lions or tigers, just donkeys . . . Do you promise to come back?"

"Yes."

"We'll have retired by then, we'll have given up all work. You'll have translated half the books published on the planet and I'll have sold thousands of newspapers. No one will care about us when we're old . . . Sure, I'm slightly ahead of you on this . . ."

"I'll catch up with you, don't you worry."

After we'd had our coffee we decided to walk around the village a bit and go to the *Domus de Janas*. People like remembering because when they do, they can see how far they've come. From home to the *Domus*. From the *Domus* to the book I was translating. Years to reformulate, trying to understand how another person thinks, saying nearly the same thing. Years with Jessica until the abyss. The number three was impossible. Luckily, there was Alessandra.

I walked with Fabrizio back to the newspaper kiosk, where his father had been waiting for quite a while. I'd never seen the old man give his son a hard time, always sparing him any trouble where he could. So, even though he'd been waiting three times longer than planned, he just said, "You shouldn't have hurried, I've got plenty of time."

* * *

Alessandra and I had arranged to meet in the middle of the village, by the church where the weekly market was held. There was quite a crowd and I had to elbow my way through. People jostled for some artichokes or a suckling pig reared to be slaughtered and eaten. I stood on the steps to the church. I was the first to arrive and thought of Roland Barthes again. The one who waits is the one who loves. Among the passers-by I recognized the Captain, accompanied by the fisherman. He was pulling a multicoloured shopping trolley, and stopped at every stall. He looked happy. The stallholders smiled at him (well, they smiled at everyone) and were happy to sell him almost everything they had on show. The trolley started to swell like Dr. Ignazio's calves and the Captain found it more and more difficult to steer. He crushed one person's foot, bashed into someone else . . . as people rolled their eyes and puffed out their chests to show their irritation. Every Sunday the market square turned into an open-air theatre. It was an exuberant kerfuffle and the Captain had a major role while I had a prime seat in a box. And was still waiting.

A van suddenly started reversing and nearly ran over some shoppers, including the Captain. He instinctively protected himself with his shopping trolley which, luckily, was full. Screams and people thumping on the van alerted the driver, who lurched to a stop. The Captain walked over to him and brandished his fist, causing the driver to freeze in terror. The Captain's face was red with anger and loathing, and certainly didn't encourage the man to get out of his van. The old soldier wore an expression I'd often imagined but never seen: total fury.

Roland Barthes was hit by a van once on his way to the Collège de France. He died shortly afterwards. Some day it would be worth looking into the effects of road-traffic accidents on culture. Giacometti was knocked down by a car – leaving him with a limp – and so was Jean-Michel Basquiat, while Albert Camus died in a car crash. There was something absurd about it all. Intelligence virtually swept aside by hunks of metal. What could be more pointless and stupid than metal? Everyone always knew the identity of the victim, but rarely that of the culprit. In Basquiat's case and Giacometti's, the accident had even inspired their work. When Basquiat was in hospital as a child he was given a book on anatomy. He would use it for inspiration, constantly pulling people to pieces. Giacometti had a limp until his dying day, his sculptures did the walking for him. But the Captain wouldn't end up like them, thanks to his shopping trolley. We'd narrowly avoided an accident on the market place but perhaps at the same time we'd also missed an opportunity to bring to light a writer, a painter or a sculptor.

I spotted Alessandra in the distance. She was looking in my direction but hadn't recognized me because of the sun in her eyes. I watched her walk towards this stranger who came to see her every day. She must have been unsure if I'd show up because she kept looking left and right, screwing up her eyes and raising her right hand to block out the sunlight. It was no good, she couldn't see, her eyes must have been tearing up with pain. It would have been rude of me to whistle to attract her attention, or make an idiot of myself jumping up and down and shouting. We weren't close enough. Emotionally. Physically, though, things were looking up because Alessandra was getting nearer. In the end she recognized me and put a hand up and waved. I could have done that but hadn't thought of it. Just putting up a hand. "I'm here." The fact was, I was paralysed by the thought of looking ridiculous.

My first meeting with Alessandra had been chaotic because I'd fallen at her feet. My legs had given way like the spaghetti in my mother's huge saucepan. A grey saucepan big enough to fit two little boys like me. Standing up. At first the pasta looked firm but when it came in contact with the boiling water, it gave way. One time when my mother had invited Gavino to dinner, he pretended to drop me into the saucepan for a laugh. I was five years old and after this suggested immersion in a hostile environment, I hadn't eaten spaghetti for many months. If you lived anywhere else on the planet, having a spaghetti phobia would be manageable, but in Italy . . . Whenever we were invited to go round to other members of the family, I dreaded the meal. I prayed silently when the pasta appeared. "Please don't let it be spaghetti! Let it be gnocchi, please, make it be gnocchi!" My prayers were often pointless because, for whatever reason, it was very often spaghetti that was served. No one up there was listening to my supplications and my longing for gnocchi. When Gavino saw that haunted look spread

over my face, he would rub his stomach. He relished my fear
of the spaghetti (which would soon be in his tummy). An ogre
confronting a little boy.

Alessandra knew nothing of all this when she came up to
me. She thought me sufficiently interesting to grant me a day
in her company. I just hoped she didn't order spaghetti at the
restaurant. In any event, on this occasion my legs had no trouble
supporting me and I had every intention of staying on my feet
for the rest of the day.

*   *   *

Do place names influence our lives? That's a logical question
to ask if you decide to spend a while on an island called Caprera.
Goat Island. Not Seagull Island, which would instantly have
conjured seaside holiday images. Not Flamingo Island, which
sounded so poetic and colourful. Not Bear Island, probably
because there weren't any bears, though that would have cast
me in the role of a courageous huntsman. Not Wild Horse
Island, a thought that almost instantly made my hair fly in the
wind and made me – in my imagination, at least – vault bare-
back onto a glorious mount. No, we were stuck with Goat
Island. Which had less gratifying connotations. When we hear
the word "goat" our brains immediately conjure the image of
a small white animal with a bit of beard. And maybe cheese.
And bleating noises. Unpleasant smells. So when I mentioned
Caprera to Alessandra, I knew that this wave of negative (the
smell) and ridiculous (the little beard) elements mustn't get in
the way of us getting along.

I told her about Garibaldi, who came from Caprera. When
Italians hear the name "Garibaldi" our brains conjure the image
of a very serious bearded man with a sabre in one hand and
an Italian flag in the other. The image that school imprints in
our minds, forcefully, so that it stays there. To my left, a goat.
To my right, Garibaldi. Alessandra was starting to break into
a smile at the name Caprera. Doctors also laugh at the silliest

things. And then Garibaldi came out of my mouth, and the smile never broke. You don't laugh about Garibaldi, he's the symbol of Italian national unity.

To get to Caprera we took the boat that went as far as the island of Maddalena. A battered boat devoid of charm, wearied by endless trips without rest. We stayed up on deck for the whole crossing.

"You should put something round your throat, Giacomo."

"It's summer."

"It's in summer that people get ill. Sore throats don't care what time of year it is."

Alessandra's reasoning was like my mother's, which I didn't find reassuring. At home I'd seen the ravages of time on an overprotective mind. At first things were said calmly, then over the years (although I didn't know whether the concept of "years" would ever have any meaning in my relationship with Alessandra) this calm turned into scolding and scolding into real anger. If Alessandra and I made this trip again after ten years of living together, the conversation might have a very different ring to it:

"Cover yourself up, for goodness' sake."

"It's summer."

"Well, don't come running to me if you get a sore throat."

And twenty years later?

"You really don't understand anything, do you?"

"What makes you say that?"

"You think you're a young man, scruffily dressed like that. I'll be laughing, when you're stuck in bed with a throat infection."

Thirty years after this first conversation about the risk of catching cold, there would be no conversation at all. All gone:

". . ."

". . ."

We shouldn't project ourselves into the future, it would stop us from doing anything.

After alighting from the boat we hired two bikes to get to the island, which was accessible only by a bridge designed by first-year civil engineering students. I say first-year because the construction didn't exactly inspire confidence. It felt as if it might collapse into the Mediterranean at any moment. Crossing this bridge brought me no pleasure, just apprehension, made worse by the fact that we were on bikes and it would take us a lot longer to get to the other side than the gleaming cars that overtook us and nearly sent us toppling over the edge in the process. I closed my eyes with every passing vehicle, praying to the heavens (which I no longer believed in) to keep me safe till we reached our destination. Alessandra kept getting really close to the right-hand side of the bridge, and I followed her as best I could.

I'd never been great at cycling, or any activity where balance plays an important role. As I child I would fall off my bike constantly, and more than once, in order to keep me in one piece, my father resorted to puncturing my tyres to stop me riding around the village. After about ten consecutive punctures, suspicions had crept into my mind: there must have been an explanation for these problems with my inner tubes. I very naturally thought Gavino was the guilty party, given how much he enjoyed making my life difficult. One morning when Mama was still asleep, I heard little noises coming from the garage. I opened the door quietly and saw Papa methodically screwing a screw into my front tyre, whistling contentedly as he turned his Philips screwdriver. Once the job was done, he worked the screw back out and put it and the screwdriver away into his red toolbox. Blue and red. I remember the colours of that puncture perfectly. I didn't say anything to my father, I was far too upset for that. He was calling into question my cyclistic abilities – not that the word existed, but it perfectly suited the situation. Papa had the right to puncture my tyre, so I had every right to invent a word. "Cyclistic", a blue-and-red word, for the blood and bruises on my knees.

I'd opted for a cycling date with Alessandra because I felt that it had a certain romance to it. I hadn't ridden a bike for years but I felt strong enough to guide my new friend. At the hire place I pretended to know all the different models and their various features, and I prodded and handled them to check their sturdiness. This of course betrayed what an amateur I was because, seeing me doing the same thing to all his bikes, the hire man eventually smiled and said, "You'll end up letting the air out of the saddle."

I was supposed to lead the way, which I did for the first minute, until, seeing how ungainly I was, Alessandra quickly overtook me and suggested she lead the dance instead. She was probably worried about all the wobbling she'd had plenty of opportunity to witness during my minute in front, so I had to be sensible and accept my demotion. Besides, if I fell, she wouldn't see it. Cycling is romantic, but only if you have a good sense of balance.

* * *

Luckily for me, the bike ride wasn't the main aim of the day. The idea was to get to an almost inaccessible but truly incredible place: a creek with crystalline waters, Cala Coticcio. It would be thanks to me that Alessandra would see it. My father had always told me that it was one of the most beautiful places in the world. In his world, certainly, because he hadn't travelled much. But in mine too because, despite my many travels, I'd rarely seen anything like it. Papa had once told me, "If you ever want to charm a girl, take her to Cala Coticcio, she'll love you forever."

He'd tried with Mama and the first part of his assertion was confirmed: Mama was charmed. As for eternal love, I was less convinced. I never took a girlfriend to Coticcio during my rebellious teenage years, because I didn't want to follow any parental advice. And because if that advice was right, then I'd have to spend my whole life with the same girl. That was risky. One day, many years later, Papa mentioned the creek to Jessica, and so I took her there. She liked it and we did a lot of kissing there. It was an important point in our relationship, and I proposed to her shortly afterwards. Seduction clung to Coticcio the way a *candiru*, a parasitic fish, clings to its prey to suck its blood. As for the longevity of love, that was another subject. Mama may have stayed with Papa but Jessica and I had divorced. The *candiru* eats its prey, it doesn't spend the rest of its days harnessed to its gills. Now, if it had set its sights on Moby Dick . . .

As Alessandra was cycling ahead of me, I called out directions to the path that led to the creek. Our roles had ended up being reversed, she was the one taking me there. In a rush of masculinity, I decided to pedal as fast as I could in order to reclaim the position I felt I should have in this sort of situation. My calves burned, indicating they would soon stop working altogether, but Alessandra was still ahead of me. I refused to give up, so I stood on the pedals and accelerated. As if by magic, Alessandra's back seemed to grow clearer and clearer, closer and closer. And so did everything else. They say you never forget how to ride a bike, and I was living proof of this: I could easily catch up with Alessandra . . . but the truth was, she was waiting for me by the side of the road.

"Are you having trouble, Giacomo?"

"No, everything's fine, but I think the chain needs oiling. It's tricky changing gears."

"I see. Anyway, are we nearly there?"

"Yes, it's another 500 metres to the right. There's a little car park where we can leave the bikes. Then we have to walk a little way, and we'll get to Coticcio."

"Perfect! I really can't wait to see this place."

We chained the bikes together at the car park – the two of us close together for the first time. Only symbolically, perhaps, but close all the same. I was happy that it was Alessandra who suggested it. As a literary type, I have a tendency to see symbols in everything. Every gesture and every word means more than meets the eye. They need analysing to reveal their deeper meaning. The bicycles weren't just bicycles, they represented us, and the chain binding them together referred to a strong union, a serious relationship. I was thinking about all this when

Alessandra pointed to the two bikes and said, "There, no one can take them now."

The operation was actually intended to thwart anyone who might want to steal our bikes. And Alessandra went on to say, "You just try carrying two mountain bikes at the same time!" My interpretation of the signs was proving inaccurate. I was a translator, not a semiologist.

"I hope you don't mind heights, because it's quite a steep climb down."

"Don't worry, I used to do a lot of walking in Rome."

"*Can* you walk in Rome?"

"You can walk anywhere! There are wonderful walks in the hills around Rome."

"They'll be nothing compared to what you're about to see today. Please let me know if I'm walking too quickly or you're finding it tricky."

Alessandra thought I was joking because there was such a discrepancy between the way I'd said this and what she knew of me. I could barely ride a bike and now I was talking like someone who'd been up K2 several times. Discrepancy is detrimental to human relationships: I should have opted for a more neutral tone, something more in keeping with the real me – a flatter tone, then, but because I'd always been told that a man should be helpful to ladies, I'd chosen words that promoted me beyond my own design specifications.

"We'll go down slowly, Giacomo. And yes, if I need your help, I'll let you know."

She was being a little sarcastic and I had no trouble spotting it. Her "I'll let you know" meant more than this simple combination of words. A longer, more complex phrase, something like, "You poor thing, given how adept you are on a bicycle, you're obviously going to break an ankle on this path."

It was a very steep climb down to the beach and Alessandra was amazed to see families undertaking the descent, carrying children and cool-boxes the size of fridges. I wasn't surprised because I'd seen convoys like this several times before. The cool-box was the father's hiking pole. Always. A man had to be laden like a mule, carrying as much as he could, be it live beings (his children) or inanimate objects (things for the beach). I meanwhile had prepared a few sandwiches but had not allowed myself to bring a cool-box, even though Mama had pestered me to. "The water will be scalding if you don't take a cool-box," she'd said. "Your father always thought of everything when he took me on outings." I wasn't my father, and I couldn't picture myself greeting Alessandra with a cool-box in my hand. Cycling was romantic. Cool-boxes weren't.

"Would you like me to put something together for you and your friend? Maybe some cold spaghetti. It's delicious for picnics. With a trickle of olive oil and a hint of garlic. And it's healthy too. Garlic cleans the blood, I heard that on the radio the other day." Mama had definitely lost all concept of seduction. I thought of her huge saucepan and the terrifying consequences of garlic in my mouth. As for my blood, it would take an awful lot more than a clove of garlic to clean it.

"These people are crazy! Making their family take risks like this."

"This is their homeland, they can't believe it would ever hurt them. It's in their blood. But they're wrong. They should be made to eat garlic . . ."

"Pardon?"

"Nothing, I was joking."

"Does everyone who lives on the island believe that?"

"No, I don't."

"But you don't live on the island, do you?"

"You're right."

★ ★ ★

I didn't twist my ankle as I showed Alessandra the way to the beach. And of course she thought the place was amazing – I wasn't taking much of a risk by bringing her here. What I hadn't anticipated was that she would ask me dozens and dozens of questions all through the day. You'd have thought she could only speak in the interrogative. When I ventured a question, she'd ping one straight back at me. I was experiencing the frustrations of an outing with a doctor; I was the patient confronted with the doctor's investigation, without the option of cancelling the appointment. And no possibility of a refund. The Captain had the failing of talking about himself far too much, but Alessandra excelled in the art of getting other people to talk. I hated talking about myself. Sardinian men aren't great talkers, it's traditional. Even if you're born talkative, time on the island soon teaches you that talking is a lack of control. I genuinely didn't know whether half the men in my village were mute due to some handicap or simply out of restraint. Every evening, summer and winter, men walked silently through the streets together without uttering a single word. It was quite strange, I couldn't see the logic in meeting up in order not to talk. Well, people communicate differently here. Rather like the trees.

While we had our lunch we noticed a lively to and fro of Canadair firefighter planes in the sky: orange-and-red planes taking turns dropping down to refill their water tanks from the sea. We watched the pilots' manoeuvres happily and with considerable admiration. And while this was going on Alessandra didn't ask me any personal questions, she was more interested in the planes.

"Do you think they have one pilot or two? How many round-trips do you think a pilot makes in a day? Would you say all these planes are from Sardinia? . . ."

I don't know everything about everything, so my answers were a little impenetrable:

One pilot.

No idea.

Some are from Corsica.

The other walkers who'd come to the beach seemed to have decided to pack away their things. You could tell that they found the planes unsettling. As the cool-boxes started their return trip,

Alessandra and I soon found ourselves watching the planes alone. A good opportunity to try getting closer to her . . . symbolically.

I looked into her eyes and held her gaze a moment.

"Do you think the fire is far from here?" she asked, still looking me in the eye.

"No idea."

"We don't want to get cut off. Do you know a quicker way out?" she asked, looking away.

When a symbolic boundary has been crossed like this, the former mode sometimes reappears, like a distant past resurfacing, only to endorse the new understanding. The person who lapsed back sometimes then adds real emphasis to the new state of affairs.

"So, Giacomo," she said, briefly touching my arm, "do you know a quicker way out?"

"There isn't another way out. The fire must be a long way away, though, don't worry."

Truth be told, I knew nothing about wildfires. I'd witnessed them several times in my life but never really taken an interest. They regularly destroyed whole swathes of the island. The scrubland burned, leaving the landscape dark and pitted like the surface of the moon. Very black and very ugly. A smouldering barbecue smell replaced the scent of shrubs. Spectacular images were shown on television and occasionally people lamented the death of a shepherd who couldn't bear to abandon his flock to the flames.

Manuella's father had died like that. She'd told us about it on the way to an away game. He used to live a good part of the year in a stone-built house in the middle of nowhere – a dream for anyone who preferred the company of sheep to people. Her father liked being alone, she'd told us, and didn't come home much. I couldn't understand this remoteness. How could anyone prefer sheep to Manuella? Personally, if I'd been able to get close to the grocer's wife, sheep definitely wouldn't have tipped the scales. She was so much more beautiful.

When you're beside the sea, you look out to sea, so we sat

looking at the sea and didn't notice the smoke coming down the path. I only saw it when I got up to shake out my towel and watched the sand whipped up on the wind. Not just sand, in fact. There were also tiny particles of ash. When I looked up the mountainside that we'd come down, it was obvious we couldn't go back that way. It turned out the people with their cool-boxes had been much more sensible than I had.

I didn't tell Alessandra straight away because I had to analyse the situation. Escaping by sea seemed impossible because my swimming talents were fairly limited. Floating on my back wouldn't be a problem but ploughing through the water like a love-struck teenager was out of the question. We'd had a swim when we arrived, and I'd noticed that Alessandra was a really good swimmer. And no, I wasn't just seeing everything about her through rose-tinted spectacles. She swam quickly and neatly, without looking effortful. That's what I'd always lacked as a swimmer, that ease. I was cumbersome – not physically, because my physique was perfectly acceptable for a man my age; no, I was cumbersome in other ways, almost magically so because my weightiness was not something you saw in most people. I could float but I never got anywhere. I had a few swimming lessons in Marseille. To no avail. The instructor soon grasped he'd never get anywhere with me. I was a sort of floating beacon.

I hadn't stayed in the water long so Alessandra didn't have an opportunity to notice my terrible swimming skills. First the bike, then swimming. All that was missing now was the spaghetti and garlic. If the situation got really critical, Alessandra would have to help me swim . . . I felt ashamed just contemplating that eventuality. If only Moby Dick could have swum past, I'd have asked him for a hand. Meanwhile the mountain loomed over the Mediterranean and grew blacker by the minute.

"We're going to have a bit of a problem."

"What?"

"The fire's coming down the track."

Alessandra spun round and looked up.

"We've had it!"

"No we haven't. The emergency services will come and get us. Look, the Canadair pilots can see us."

They were actually concentrating entirely on the necessary manoeuvres to draw up water without crashing into the surface. Human beings need to be really cornered before they'll relax entrenched habits and do things they never normally do: it's the survival instinct.

"I'm going to call my mother."

"Will she come and get us?"

"No, but she'll know what to do."

All Italians have a problem with their mothers. I fought this rather stupid prejudice for a long time. With my friends in Marseille I put up a daily battle against the notion that dogged men from my country. I was wrong to. I should have said yes, they were absolutely right and, whatever our outward show of confidence, Italian men are just little boys who are lost without their mamas.

"Mama? It's me."

"Hello, darling. Have you had a good lunch?"

"Yes, but that's not what I'm calling about. We're at Coticcio."

"I know."

"We're stuck on the beach. There's a fire in the mountains."

"Oh God! I'm on my way!"

"You can't get here. The path's blocked."

"Have you called the emergency services?"

"No. Just you."

I sensed a certain satisfaction in my mother. She was frightened, obviously. But the fact that she'd been called before the emergency services conferred considerable status on her. First place.

"Call them right now. How's your friend coping?"

"Very well."

"Wonderful things always rise from the ashes."

"Thank you for that poetic thought, Mama."

"Hang up, Giacomo."

On my mother's advice, I immediately called the fire brigade.

"We're at Coticcio and we can't get off the beach because of the fire."

"I know."

"You know we're trapped?"

"No, I know the beach is surrounded by flames."

"We need help."

"How many of you are there?"

"Two."

"Just two?"

"One would be one too many."

"Two adults?"

"Yes."

"Could I have your names."

It felt like trying to buy a train ticket from a grumpy salesperson.

"Will you come and get us?"

"Of course, when I've filled in the forms."

I gave him all the information he asked for. If the flames had been more virulent, our lives would have come to an end on that parcel of paradise. Which was now blue, ochre and black.

"I'll send a boat to pick you up. Don't panic."

"One last thing, if I may."

"Tell me."

"What do we do about the bikes?"

"What bikes?"

"The bikes I hired to get to the car park."

"What can I say, we're not going to send a team out to salvage a couple of bikes."

"I put a big deposit down on them."

"You'll have to sort that out with the hire company."

"That's a real shame."

"Would you rather we saved you, then, or the bikes?"

"Well, given the fact I made out a cheque for 500 euros, I'm beginning to wonder."

"Are you joking?"

"I don't know."

Alessandra was reassured when I told her they would be coming to get us soon. She must have been thinking this sort of thing never happened in Rome. She told me she'd think twice before going walking in Sardinia again. The comment stung me like a slap in the face and my expression darkened. I couldn't hide how I felt.

"Don't worry, I don't blame you, Giacomo. Don't sulk!"

"I'm not sulking."

"What about the bikes? You left a deposit, didn't you?"

"Never mind about that. What matters is we're safe."

Sometimes in a (budding) relationship it's best to keep some thoughts to yourself.

* * *

We didn't perish at Coticcio. We ended where everything was meant to begin, but nothing really got started. On the boat back to the harbour, Alessandra chatted for ages with the first-response team. She knew some of them. She didn't ask any questions. I stayed in my little corner of the boat and enjoyed the glorious view. I'd never seen that part of the island from the sea. I left them to talk. Alessandra was still just as pretty but I no longer knew what I wanted. To burden her or not to burden her with my endless procrastinations? Jessica would never have left me and gone to talk to a bunch of firemen. She would have stayed with me on this secluded part of the deck, and we would have watched as the flames ravaged the land. At first we faced our problems together, when they started, as they evolved and afterwards. But eventually the flames got too aggressive. Then came that evening when I took her to hospital. There were first-response teams there too, but she didn't give a damn about them, not Jessica.

I saw Alessandra back to her car before calling the bike hire man to explain what had happened. He assured me he wouldn't keep the deposit and would go and fetch the bikes as soon as the firefighters had reopened the road. Everything was falling into place, almost. The day I'd been so looking forward to hadn't gone as planned.

Mama was waiting for me on the doorstep; I'd managed to set her mind at rest over the phone but she wanted to be sure I was all in one piece. She was holding a plastic container, which didn't stop her giving me a huge hug. The container felt hot against my back. I tried to pull away, but found that I couldn't. She hauled me back. "I'd have gone mad if anything bad had happened to you." I didn't venture to tell her that madness was a subjective concept and, in my opinion, some of her behaviour (like waiting outside the house for me with a scalding-hot plastic container or threatening to leave the marital home over one tiny comment taken the wrong way) could be attributed to it. "You should have brought your friend back. We could all have had dinner together. You must both be very hungry after all that." Mama opened the container. It was full of gnocchi. Another source of pride on the island.

"She had to go home, she's working this evening."

"Does she work in a restaurant?"

"Restaurants aren't the only places where people work in the evening . . . or at night."

"At night too? I can't think of many night jobs. Please tell me, Giacomo, it is decent work, is it?"

"It couldn't be more decent."

"Well, tell me, for goodness' sake! Why are you keeping me on tenterhooks about this young woman?"

"She's the doctor who looked after Grandma."

"Ignazio?"

"Mama, Ignazio's not the only member of the medical profession. And she's a woman! The doctor at the hospital, young, dark hair . . ."

"How wonderful! My son with a doctor!"

"We're just friends, that's all."

Mama was so proud, she'd forgotten about the gnocchi that were going cold. She looked left and right to check whether my father was anywhere near because she was dying to reveal my friend's identity to him, but Papa had headed off in another direction.

"Call her!"

"Why?"

"To invite her to dinner."

"I told you, she's working."

"Are you ashamed of us?"

"Not at all, she's on duty this evening."

"Let me speak to her!"

"But I haven't got her on the phone, how am I supposed to . . ."

"We're not educated enough. I see."

"Mama!"

"I'll go back to my course at Cagliari University, then you won't be ashamed."

"What course?"

"I started studying history when I left school."

"I didn't know that."

"Will you call her, then?"

"Mama!"

"And your father can study history of art. History of art, that does sound good."

"Mama!"

"Mama, what?"

"You're mad!"

* * *

It wasn't easy for two adults to get inside the *Domus* on my street, even though Fabrizio and I weren't very tall, but we'd decided to spend some of the night in this tiny space, as we used to when we were boys. I'd slipped out of the house very quietly so that my parents wouldn't notice. The maternal radar that once detected the tiniest movement in the air was beginning to lose its touch.

There were shards of glass on the floor of the *Domus* and a consummately unpleasant smell that could not be put down to the Nuragic civilization. Fabrizio had planned everything and brought a small blanket and two scented candles – which we had to light carefully to avoid burning ourselves in such a cramped space. Our knees touched. I'd taken care of the drinks: Sardinian beer, Ichnusa, the pride of the island, whose name derives from *Hyknusa*, the Greek name for Sardinia. We were doing something – sitting huddled together in the fairy house – that our ancestors had done for centuries before us. They had hoped for reassurance because there was total darkness outside and they knew nothing about anything: day and night were yet to be explained. And beer hadn't been invented to help them forget their ignorance.

"The fairies must be happy to have an old man like me in their house. It's a good thing you're here!"

"The fairies only like children, not adults."

"Shame, I'd have liked to ask them to turn me into Prince Charming. Just for a day, or even a night. Fabrizio, with brand-new skin. How about you, what would you ask for?"

"Can't you guess?"

"Yes, of course I can. We'd ask for things that would change our lives. Just our bad luck the fairies left the building years ago. I'm stuck with my skin and you with your heartache."

"What if we could ask them something reasonable and not too complicated . . . ?"

"Like finding love?"

"Exactly!"

"Well then, I'd ask them for permission to love myself."

"Don't you give yourself permission?"

"I don't want to foist my problems on anyone else. But I've had enough of being on my own. The only woman I talk to, bar the odd customer who comes to buy a paper, is my mother! I love her, you know that, but I can't take her any more. Mama here, Mama there, she's everywhere. Supermama! Just imagine my mother in a superhero outfit, chasing after me all day long. 'Look after your skin, Fabrizio, be careful, don't stay too long in the sun!'"

There we were in a dirty, smelly place laughing heartily about childish nonsense.

"She's right, though, the sun does damage the skin."

"I don't need any help from the sun, my skin's doing a good job of being damaged on its own!"

I don't usually drink much because I like to be in control of my thoughts and actions, but that evening, the beers just kept on coming, as if the fairies had opened a free bar. The cans on the blanket mimicked the shape of the island, and the smell of the island's beer at our feet overpowered the much lighter fragrance of the candles Fabrizio had brought. Our laughter was interrupted by a stray dog popping its head into the *Domus*. This must have been its chosen kennel. It stood staring at us for a few seconds, then slunk off without even baring its teeth at us. It had clearly grasped that the two drunken humans would be staying put for the night, and it would have to find another bed to sleep in.

"Poor dog, we could have invited it in for a beer."

"Do dogs drink alcohol?"

"They do nowadays, I think . . . That's the modern world! They're just like us."

"So we've succeeded in corrupting dogs . . ."

"And cats too. My grandmother's cat is obese, as fat as that man who couldn't get out of his house."

"You'd never get something like that in the natural world."

"Mankind's ruined everything . . . even the walls in the village!"

"Do you mean the paintings?"

"Yes, they're all over the place and they get uglier and uglier, all wrinkled . . ."

"Like my skin."

Fabrizio managed to laugh about his condition, he was so familiar with it, having lived with it for all those years.

"Do you want a cigarette, Giacomo?"

"I've never smoked . . ."

"Really? You're a good boy, aren't you? Top of the class, with his parting on the right and his hair always neat. Goody Two Shoes!"

"Pass me one, then!"

Of course I choked on the first puff. Can you start smoking at thirty-six? It was now or never. Fabrizio mimed what to do, exaggerating every action so that I could copy him, his lips reaching droopily towards an imaginary cigarette.

"The doctors won't let me smoke, the fools. It's easy for them to tell me what I can and can't do, dishing out rules that have to be followed. 'You mustn't, you shouldn't, we wouldn't advise . . .' I don't give a stuff! Let them spend a day in my shoes, then they'll understand."

We spent a good part of the night laughing idiotically together. The fairies didn't come and disturb us, but neither did they offer to grant us a wish. We were in their house, but they weren't home. Fabrizio walked me back to my place, even though it was very nearby, because I'd set off in the wrong direction when we came out of the *Domus*.

"Are you going down to the harbour?" he asked, laughing.

He was looking out for me. I'd be gone soon.

* * *

In my dream, Moby Dick is coming up to the beach where I'm trapped. Alessandra has already left and I'm ankle deep in the water when the animal raises its eyes and teeth above the surface. Not aggressively.

"Do you have news of Ahab, Giacomo?"

"I saw him on my way home last night."

"How was he?"

"He was very annoyed about you. I think he wants to hurt you."

"What harm can he do me? A captain against a sperm whale . . . pah! . . ."

"Still, be careful."

"What about you, how are you?"

"I've had some tough times the last few days."

"Really?"

"Problems with family, work, relationships . . ."

"Ah, I've had some issues too, but things always sort themselves out, believe me. Do you think this Alessandra is for you, Giacomo?"

"I don't know."

"I thought so. She's very kind, very pretty. I may be a whale but I can see the charms of a beautiful woman. You live in Marseille and she lives in Sardinia."

"Yes, but I could make arrangements."

"With Carlo? Have you seen how the man hassles you? He's your very own Ahab. Don't complicate your life, you know all about pain."

"I didn't know whales did oracle work on the side."

"Whales have many powers. Men only see what they want to see in animals. And in my case that's a huge lump of aggression. But have you looked at my eyes? Look how expressive they are, they show how sensitive I am."

"You're right. We don't see anything. We only see what suits us."

"What about your Captain, are you still meeting up with him?"

"Sometimes."

"Are you disappointed with that reunion?"

"I thought we'd have more to say to each other."

"He talks too much."

"Probably."

"And you don't talk enough! Have you finished your translation?"

"Yes, at last!"

"And now what?"

"I'm going back home, to Marseille."

"Home? I thought this island was your home."

"Not completely. Not anymore. How about you, what are your plans?"

"I'm leaving too. I came to say goodbye. I'm also heading north. I've really enjoyed my time on this wild coastline."

"It's a magical island."

"I must leave you. It's a long journey. The emergency services are coming to pick you up, I can hear them."

★ ★ ★

My translation was finished. Ahab was standing tall on the whale. Carlo would be pleased but I hadn't told him yet – it was my translator's revenge on the editor. I knew he would be waiting to hear from me, he must have been clinging to his phone all day long, his publicity plan was all set, the only thing missing being the text . . . and I had it. Saying nearly the same thing in a different language was a complex and mostly misunderstood process. Within a few weeks, news of this new manuscript would go around the world and back. There would be a lot of talk about Herman Melville. Carlo would give the press interviews, with a smile on his lips. He would pose in his office, more specifically on the sofa under the portrait of himself he had commissioned from an obscure painter, which depicted a languid Carlo on his bed, in pyjamas. I'd never understood what the artist was trying to do, or the client for that matter, because the painting didn't do either of them any favours . . . Carlo would put on his orange trousers and emerald-green shirts for the journalists, signs that he still had some Sardinian blood in him. I mean, who else but a Sardinian would wear colours like that? He would also parade his very white teeth and prolific hairiness. Come to think of it, he could audition for a part in *The Bold and the Beautiful* . . . a new lover for Brooke. Grandma would be thrilled.

Meanwhile, no one would talk about me. They wouldn't give a damn who'd translated this fascinating manuscript. A little translator lost on a hostile island. It was always the same. Who knew about Daryl Stuermer, the lyricist behind Phil Collins's songs? Not the singer on the boat or his audience who shimmied to the former Genesis man's hits.

Keeping the text to myself meant I could enjoy a moment of calm before the media storm. Before a new adventure began. Simenon or another author, male or female, who knew? And then I would have to immerse myself in their work, understand a whole new world, another way of seeing things, because literature was nothing other than one person's vision of existence. Stendhal described novels as a mirror carried along the path we tread. He was right. But I would have added a few adjectives to the noun, to that path: bumpy, steep or even burnt . . .

★ ★ ★

Alessandra and I decided, politely, not to see each other again. Politely because we were both reasonable people. My head was all over the place, I couldn't be sure about anything and Alessandra apparently preferred first-aiders to translators. She hadn't said it in so many words, but I was sure of it nonetheless. You can immediately tell when someone's attracted to the guy sitting next to you. The one talking loudly and who, at first, at least, is endlessly confident. The one whose path is gentle, pleasant and edged with flowers. Alessandra hadn't been on duty that evening after the fire. I'd lied to my mother to avoid telling her that her hopes of seeing her child happy again had been blown away with the smoke into the blue-and-grey Sardinian sky.

All that was left to do now was to go home to Marseille. Grandma still hadn't died – in fact she was very well. I promised to come back and see her soon. We always make promises to come back, it's terrifying. I couldn't help myself.

"Come back soon, my little one. I don't have much time left."

"You can't leave us halfway through a season of *The Bold and the Beautiful*! You need to know what happens next year."

"If I wait till the end of that series I won't die for thirty years and I think people will soon be fed up with waiting for me to go. Death does need to come along. For our own sakes, of course, but mostly for other people's."

"Don't give them the satisfaction! Wait till I'm back!"

"You've always been brave, Giacomo, even when life's been hard on you."

"On us, Grandma, hard on us."

"Give Jessica a hug from me when you see her. I was very fond of her. I thought she was a lovely, charming girl. I'd happily have traded her in for Gavino! What am I saying, I'd even have paid him off to get rid of him . . . But, what can you do, we don't get to swap our children."

Grandma still had her sardonic side. I'd be seeing her for a good while yet in her armchair or on the stone bench that Papa had built next to the house. A bench to watch our street from. A bench that would be there for years to come and on which I hoped – and why shouldn't I? – I might sit as an old man. It might be wobbly and uncomfortable, but it afforded a view of our world like no other. A bench for watching the world go by.

I went to the newspaper kiosk to let Fabrizio know I was leaving soon. He'd helped and supported me during my time here, as he always had. There were a few tourists buying the French magazines that Fabrizio ordered in during the summer months. Nothing very high-brow, scandal-mongering magazines that no one admitted to buying or reading but which sold nonetheless by the tens of thousands. A rather guilty pleasure but it did their readers good, when they were abroad. Having a taste of France from mildly diverting magazines. A half-naked reality-TV starlet on a beach had pride of place on the whole range of weeklies. What a scandal! What a scoop! The real news would have been seeing her with her clothes on. Fabrizio was used to these pathetic publications (he had them for every country) so he didn't even notice them anymore. Like the short-lived stars themselves, who would soon fade into obscurity.

The tourists bought the whole range of French magazines that Fabrizio sold – a gold mine for my friend. A direct attack on intelligence! I used to witness this dispiriting process when I travelled with Jessica. We occasionally bought this kind of magazine ourselves. Shamelessly. We read them on the beach or at the hotel before leaving them deliberately on our deck-chairs. There was no question of taking them home in our luggage, they were proof of our passing idiocy. The art of reading was being lost, intellectuals claimed. Wrongly. The number of people reading books was growing all the time, I had first-hand evidence of that. People were reading more and more, particularly on holiday, never mind the quality. I understood those who said people read nothing but rubbish nowadays. Perhaps the solution was to put passages of worthier material into these magazines. An article about a pseudo-star immediately followed by a short story by Maupassant or Joyce, or something by Jack London. Readers would get a taste for it because we can't help getting used to beauty and luxury. A bit of Kafkaesque caviar following on from a piece about a summer holiday break-up. *K*'s arrival in America to publish the heartbreak of the actor who died tragically in a selfie competition on a precipice. I would touch on this idea with Carlo once I was back. Scope out whether he might want to get into innovative trashy magazine publishing . . .

"Are you looking for something, Giacomo? I'm afraid I've completely run out of French sensationalist magazines, sorry!"

"I'll find plenty in Marseille, don't you worry."

"I'm sure you will, my friend."

"I'm leaving soon."

"Are you abandoning me?"

"I came for a few days, and suddenly the weeks have flown by."

"Do you regret that?"

"No, I've enjoyed spending a bit of time with you."

"So've I. People always end up coming back, it's just what happens. I know you'll be back sometime to see your old – very old – teammate."

"Of course I will."

"Before you leave, you should go and see the Captain. I've heard he's not in very good shape."

"Who told you that?"

"Dr. Ignazio. The Captain had an appointment with him the other day."

"Is Dr. Ignazio still working?"

"He's like a weed you can't get rid of. He once told me, 'When you're a doctor, you're a doctor for life,' as if it was an incurable disease. Like me saying, 'When you have *cutis laxa*, it's for life.'"

"So will you never get rid of it?"

"Never, Giacomo. Even in my coffin, it'll be there with me. The maggots will think they're eating an old man . . . that will be my revenge on them. Tricking them about the goods. Like your grandmother did with your family! Ah, we do like tricking people here. Maybe you lost that, Giacomo, by leaving so young."

"I don't know . . . I'll drop in on the Captain before I go."

I'd changed the subject because I didn't know what to say to Fabrizio. We all do it. When a conversation gets too awkward, you have to divert the other person's attention, even if you know it's an illusion. Fabrizio was well aware of his circumstances, and he accepted them. I didn't. He didn't pursue it, accepting the new turn I'd just given to our chat. I gave him a hug but didn't squeeze too tightly because I could feel how weak his body was.

★ ★ ★

The night before I left I went up to the attic to fetch my father's paint sprays and a floodlight. The fresco he'd made after the young demonstrator died had almost disappeared. I had no gift for drawing – a disaster for an inhabitant of a village whose walls looked like an open-air graphic novel. I had a few hours in hand to come up with something. Starting with washing away traces of the original painting. My palimpsest. Fabrizio was meant to be coming to help but cancelled at the last minute, too tired to join me. I wasn't annoyed with him. We all do the best we can with the lives we have. And anyway, Fabrizio was no more of an artist than I was, so his absence wasn't all that much of a loss. Obviously my parents knew nothing about this.

I'd opted for a simple shape but one with a wealth of symbolism. A vertical shape. Painting is no more than a combination of horizontals and verticals; no painter escapes that law. A vertical shape, then, and three colours: brown, green (the emerald coast had given our island its reputation) and blue. Nothing else. It had to be simple. And even if my design looked like a child's, I wasn't in the least ashamed of it. Jean-Michel Basquiat, one of the most highly rated painters in the world, had a naïve style, and did anyone find that offensive, apart from a few brainless idiots who always wanted to explain everything? Comparing myself to him might seem a little over the top, but artists need models. The creative process has to start with something. So in my case it was Basquiat.

The wall didn't help much because it was such a rough surface. Still, I started by marking the outline, the silhouette of my subject, with the help of a badly printed photo, its quality ruined by the pixilation. My parents had had the same printer for years. They didn't care about technological advances because they used it once a year to print out the lyrics of the songs they needed to learn for the procession in April. The printer had been so surprised someone wanted to use it in the summer that it had made a terrible noise in the middle of the night, like a person being woken by someone playing a prank on them.

Luckily my parents and grandmother hadn't stirred. Only Mila the cat came to have a look, probably thinking the noise was in some way connected to food. "Maybe Giacomo's carving up a shark with the chainsaw." Disappointed, she stalked back to her cushion with that disdain peculiar to cats.

As time went by, I concentrated hard and the vertical shape was coming along perfectly, now dividing into several segments. After two hours I could finally start applying some colour. My work wasn't exceptional but it suited me: there was now a tree on the wall, a maritime pine on the stone. Just one because I didn't want to represent a crowd. One maritime pine, like a lone man, lost, not in his usual place. A maritime pine in the mountains, far from its kind. I needed to add some blue for the sky. No smoke this time. No grey. A light blue which I couldn't be sure of in the glow of the floodlight. I'd get a better idea in the morning, when it would be too late. I stepped back to get the overall impression, careful not to trip on uneven cobblestones.

I heard a shutter open in the street, and threw myself at the light to turn it off. No one must see my creation. People in the village were inquisitive. I hid for a few minutes. Dogs barked in the distance, claiming possession of their nocturnal territories, not that anybody cared. Once the danger had passed, I went back to my tree because there was still one thing to add: some words. I may not have been much of a one for painting, but I did know about words. I'd just translated tens of thousands of them written by Melville, but these would be my own. I picked up a special can of black spray paint, the kind used for graffiti. Working patiently, I wrote:

We always hope to come back.

I wanted to sleep now. Basquiat was asleep too. The indefatigable church clock struck three. I found Mila in my bed, she'd left me a small space where I could lie down. She obviously realized that I was leaving for a good long time. She snuggled up to me and I didn't push her away. My boat was leaving at seven – with a bit of luck no one would see the fresco before I left.

The painting had exhausted me. My hands hurt, my fingers and wrists, and my legs too because I'd been on my feet a long time. I was usually someone who sat down to work, one of the privileged. Luckily. My inspiration had gone, but not the adrenaline that was running through my veins and thrumming in my temples. I pulled the sheet up to my ears as I used to when I was a little boy, hoping to find some comfort. It didn't work this time, I couldn't stop thinking about what time I had to get up. I turned to the right, facing north because I'd heard that people sleep better in the north. There's a lot of nonsense spoken, and idiots believe it. Twenty minutes later the sheets moved and I soon felt Mama's feet next to mine. Mila jumped out of bed, she couldn't bear being disturbed. Mama slipped into the cat's place and stroked my face. She couldn't sleep either. She wanted to make the most of having her son there just a little longer.

* * *

There were always twitchy passengers out on deck, cigarettes in their mouths, phones in their hands. You'd almost think the decks of boats were there to release tension. I watched the merry-go-round of cars loading onto the ferry down below. It swallowed them all up, all the cars from the smallest and cheapest to the most glamorous. Everyone in the same garage, eroding social differences. The poorest passenger parked next to the richest, indiscriminately. Poorest and richest alike making sure no one scratched their cars. Even the most impressive lorries found a space in this floating garage. They often headed back empty because they brought supplies to the island, but never returned with any. There was some exporting, but the island's external trading mostly operated at a loss. Who wanted our gnocchi and our bread?

Smoke from the boat rose up and joined the blue of the sky, but didn't threaten to darken it. I'd been through dozens of departures and I always had the same feeling: despair to be leaving, a ludicrous longing to run back down all the levels on the ferry and out onto the quay. Everyone around me (or most of them at least) must have had the same impulse, but nobody dared do it. If one of us had taken the plunge, maybe the rest would have followed, but no one did. Not one, not ever. We had to leave. The man next to me chucked his cigarette end into the dark water, while he argued with someone on the phone. Seven o'clock in the morning and you could find someone to talk to on the phone. And to argue with.

Gavino must have been looking everywhere for his razor right now. Or his bike. Or his phone. Or whatever else. I'd been to say goodbye to him the day before. He'd taken me in his arms, as he always did when I was about to leave, struggling to disguise his pleasure that I was going. A few words of advice, a few questions about life in France, and I'd done my duty. In Sardinia, even if you hate someone, you say goodbye to them.

"I'll look after Grandma, don't you worry."

"I know you will."

"And I'll keep an eye on your parents. I know I'm sometimes a bit like a bull in a china shop but I do love every member of our family. Even you."

Gavino always said whatever came into his head, he had no filter. Like a cafetière pouring out water that didn't change when it came into contact with the coffee. What came out couldn't help being disappointing, but it didn't hurt because I was used to it. My uncle never played a part: he was just there, utterly himself.

"And Mila too, you won't forget her, will you?"

"I couldn't possibly! I'm very fond of that cat."

"I didn't know that."

"I've been giving her our leftovers for years. She can really get her knife and fork stuck into things."

"She's a cat!"

"Yes, well, I mean she's got a healthy appetite."

I pictured Mila with cutlery in her paws and a napkin around her neck, sitting at Grandma's table. And Gavino serving her leftovers. *Buon appetito!*

"I knew what you meant."

"Oh, you're always so obsessed with words! But I get it, words are your job."

"Other people's words . . ."

"Giacomo . . ."

When my uncle started a sentence with my name, that meant it was a serious subject. His face tensed and seemed to close, like the doors on a lift.

"Giacomo, I don't blame you for Grandma's lie."

"You don't? Really?"

"Well, I did at the time. That's only natural. But I don't anymore. With family, you have to forgive. Here, give us a hug! No hard feelings, Giacomo. To think your mother used to send me out to buy milk for your bottles . . . You've grown so much, my little nephew."

The ferry started to move away from the quay and Gavino slipped out of my mind to wend his way home to the village. The man beside me had finished his telephone argument and was now watching other passengers barging to find themselves a space on deck. One man, about as tall as three cans of beer one on top of the other, was blowing up a lilo for his offspring – two adorable little girls who wouldn't stand still – to sit on. If you didn't opt to take your own cabin, that only left the deck or the walkways. Unfortunately for him, his pump was showing worrying signs of exhaustion. The minute he pushed it down, the tube sprang off. He threw himself to the deck angrily and tried blowing with all his might into the tiny plastic aperture. A crazy task! His face grew steadily redder while his little girls ran all over the deck. It was a comic scene, with the father regularly interrupting his efforts to reprimand his daughters. The man next to me started laughing, openly. He was laughing because that poor father's journey was starting so badly. Was it even possible to blow up such a big lilo with such a small chest?

"Are you watching this? God, people are stupid!" he said.

I didn't reply and turned the other way. He'd nudged me in the ribs when he didn't even know me, a terrifying lack of common courtesy. Luckily for me, his phone came out with a ridiculous ringtone, perhaps a Phil Collins song. The argument started up again with renewed vigour. And there was the sea, the calm, calm sea. A little dark too, because of the boats' pollution. There were birds gliding near the funnel, waiting for passengers to drop crumbs from their breakfast. The speakers kept reminding us it was time to eat. On the boat, weary from its night crossing, the bars were beginning to open. It never stopped. The cabins had been prepared, sheets and towels changed, and floors cleaned. The staff were busy: today's passengers needed to feel they were the only passengers, never mind the thousands of people who had trundled along these walkways before them. It all kept starting over again. There was the island, still a huge bulk facing us, soon to be reduced to a memory.

* * *

An old legend has it that our ancestors built the first *Domus de Janas* where the Mediterranean now has its seabed. Boats glided over tombs under that great weight of water, like aeroplanes flying over a cemetery. I thought about this myth every time I took the ferry, little men buried so deep below and looking up to watch us from underneath. They must have shaken their heads in despair to see so many idiots throwing out whatever they got their hands on.

Someone put a hand on my shoulder.

"Aren't you staying in our cabin?"

"I'll go back in a minute, I just want to make the most of this."

"The deck can get rather rowdy."

"I'm used to rowdiness."

"I know, Captain."

My suitcase was full to bursting point for this trip home:

full of a new translation and local produce that would make the journey back to Marseille with me. And there was the Captain too. When I'd gone to his house on Fabrizio's advice, I'd found him in a very pitiful state. "I'm at death's door, Giacomo, and I've just rung the bell," he'd said flatly. People don't die that young on our island. The Captain couldn't go to sleep on his own in that empty house. We talked for a long time, him lying down and me in an armchair by the window that constantly showed his reflection. The fisherman had abandoned him in the end, just like everyone else. Once their big conversations were over, he'd found the old soldier to be a burden so he'd stopped coming to see him. Love is always impossible.

"Thank you for taking me with you, Giacomo."

"I didn't take you, Captain. You came – it's different."

"I don't have many journeys left to make but this one's warming the cockles of my heart. I haven't left the island for years. And it's taken a young man to drag me out of the place!"

"Not all that young."

"A very kind man. Forgive me for dropping you for that fisherman. I thought he was interested in my stories."

"You mustn't tell too many of them. Keep some in reserve."

"Like with love . . ."

"Like with love! A secret revealed only slowly, that's the key with love."

Mama didn't know the Captain was travelling with me, I hadn't told her anything. I so wished she would make this journey with me someday, but she never left the island either, not unless something terrible happened. The old soldier hadn't let anyone know he was going, he told me he'd looked for someone, but who could he tell in such a vacuum? As he left, he'd grabbed a small suitcase that bore the stamps of the different battalions in which he'd fought, a tiny suitcase. He said he made do with very little: very few clothes, very little food . . . When Jessica and I set off on journeys I always felt I was taking basically everything we owned, that it was only by taking everything that we wouldn't miss anything. But, Jessica, no one ever misses anything on the island. Except you, I was missing you just as the ferry settled into cruising speed.

"You have a lot of dreams. I'm sure that's a translator's failing. Always lost in your thoughts, in words. Far from the real world."

"You really do understand me. A minute ago I was talking to my ex-wife, Jessica, as if she was here beside me."

"All you've got beside you is an old soldier! But you talk about Jessica a lot. Do you still love her?"

"Probably."

"You must win her back."

"I'm not a winner. That battle was lost long since."

"Since when?"

"Since the evening I took her to hospital."

"You told me she was still alive . . . ?"

"Yes, of course. Jessica was meant to be giving birth."

"Meant to be? What happened?"

"Our baby died."

"Oh God."

"The doctors did what they could. Our relationship didn't survive it. Jessica felt guilty, and so did I. We were better off going our separate ways."

I never talked about "it". I say "it" because the words are difficult to say, and to hear. My parents came to Marseille to give us their support, but it was too late. We were buried deep down, like the *Domus* under the Mediterranean. No one could get us back out. The only journey they ever made to where I was. They were meant to be coming for a birth.

They came for a funeral.

"Why've you never said anything before?"

"Can we talk about something else, please? I shouldn't have mentioned it. I over-share everything . . . Did you know there were *Domus* under the sea?"

"I've heard there are. But do you really believe that?"

"Yes! Don't you?"

"No. I'm more the pragmatic type. I've never believed in magic and witches. Even when I was a boy."

"That's all that's left, books and magic. They're how I keep going."

When Mama arrived in Marseille she'd stopped talking. It was the first time I'd known her silent. Papa picked up and tried to do what he could. They were in an impossible situation. Children sometimes put their parents through appalling experiences. Even if they don't mean to. Meanwhile, the Captain looked devastated, he could hardly look at me. The great soldier struck down by the thought of a lost new-born. A little boy, Fernando, in homage to Pessoa. People who like reading are often tempted to give their children "literary" names. Jessica and I had hesitated between Fernando and Solal, Albert Cohen's hero. Solal or Fernando. Names full of poetry. Or Sandro because there was a novelist with that name. And one other name. The one we chose in the end. No one knew but us. The privilege of parents-to-be. The Captain kept his eyes lowered, it seemed impossible for him to look up again. It didn't take much with these men on whose shoulders our country's fate rested.

"Shall we go and have a coffee?"

"I'd love to. I've ruined your trip with my story . . ."

* * *

My baby had made up his mind not to come into the world, I was convinced. He hadn't been harmed by any illness, he'd just decided not to come. Children can sense things and my little boy could tell things weren't going well. He'd left us on our own, but I didn't hold it against him. Everyone around us ventured their own explanation, an interpretation of the heart-break when there was nothing to say but what I told them: the baby had changed his mind at the last minute. People thought I was mad and put it down to my unfathomable pain. They were wrong. It was a carefully considered opinion.

Jessica decided to go and recuperate at her parents' house

in Rome. She didn't want me to come with her. I stayed in Marseille, in the apartment where the baby's bedroom still was. Jessica couldn't bear to look at it. Having worked so hard to put the cot together, I dismantled it, much more quickly. Undertaking well in advance a job I should have done when my child was three. I wasn't careful with the nuts and hinges, just taking it apart as fast as I could. In the space of half an hour the cot was out of the bedroom. Within an hour it was inside a container at the dump. I covered the walls with two coats of white. The baby's room now only existed in my mind. The apartment's future buyers – because we would obviously sell the place – would never know it had been intended for our child. Jessica hadn't had the strength to contribute to these alterations. Or watch them, even. She was weeping at her parents' house in Rome. I didn't want to join her. It was over. It would have been unbearable to go back to being the two of us when there had been three of us.

Mama pestered me every day, saying I should go to Sardinia. "I'll look after you, my darling," she kept saying. "You won't have to worry about anything." I didn't want to be looked after. I wanted to be alone. Why not in Sardinia . . . ? That was when I remembered the lighthouse at Carloforte: Fabrizio's older brother had been in charge of it for years and had even lived in it. That was what I needed, a lighthouse on the very tip of an island. Except I needed to be invited. Fabrizio persuaded his brother to let me stay there (when Fabrizio asked for something, his family always said yes, it was an upside to his condition). His brother didn't know what to do to apologize for being healthy: he'd won in the chromosome lottery and Fabrizio had lost. I just needed to be discreet and not ransack the nineteenth-century building. So I set off for Sardinia, just as my mother wanted, but I didn't tell her my exact destination.

"You'll be the death of me, Giacomo. Where are you? Tell me and we'll be there."

"I'm in Sardinia, just like you wanted."

"Yes, but I thought you'd come home."

"I need to be alone, Mama. Please understand. I couldn't cope with the family."

"But you wouldn't have to see them!"

"They would have come to pick me up off the ferry, Mama."

"I'm worried you're going to do something stupid."

"I won't do anything stupid, I promise."

"Are you somewhere in the north of the island?"

"Bye, Mama."

The lighthouse had never been painted, the stones were ochre-coloured, blackened by the wind and the waves. No painting, no frescoes. I was in the south of the island, a long way from my illustrated village. Mama wouldn't find me, no matter how many times she questioned Fabrizio. She knew he knew, but my friend could prove as little disposed to conversation as a rabbit with a tiger. Every morning she went to the kiosk to buy a newspaper and every morning she took along some biscuits for Fabrizio. Mama thought the whole world could be corrupted with biscuits. Not Fabrizio. He accepted the gift because he was greedy, but held his tongue because he was my friend.

"Won't you tell me where my son is, Fabrizio . . . I miss him so much."

"I don't know anything about it. And if I did know, you can be sure I wouldn't tell you a thing. Your biscuits are delicious! Giacomo's often told me about them."

I spent a month at the lighthouse. Reading, working, watching passing boats, crying. There was nothing else to do. I was translating Emmanuel Bove's novel *My Friends*, a book which is both funny and sad, the story of a friendless man alone in Paris. I found the character Victor Baton endearing, and recognized myself in his loneliness. It was the right book to be translating in my circumstances. Baton helped me keep going.

Fabrizio called me one morning to tell me Gavino was looking for me. Fabrizio laughed uncontrollably, incapable of clearly formulating what he wanted to say. My uncle was prospecting in the north-east of the island and thought he'd have no trouble finding me. An acquaintance of his thought he'd seen me buying artichokes in the market in Olbia, another had seen me eating a slice of watermelon on Santa Teresa di Gullura Beach . . . Meanwhile, I stayed put in the south-west. A real police-style investigation was set in motion: the whole family was searching for me and Gavino trawled all over the island in vain. Yet another friend spotted me cycling near the mountains – me, who couldn't cycle in a straight line. This episode lightened things a little for me; I accepted the distraction gratefully and was careful to mislead Mama when I spoke to her on the phone.

"Are you doing any sport where you are?"

"Of course, Mama. It clears my headspace. So does the countryside."

"The combination of the two?"

"How do you mean?"

"Are you doing a sport that gets you out into the country-side?"

"Exactly."

"Cycling!"

"Yes. The roads near— Well, they're beautiful. Ah, you nearly got it out of me. But I'm being careful."

With this, Mama cut the conversation short, claiming she had something in the oven, even though it was the middle of the afternoon. She hung up and would probably then contact her investigator to confirm the news: her son was cycling on steep sinuous roads in the mountains.

I was sitting on an iron chair, looking out over the Mediterranean, surrounded by rocks and scrubland, in a massive lighthouse looming up into the sky. The wind, every cyclist's enemy, was my only companion.

* * *

In the bar, the singer I'd met on the way over was carefully setting up his equipment. People watching him probably didn't realize he was the performer himself – you don't often see international stars plugging in their guitars and amps and other paraphernalia. He was sweating before he even started and kept wiping himself with a hanky, always the same one, so it wasn't long before the scrap of fabric just added more sweat to his already sweaty forehead. We sat facing the small stage and the singer gave me a friendly hello. He didn't really appear to remember me but my face must have meant something to him. Since our conversation he'd seen thousands of passengers whereas I hadn't met any other singers.

"You wait, Captain, he's not bad."

"I hope more of an audience will come to watch. It's a long time since I've gone to a concert. It must be, um . . . actually, I've never been to a concert."

"Well, this will be your first."

"What does he sing?"

"Phil Collins."

"Is that all?"

"Nothing else. Do you like Phil Collins?"

"I don't know him."

"You're lucky. Well, you were lucky."

The set started while people ate their breakfast. Some chose sandwiches with Mortadella or speck instead of coffee and brioches – memories of the island for their stomachs. The sound of crumpling plastic and conversations about the temperature of their drinks smothered the opening bars. It wasn't Phil Collins. I recognized Supertramp's *Logical Song*. The singer had changed his repertoire. He sang a succession of the group's songs, without a break, without drawing breath. The sound of crisp packets opening and the grease they propelled into the air didn't stop him performing his set. Far from terra firma, suspended outside time and away from any precise location, the passengers lost all their bearings and ate whatever they laid eyes on; they needed to fill the void created by leaving.

"I'm going for a little lie-down in the cabin, Giacomo. The music's too loud."

"I'll be down later."

Maybe Phil Collins would have appealed more to the Captain but I would never know. He struggled to get up off the seat we were on and his unsteady walk didn't fill me with confidence. Our cabin was on the deck below, at the end of a dismal narrow corridor. The shark in the corridor. Could he get there on his own? I didn't dare ask him for fear of belittling him. I made as if to get up but with a wave of his hand he implied I should sit back down. "Enjoy the show," he said. "You're sadder than I am." At that precise moment I wasn't particularly sad. I had been sad, very sad. Enough to make me retch. Then I had to pick myself up. Climb back up from the depths. Because going the other way would have led straight to death. Now a soft sort of melancholy had overtaken the sadness.

A few passengers started jigging in front of the stage, much to the performer's surprise. I imagine he was rarely paid this compliment. Personally, I couldn't work out whether the dancers were dancing out of genuine enjoyment or just mocking him. English sung with an Italian accent produces strange results, a sort of linguistic hyperbole. The singer kept going though, he even encouraged the audience to clap in time but they didn't all join in – how do you clap when you're holding a scalding coffee or a dribbling sandwich? I had my hands free so I joined in willingly. He interpreted musicians' work just as I did with novelists', so a bit of recognition wouldn't do him any harm. I stood up to get more into the rhythm and my legs stepped in time with my hands. People watched me but that didn't bother me. I like Supertramp, even when sung with an Italian accent.

A few years earlier I'd translated Maupassant's novella *The Necklace* in which the lowly young Mathilde is invited to a prestigious ball. She has a wonderful time at the ball and is the star of the evening, despite her poor background and fake jewellery. The most illustrious guests only have eyes for her. I was Mathilde – well, a bit – dancing to the singer's clumsy music. More people watched me. I've always liked dancing.

Jessica and I used to have tango lessons, it was incredible. My dancing on the ferry was more instinctive though, less formalized, probably rather more ridiculous, but what did that matter? At the end of the set people had finished their breakfast so they had no trouble clapping. Some even complimented me as they did so.

"Thank you for keeping me company."

"Not at all, it was my pleasure."

"We've met before, haven't we?"

"You've got a good memory. I'm a translator."

"Yes! The one who says 'nearly' the same thing. I remember."

"No more Phil Collins, then?"

"I needed to move on from him. There were no surprises with him anymore. It's like having a different haircut, it changes everything. The way we see things depends on how other people see them. You must feel it when you start translating a new book or a different author."

"Do the audiences like Supertramp a bit more?"

"Definitely! But, tell me, your father left in the middle of the set. Didn't he like it?"

"He's not my father, just a friend."

"Oh, sorry."

"He was tired. He's quite old. Actually, I must go down to the cabin to check he's okay."

"I'll be singing again in two hours' time."

"I'll come along."

"It'll be the same stuff. Well, almost. I'm going to have a go at Depeche Mode next year, then it'll be Duran Duran . . . I'll have to grow my hair long!"

And he started singing the opening lyrics of *Just Can't Get Enough*, sprinkling them with Italian sunshine.

★ ★ ★

Carlo whooped for joy when I told him the translation was finished. He put down the phone and broke off our conversation for at least a minute. I'd seen him do this: he ran dementedly around his office, like the grocer's dog when he knew he was getting the leftovers of a meal. Racing about, watched by his own portrait on the wall. Carlos everywhere. He told me he loved me, which is what he usually did when I delivered work. "I love you, Giacomo. You know I do. We're brothers." Exaggeration was part of his personality. "If I had you here in front of me, I'd take you in my arms and smother you with kisses." He forgot his own lethal aversion to any suggestion of homosexuality. His happiness swept everything else aside and I could have asked him to come to Sweden with me so we could get married. *Moby Dick* erased all negative waves and slightly shameful prejudices.

I met his assault of good humour with relative equanimity, knowing that his mood was only temporary, like a bad bout of flu, and it would soon be time for another job and more threats. "Things are going to explode for the company! People will be talking about us all over the world, my brother! Can you imagine?" The question I couldn't help pondering was: Are readers still interested in *Moby Dick*? The book was long, acerbic, perhaps not really suited to modern tastes. A love story between a man and a whale . . . I thought the pitch a bit outlandish, disturbing. I hoped Carlo wasn't wrong about this. He had such big dreams for this text.

"And then we'll find you something else, Giacomo. I've got some leads."

"What sort of leads?"

"I'd like to specialize in unpublished famous works."

"Unpublished and famous, you've lost me there, Carlo."

"I met a man who says he can supply me with unpublished manuscripts from famous authors from all around the world. He's got an unpublished version of *Les Misérables* up his sleeve."

"What are you talking about? There's only one version of *Les Misérables*."

"That's what everyone thinks, but we can come to an arrangement."

"An arrangement?"

"We can come to an arrangement with the truth. People are hungry for novelty, new discoveries . . . Put yourself in their shoes, they're constantly being peddled the same thing."

"Is this man you're talking about a forger?"

"Oh, such big words so quickly! Let's say he wants to make readers happy. He's a real craftsman, you know. He works on period paper, uses special inks . . . he's an artist, my friend!"

"He's a forger! You'll end up in prison, cheating people like that. Don't expect any help from me."

"Don't say that, Giacomo, my brother. You'll be rich and famous."

"Han van Meegeren!"

"What?"

"He was the forger who launched Vermeer's popularity. He had the most fascinating, exciting life. There's a very good book about it, I'll give you the details. It didn't end well . . ."

"There's nothing fascinating about the man I'm talking about, he's an ordinary man, unbelievably talented but ordinary. You're keen on Victor Hugo, aren't you?"

"Victor Hugo's not the problem. It's the principle that bothers me."

"If you'd rather, he's also offered me some Voltaire."

"Carlo, you've gone mad, I'm convinced you have. So tell me, is the *Moby Dick* manuscript real?"

"You're breaking up, Giacomo."

The conversation ended there. I tried to call Carlo back at least ten times but it kept going straight to voicemail, so I wouldn't get an answer until I saw him. Perhaps I'd been working on a fake. The idea upset me but there was nothing I could do about it now. I'd sent the translation off by email just before our telephone conversation. We southerners were often suspected of dishonesty. With good reason in this instance. Carlo wanted fame; morality and truth didn't really matter to him. The chair of convictions I'd been sitting on for months had suddenly been snatched from under me. I stayed suspended in the air

for a few seconds, like a cartoon character, before thumping
to the floor. If I could have teleported myself I would have
done it instantly, straight to Carlo's office. I'd have put my
hands around his neck and squeezed hard enough to get the
truth out of him. But teleportation only happens in fiction and
a couple of science laboratories: they can move light by a couple
of metres, but only in exceptional circumstances. And it's a
little further than that from Sardinia to Rome.

I thought about Vermeer's forger again, the man who
managed to fool the Nazis during World War II. Cheating
monsters wasn't reprehensible. Quite the opposite. Cheating
credulous readers seemed less acceptable to me. In prison Han
Van Meegeren had painted a "new Vermeer", *Christ in the
Temple*, in front of witnesses. Proof that he could bring the dead
painter back to life and add to his body of work.

I'd painted a fresco on the walls of my parents' house, but
hadn't signed it. I'd have to do that next time I went to the
island, I wouldn't want anyone laying claim to my work. Gavino
was dishonest enough to sign it in his name. I would use a
pseudonym. Banksy, for example.

1789. The number was clear to see on the key card the receptionist
had given me. 1789. The French Revolution. 1789 but I couldn't
open the cabin. The door must have dated back to the eighteenth
century itself, it looked so drab and weary after what I'd just
inflicted on it, bashing it with my shoulder. I hadn't gone as far
as kicking, that was for real emergencies. The Captain must have
been asleep inside and couldn't hear my attempts to get in. The
calm and the storm separated by a door. I threw myself at it
several times, being careful not to injure myself. It was thin, like
all cabin doors, it wouldn't hold out for long! I leant on the one
opposite, number 1791, about a metre away, and noticed that it
moved easily and felt as if it was about to give way. It turned out
it wasn't locked. I cast an eye around discreetly to check the cabin
wasn't occupied. It was empty but there was a strong rancid
smell. I went to the far end of the cabin, between the two beds,

to give myself a much longer run-up. 1789 wouldn't stand up to that. I threw myself at it once, then twice but still it held out.

My actions were now accompanied by swearing; swearing and then pleading because the former wasn't producing the desired effect. "Open up for pity's sake," as if the door could hear me and pay specific attention to my request. As I launched another assault that I hoped would clinch it, I heard a man say, "Wait, you'll hurt yourself." Like an athlete called back by the starter, I stopped in my tracks. A head appeared. An imposing head, leaning around the corner, disembodied. The man was frightened I'd knock him over, which was why he revealed only this part of his body. Survival instinct . . . When he was sure I wouldn't launch myself at him, the rest of his body appeared. He was a member of staff. He doubted my ability to open the door, which was understandable when he said, "I've been watching you for five minutes, you'll never do it." I desperately wanted to ask him why he'd let me make a fool of myself like that, but didn't. A vestige of pride perhaps.

"These doors open with key cards, not shoulders!"

"I know, but mine's not working."

"Could I have it, please?"

I handed him the card, and he came over to cabin 1789. With a calm, gentle, almost ladylike action (if there is such a thing as a ladylike action), he swiped the card and a green light came on – evidence that it was working perfectly normally. Open sesame! The door was unlocked.

"Doors are like women, you have to handle them gently."

When I heard this proverbial pronouncement, Manuella's, Jessica's and Alessandra's faces resurfaced right there, halfway across the sea. Raphael's *Three Graces* on a ferry. These women who meant something to me weren't doors, not one of them deserved the analogy (nor did any woman, in fact). Personally, I'd have compared the door with a seat belt: when the belt is stuck, forcing it is no help at all. You have to release it gently or it braces harder. Doors are like safety belts, you have to handle them gently.

People often say sailors are a bit crude, dripping with machismo, and I don't usually join in this tendency of negative stereotyping. I think it's unfair to catalogue people when you don't know them. Still, after this man's comment, he now fell straight into the "crude sailor" category. He'd be completely at home there.

Meanwhile he had plenty more uncouth behaviour to offer and indiscreetly opened wide the door to my cabin. The Captain was fast asleep.

"You nearly woke your father."

"He's not my father, he's a friend."

"Oh, I see. You know, we do have cabins with double beds."

"Twin beds suit us just fine."

"They're not much more expensive . . . anyway, I'll leave you to it. Have a good trip."

He looked at me, gave me a meaningful wink and sauntered off whistling.

The Captain was asleep on his back, snoring so loudly it was difficult to hear the information being relayed through the public address system. There was a book open on his chest, the copy of *Moby Dick* I'd lent him for the journey. I picked it up and leafed through it. The book's opening is distinctive, grabbing the reader. The first page, the first line: "Call me Ishmael." The Captain had underlined it in pencil. When he and I had first met under that scorching bus shelter, years before Jessica, years before heartbreak, that was how he'd introduced himself to us: "Call me Captain." Did he know Melville's book? He'd never told me he did. Was it the sheer power of literature which could sneak its way into real life? Altering it, making it a never-ending narrative?

I put the book on the bedside table halfway along the wall. It was going to be a long crossing, the Captain would have plenty of time to read it. In the meantime I decided not to stay in the cabin because I wanted to read but his snoring was distracting.

The singer was performing again so I couldn't sit in the bar.

I needed to find somewhere else; finding a quiet spot was a challenge, on a boat or anywhere else. There were people talking loudly everywhere, children shrieking and running . . . Why hadn't they set aside a space where people could be quiet? Was it that no one wanted peace and quiet? I found a chair near the swimming pool. The boat's designer may not have thought of a quiet room but he had come up with a tiny and peculiarly deep pool, a sort of upgraded bath. It was ten o'clock in the morning, no one had taken the plunge into it yet, so I could start reading Milena Agus's *From the Land of the Moon* in peace. This Sardinian author was much talked about in France, considerably less so in Italy. She lived in Cagliari and moved in literary circles like a ghost moving about a haunted castle. She was occasionally seen and sometimes heard but was still elusive. Reading a book that describes the island you've just left when you're sailing away from it smacks of sadism. Her writing glorified Sardinia, every word of it, even the spaces between them. The punctuation too. The full stops, the commas, all of it was Sardinian. Agus had a gift for making you love our island. Or loathe it, if you'd had a painful experience there. There's a pastry they make in France called a *gâteau saint-honoré*. When I first moved to Marseille I adored it, my love for it knew no bounds. I'd buy a slice of it every day from a patisserie near my apartment (I wasn't interested in healthy eating, all that mattered was the pleasure of it). This went on until one of these delightful cakes made me ill. So ill I couldn't even leave the house. All that for a patisserie . . . Ever since, I've rejected everything remotely associated with the cake: cream, choux pastry and caramel. It was unfair because there was clearly only one guilty party.

Reading Milena Agus when you've suffered some form of pain in Sardinia should have more or less the same effect. A total – if unwarranted – aversion to the island.

My mind was focused on my theory about Milena Agus when I was hit full in the face by a ball, one of those balls featuring the Sardinian flag and sold on the island's beaches.

The sort of thing I would have bought for my son to take home to France. Pride stamped onto imitation leather. My sunglasses flew off and the Milena Agus book, perhaps responding to a delayed self-defence reflex, ended up in the pool. A young teenage boy came up to me and apologized: "I'm really sorry. I'll get your book for you." He took off his T-shirt and threw himself clumsily into the water to retrieve Milena who was floating like a cork. He climbed out of the pool and shook himself, spattering me with icy droplets carried on the wind.

"Here, it just needs to dry. I think you'll be reading again in about fifteen minutes."

"Thanks for the advice."

"If not, my dad'll pay for it. Look, he's over there, the tall one in the blue shirt."

"Don't worry about it."

"Here, here are your glasses . . . Oops, they're a bit battered . . . Hey, weren't you on the beach the other day? The guy with the injury."

"Injury?"

"Yes, you couldn't play football with us because you said you'd damaged a ligament. The scar on your knee."

"Yes, you're absolutely right, that was me."

"It's good to see you again. Is it any better?"

"Getting better and better, thanks."

"If you like we could play football together later."

"It's still a bit soon. I'd rather read, I think. But there's something I'd like to ask you. Will you do something for me?"

"After what I've just done I can't refuse."

"When you get home, promise you'll buy a copy of the book you've just sent flying into the pool."

"If you like. And what about the glasses?"

"Don't worry about them."

"What's the book called?"

"*From the Land of the Moon*, it's by Milena Agus."

The boy took his phone from his backpack and made a note of the book.

"Is there an H in Agus?"

"No, it's A, G, U, S. Will you read it?"

"I promise."

"It's definitely worth more than a pair of sunglasses."

"What's it about?"

"Sardinia."

* * *

The first few times the Captain took us down to the beach, he bought us each an ice-cream. I was a bit embarrassed because Mama had always told me never to accept anything from strangers. He may have been a rather famous stranger from our village, but he was a stranger all the same. To avoid disobeying her straight away, I adopted the initial-refusal technique, keeping my eyes on the ground.

"Would you like an ice-cream, Giacomo?"

"No thank you, Captain."

"Really?"

"Well, if you're sure, it *is* very hot. Yes, I'd love one."

My eyes opened wide, my head tilted upwards, and the list of ice-creams appeared like a mirage; eighty whole centimetres of cornets, ice lollies and frozen treats. I chose a red, hand-shaped ice-cream, the kind that is guaranteed to be stuffed full of chemicals. My friends varied their choices from week to week but I never did, I needed reassurance, and children find repetition reassuring. The hand-shaped ice-cream passed from the Captain's hands to mine. And all the others, all those multicoloured confections, followed the same route. The ice-cream seller, in his lemon-shaped booth, was so happy when he saw us coming over to boost his business. Ten or so of us jumped up and down outside his plastic lemon. We associated the beach with ice-creams and waited feverishly for the old soldier to point to the booth. That was the signal: time for our assault on the lemon. When we'd all been served, we gave the Captain a huge thank you in unison, a unanimous Sardinian people's vote that delighted him. He pretended to give a little bow to show his appreciation.

Sadly, old habits are always eventually caught out by the stumbling block of time: you can take the stairs three steps at a time, you have no trouble carrying three bags of shopping . . . and then the time comes when you can't do these things anymore.

One day the Captain told us solemnly that he would only buy ice-creams for half of the group, so just for five of us. The others would get one the following week. This new arrangement shook us up because we all wanted to be in the group who got an ice-cream; no one wanted to wait till the next time. Realizing how much this idea had upset us, the Captain suggested tossing a coin. Of course, I lost and was relegated to the second group. I always lose. Fabrizio does too. My four partners in misfortune and I watched miserably as the five winners enjoyed their ice-creams. As I've said, the Captain didn't understand how children worked. He might be able to master weapons, survival and combat, but not children.

It was our turn the next week and I took malicious delight in eating my hand-shaped ice-cream in front of my former friends. They'd stopped being my friends when they won at heads or tails. We'd stopped talking to each other and the old soldier hadn't even noticed. He didn't notice the gloom that descended on the children without ice-creams. He would say glibly, "If you want a bit of colour, look at my shirts, they'll give you plenty of colour." Taking consolation for not having an ice-cream by looking at a colourful shirt – what torture, what a ludicrous idea. Multicoloured shirts weren't even in fashion.

Interestingly, though, the Captain's bright colours gradually became scarcer. We children couldn't really understand why blues became grey and reds evolved towards black. Symbols are a mystery to most humans. Another time, almost before we'd all found seats on the bus, the Captain stood up in front of the whole group and said, "There won't be ice-creams for any of you today. That's just the way it is." He sat back down so all we could see of him was his neck and the back of his head. We weren't in the habit of questioning his orders – out of respect and fear – so we behaved as if this news was of no consequence. Just an optical illusion. Sadly, it was my group's turn to have an ice-cream. The other group looked at us, gloating. They mimed licking ice-creams with unedifying vulgarity. Future sailors, no doubt. Still, we enjoyed being by the sea, gradually forgetting our disappointment and the list of delights taunting us from outside the plastic lemon. Swimming replaced the sugar rush. In the middle of a ball game in the water I got a cramp and decided to limp back to the beach. The Captain had his back to me and didn't see me coming. He was chatting to the bus driver.

"The state has cut my war pension by half."

"How do you mean?"

"Old soldiers aren't needed anymore. We were handsome and useful once, but no longer. So I officially need to scrimp and save . . . I can't even buy the children ice-cream now."

"They'll get over it."

"It'll be harder for me. I haven't dared tell them the truth. They've got so much respect for me, I feel it would be letting them down."

"But they'd understand. They'll still respect you."

"Things are going to get tricky."

"How will you cope?"

"I've already thought of selling my medals and uniforms. There are collectors all over the country prepared to pay a fortune for my ribbons and clothes. Even if they're not in tip-top condition."

"You wouldn't!"

"I would, I don't have a choice. All I've got is memories no one's interested in anymore. I think maybe—"

The driver gestured to the Captain to warn him there was someone behind him. He broke off mid-sentence.

"What's going on, Giacomo?"

"I've got cramp."

"You lie down here, I'll take care of that."

He stretched out my leg gently, and the cramp eased away in his hands. His eyes seemed to be watering and the sea breeze had nothing to do with it. Our unified country could no longer be bothered with its soldiers, they were in the way.

"Is that better?"

"Thank you, Captain. I've got a bit of money at home, you know. I helped my grandma tidy her attic and she paid me. I could give it to you if you like. We won't tell the others anything."

I was very frightened about how he'd react. Lying there with my leg stretched out, my fingers started to tense, as they did at the dentist when he scraped off the tartar with a sharp instrument. My fingernails dug into my palms.

"I'm really touched by your offer, Giacomo. But I can cope on my own, don't you worry about me."

"If you change your mind, feel free to come round to my house. Mama will be happy to see you. And Papa."

"Go on, off you go and have fun with your friends."

My fingers had released their grip and were now straightening. I ran and threw myself in the water, scattering sand on towels as I ran past. Grandma had given me a few coins for my work and I'd hidden them inside a book for fear of having them taken away again. Which book, I wonder? Probably *Moby Dick*.

* * *

I now didn't have a book to read, so I went into one of the shops where they sold light fiction – very light, in fact – the sort of thing that flew away as soon as you finished the last page. Stories about cleaning ladies marrying rich and powerful men; covers featuring horses and faces in close-up surrounded by clouds of roses, all in soft, appealing colours. Yes, we definitely were surrounded by colour. On walls and on books. The saleswoman didn't pay any attention to me, she was busy folding

T-shirts with the Four Moors flag printed on them. The Sardinian flag was endemic on our island, like argan trees around Agadir. I didn't see the famous tricolour much in France, it was only brought out on very rare occasions, but in Sardinia our flag was plastered over clothes and the windows of houses. Four Moors turning to look to the right – since an official decision was made. They used to look to the left and wore a blindfold over their eyes, a sign of their submission to the nation they'd tried and failed to defeat. The saying went that their heads had been cut off. Up until the early 2000s children still wore T-shirts with severed heads on them.

"Are you looking for something?"

"I've read all of them."

"Wait, have a look down at the bottom, behind the magazines."

I leant over and moved aside a pile of magazines and sure enough, there were two paperback books behind them lying haphazardly across the shelf. I grabbed them and stood back up.

"There you are, you see. I was sure I had some other ones left. I put them there because no one's interested in them. Everybody writes nowadays, even people with no talent at all . . ."

She sounded sad about this state of affairs. The books I'd exhumed were identical, an ugly edition of Rimbaud's poetry with a green cover. A disgusting green, a far cry from the emerald of our coastline. Anyone not familiar with the contents wouldn't be tempted to dive in.

"I'll take one."

"But not the other?"

"They're the same."

"Are you sure?"

"Yes, look."

I showed her the spines, holding them right next to each other, making a sort of long, green Rimbaud sandwich. The woman started reading the one on the left, then shifted to the one on the right.

"Rimbaud, *Poems* and Rimbaud, *Poems.* You're right, they're the same. So you like poetry."

"This poetry, yes."

"Have you already read it?"

"Yes."

"Why buy it again, then? Wouldn't it be better to pick a book you don't know?"

"I'm buying it because I know what I'll find in it. Look, have a read of this."

I handed her the collection and she started reading out loud:

"*In winter we'll travel in a little pink railway carriage / With cushions of blue. / We'll be happy there. In every cosy corner a nest of wild kisses / Lies waiting for you.* A nest of wild kisses lies waiting in every cosy corner . . . sensual stuff."

She pretended to fan herself with her left hand and rolled her eyes skywards.

"Very."

She kept reading, pronouncing each phrase perfectly. The blue-and-white boat was transformed into that pink train. Other customers listened attentively, no one moved. The magic of poetry. An incursion into human time.

"*And you will tilt your head at me and say 'fi—'*"

A man's voice interrupted her mid-sentence. A man dressed all in white, the sailor who'd stopped me forcing the cabin door.

"Oi, Nina, are you doing readings for customers now? Back to work, please."

"Okay, boss. That's seven euros, sir."

I paid and made way for the next customer, who dropped her voice as I brushed past her to say, "That was so beautiful. I'm going to buy the other copy."

"Oh, don't mind me!" the man said sarcastically. "She's pretty, our Nina is."

"I was only buying a book from her."

"Just like you were trying to open your cabin door with brute strength. Go on, out of here, you rascal!"

I was thirty-six and it was the first time I'd been called a rascal in public. A rascal because I'd got a young woman to read a poem. I hadn't intended to chat her up, just introduce her to incredible poetry written by a boy when he was half my age.

"The poem was wonderful."

"So you're a poetry lover, that's a bonus in the seduction game."

"Your colleague is delightful but I just wanted to buy a book."

"Well, you would say that . . . but be careful, she may look easy on the outside but Nina's always got an answer to everything."

Rimbaud's poetry cut right to the essence of things. It was full of rebellion and pleasure. And accessible to everyone, except the odd idiot dressed in white.

Your breast against mine,
Our voices mingling,
We would slowly reach the ravine,
Then the deep woods! . . .

* * *

Jessica and I nearly stopped talking to each other altogether. It's all about the nearly. Contact between us had melted away like an ice-cream left in the sun. We called each other from time to time about some administrative problem still kicking about in our lives. An old bill, a contract cancellation, small traces that brought so many memories with them. Where work was concerned, Carlo made sure he didn't ask to see us at the publishing company at the same time. He knew how we had got to this situation. Still, we did occasionally cross paths. It always felt strange seeing the woman who was meant to be my wife for life (that's what we'd told the priest) and the mother of my child. She was a mother for just over eight months. A long time and hardly anything. Eight months to translate a book seemed like an interminable ordeal. Eight months of motherhood, a drop in the waters of the Mediterranean. Every time we met I noticed that Jessica was growing steadily paler. This woman whose skin was never white now seemed to come from some Nordic country. "I'm always cold," she once told me at Carlo's office. "I'll never feel warm again."

Jessica's face came to me as I was falling asleep in a deckchair on the boat, a sun-kissed dream because she was tanned. My dry lips woke me. I felt uncomfortable and my eyes were misty. I drank some water, now sun-warmed, that I'd bought before settling in the chair. I couldn't get Jessica out of my mind, there was no antidote to it: her face appeared on every woman strolling on deck. The young woman diving into the ridiculously small swimming pool; the mother vigorously drying her daughter; the stylish old lady sipping a Campari. Jessica's face was even on the poster extolling the merits of "Aqua di Sardegna" perfume. My phone started to vibrate in my pocket, it must have been her. I saw Alessandra's name on the screen. Another name ending in A. The *Dottoressa*. I didn't answer. I only wanted Jessica. I had to call her, that was all there was to it.

"Jessica, it's me."

"I know. The caller's name's been coming up on mobile screens for several years now."

"I'm an idiot."

"What do you want?"

"I keep seeing you everywhere."

"Are you drunk?"

"No, not at all. Or if I am, I'm drunk on water. I'm surrounded by water."

"Giacomo, you sound as if things aren't . . ."

"I keep seeing you everywhere, Jessica. Every woman on the boat has got your face."

"You're on a boat?"

"Yes, I'm on my way back from Sardinia."

"I thought you were in France working on the *Moby Dick* translation."

"I had to come over for Grandma."

"Has something happened to her?"

"She was at death's door. I came over as an emergency."

"And?"

"And she's watching *The Bold and the Beautiful* . . ."

"She's what?"

"She didn't die. I stayed longer than planned. You see, she was meant to die. It's a long story."

"You always have a good excuse to go back to your island."

For years I'd used every possible pretext to go to Sardinia with Jessica. In the early days it only affected our summers, then it included a late-October break to make the most of the autumn, then the Christmas holidays because Sardinia's warm in winter, and lastly our spring breaks because there's nowhere prettier at blossom time. Jessica had had too much of it by the end. She felt sick in the car on the way to the port and sick on the boat that wouldn't stop pitching. All that was missing was me giving her a copy of Milena Agus's book.

"There's something else."

"Some paperwork? Bills?"

"No, a more important something else."

"Tell me."

"I've been thinking about the baby a lot recently."

"Are you joking? Well, I've thought about him every day since it happened, not just recently! Is that what you're calling me about?"

"I'm in pain too, you know. You're not the only one in this terrible business. What I mean is, I've been thinking about him more than usual the last few days. You see, I just don't accept it! I'll never accept it! Grandma will live to a hundred and our little boy never breathed the same air as us. I can't take it, Jessica. I never told you this before, but I can't take it. I work, meet up with friends, travel . . . but I can't take it. He's everywhere."

"You don't have to keep saying 'he', Giacomo. Say his name for once, maybe for the first time. I want to hear it."

"Ishmael . . ." I managed quietly.

"Our little Ishmael."

"Don't cry, I didn't want to make you cry."

"Well, that worked," she sniffed.

This was why we'd avoided talking to each other for months. Words were impossible, in the same way that love was impossible for the Captain. The women around me had got their own faces back. People were sunning themselves peacefully on the sun deck, the see breeze tricking them about how powerful the rays were. They'd realize come night-time when the burning stopped them sleeping.

"How's your mama?"

"She's well. She's always sad when I leave, but she knows I'll be back."

"You always go back . . ."

"Have you heard from Carlo?"

"Yes, I've spoken to him on the phone quite a lot, actually."

"Really? For work?"

"Not just work. We talk a lot."

"You be careful. He's a smooth talker."

"Like everyone from your island."

"Maybe so."

Carlo was good at listening to people and reeling them in with his own bizarre stories. He must have told her about this forger who was going to make him famous. Jessica didn't need a guru, but she was fragile enough to be manipulated.

"I must have a word with Carlo."

"Why, are you jealous? We're not married anymore."

"I'm not jealous. I just meant I need to talk to him about work, that's all."

The first time Carlo had met Jessica, he'd told me she had a perfect backside, like something drawn by a painter. It was a coarse comment, worthy of a sailor, but with an artistic reference thrown in – the editor's touch.

Lying on my deckchair, I was sandwiched between the blue of the sky and that of the sea. The phone signal had gone. Perhaps Ishmael was up there, looking at me. Or down below, in the other blue, hidden deep in a *Domus de Janas*. He could definitely see me and hear me!

God, on the other hand, hadn't heard a thing, even though people on my island talked to him a lot. The church bell set the rhythm to our days and nights, no one must ever forget that God was always somewhere nearby. When we were learning our catechism, the priest never stopped telling us that our Father loved our land, and loved it more than all other lands in his creation. Of course he never gave us any further reasoning. He probably knew this because God had told him: God loved Sardinia, God was Sardinian, yes! He spoke these words with terrifying intensity. His eyes shone so brightly, I thought there must be a couple of halogen lamps behind them.

According to him, the Garden of Eden had been near a small village in the centre of the island. Near a huge forest, perfect for fruit trees to flourish, and fed by many rivers. There were even snakes there. It all fell into place. We were too young to question what a man of the church said. Convinced by affirmations, we used to ask him every week to take us to this sacred place because we felt important, chosen by He who chooses everything. The priest didn't refuse but kept deferring our pilgrimage, and we accepted this: a priest doesn't make decisions alone, he needed God's support. What we actually thought was that *Dio* wanted to give us a special welcome (we were from the same place as Him, after all). When I talked to Mama about it, she told me to be patient and said we would soon be rewarded.

"But, Mama, is it true that God's Sardinian?"

"Who told you that?"

"The priest."

"The priest is always right."

The priest is always right, especially when he raps children's fingers with a ruler.

Either way, in our particular case and whether He was Sardinian or not, God hadn't heard a thing. He hadn't heard how miserable we were and that playing this terrible trick on us was the worst abomination Jessica and I could have suffered. Etymologically, Ishmael means "God will hear" because in the Bible he is the product of forbidden love. Abraham was married to Sarah but she couldn't give him any children. So the couple decided that their servant Agar would use her womb to carry little Ishmael. After the baby was born the two women tore each other apart and the Bible story became as complicated as a whole season of *The Bold and the Beautiful*. When Jessica suggested the name Ishmael to me, I immediately thought of all that family strife in the Bible but she couldn't care less about that, or that the name featured in Melville's novel, for that matter. Jessica liked the name's exotic resonance and the fact that people would struggle to work out where it was from. My uncle was called Gavino and everyone knew he was Sardinian; Ishmael was a more enigmatic name. I didn't try to go against her or make any malicious comments. I didn't say anything, and God didn't hear anything.

The Captain was sound asleep and the ferry was still a long way off docking.

I really did have nothing to do on that boat. People started gathering on the left-hand side – port or starboard, I'd never known. Children came rushing over, jumping into their parents' arms because someone had seen a dolphin. Or rather a dolphin's fin because when I went over and scanned the water, I couldn't see anything except for some small waves that could have been left behind by a dolphin. The vulgar sailor came over, still smiling. With his sunglasses clamped on his face, he gave the children a conspiratorial thumbs up. In fact he seemed to spend his whole time performing. Perhaps I'd been wrong about his job – an activities leader rather than a sailor. I didn't feel like asking him.

"Kids always love dolphins. Do you have any children?" he asked, leaning against my shoulder.

"I had one."

Grammatically speaking, that straightforward question required a yes or no answer. My peculiar and awkward reply completely astonished the sailor. He repeated the question, hoping for some clarification from me.

"So you have one, then?"

"I did have."

"And I bet you showed them dolphins."

"No, never. He never saw any dolphins. Well, I'm not so sure anymore."

"Even in books?"

"Definitely not in books. I wanted to ask you something."

"Go ahead, it's what I'm here for."

"What's your job on this ferry?"

"I take care of the passengers' well-being. I make sure their crossing goes without a hitch."

"That's a nice job."

"Thank you."

"What if one of them fell overboard, what would you do?"

"Well, if I was there at the time, I'd jump straight in to help them."

"Has that ever happened?"

"Never. There are sometimes incidents, but nothing serious. Never any divers!"

He took off his sunglasses to give a wink worthy of an American actor in a commercial, then put his glasses straight back on. He probably had weak eyes, given that he spent most of his time on a boat in blazing sunshine. He reminded me of a taxi driver I'd met when I was in Naples once, a man who kept a Captain America shield on his passenger seat. It was a plastic toy which he said discouraged criminals from attacking him. I'd been amazed by this line of reasoning because no toy had ever stopped a mugger, but he claimed that the fools were terrified by this symbol of the superhero. And plenty of other people were too. "Everyone's frightened of Captain America, he's the size of a dustbin lorry. I never go anywhere without it. And, you never know, people might end up thinking I'm Captain America . . . *Di Napoli!*"

When Jessica left the maternity ward she no longer had her protruding tummy. Or a baby. She wouldn't take off her sunglasses despite the grey skies and the incessant rain. I carried her small overnight bag and tried to avoid stepping in puddles. The car was parked quite a long way from the hospital because the architect hadn't thought to put a car park nearer the building. If Ishmael had been with us, he'd have been soaked. A disastrous first outing . . . But he wasn't with us.

I was holding a copy of Rimbaud's poetry. *The Drunken Boat.*

> *Lighter than a cork, I danced upon the waves so high,*
> *Waves called eternal rollers of victims,*
> *Ten nights, never sorry to be far from the lighthouse's stupid eye!*

The sailor noticed a young woman coming over to us, and turned towards her with undisguised pleasure.

"How can I help you, madam?"

"Do you know what time we'll arrive?"

"At about five o'clock. Nothing's ever guaranteed at sea. I've been sailing for twenty years, you can believe me . . ."

All passengers always asked the crew this same question. It was traditional. Even though the arrival time was printed on the tickets they all had; but that didn't matter, they had to ask when we'd arrive. Human beings need to know the time, even if it ends up killing them. I stepped over the partly rusted railings. The flaking paint broke away at the slightest contact, it would be all over my trousers – white trousers, which were a bad choice, given the circumstances . . . You can see through them when they're wet. The young woman screamed and the sailor spun round. The steel barrier stood between us.

"What's got into you? Stop!"

"*Lighter than a cork, I danced upon the waves so high, | Waves called eternal rollers of victims, / Ten nights, never sorry to be far from the lighthouse's stupid eye!"*

The water temperature out at sea is appreciably lower than by a beach. That's probably why people rarely swim there. The noise that accompanied my entry into the Mediterranean was impressive. To my ears, at least. Water poured into them and it felt as if the sea was filling me up like an empty bottle. A bottle of Sardinian water, of course. When my head resurfaced I heard shouting from the deck but I couldn't see anything clearly. A loud sound rang out, the distress signal sent out by the ferry. Then another, from a man who'd taken the same route as me.

"Moron, moron, moron!"

Someone was swimming towards me, cursing at me. I adopted my favourite pose, floating on my back. I didn't exactly dance over the waves but let them carry me like a cork, the swell lifting and lowering my body. Now that I was used to the temperature, I felt completely relaxed on the open sea. I wasn't planning on making any movements, just letting myself go. My son might be there, right underneath me, watching me. He might even be proud of his father who'd played a nasty trick on the coarse sailor. Deep in his seabed *Domus*, he must have had the beginnings of a satisfied smile. His father wasn't a nobody: a whole ferry-load of people was watching him, shouting at him, encouraging him to float, not to go under, not to sink.

But if I did sink I might see Ishmael. My one, my child. Or Melville's. Who knows? And what about the whale, would it come to see me? And Ahab? I'd spent weeks on end in their company, they owed me that at least! The water flowed over my face and I wasn't at all frightened. At swimming pools I always dreaded having to put my head under water. Afraid of drowning, afraid of dying. I didn't feel any fear now, though.

"Aargh! I won't let you get away now!"

An arm gripped me firmly between my head and shoulders, not that anyone had asked my permission.

"You kept your word."

"What?"

"You said you'd dive in if someone fell in the water."

"But you didn't fall in, you jumped. Don't try to talk, they'll come and get you in the Zodiac."

"I'm sure my boy saw me, you know."

"Please, don't talk."

"He's right at the bottom."

"Be quiet, or I'll leave you to drown."

"I won't drown, I'm floating. I'm so happy floating here. Let go of me."

I broke away from him and lay on my back again. The sailor was starting to tire and didn't put up much resistance. He wasn't very fit – looking at pretty women all day doesn't work the heart muscles.

"Look at me floating, I really am like a cork. Go on, you have a go, lie on your back."

"You're out of your mind."

"Come on, don't be a fool, on your back. The rescue squad will have us back in no time. Might as well make the most of what little quiet we've got left."

In the end he complied with my recommendations and revealed his paunch, which rose above the waterline. All things considered, I wasn't that bad for my age.

"How old are you?"

"Forty."

"I'm thirty-six. Did you know there are sharks in the Mediterranean? They're harmless. They're even shyer than dolphins, that's why you never see them."

"Thank goodness."

"Let's hold hands, it'll help us stay together."

I reached for his left hand and held it firmly enough so he couldn't shake me off. From above we must have looked like a sort of misshapen starfish. An aquatic ballet for the passengers watching us from further and further away. Jessica loved synchronized swimming, she spent hours watching international competitions. Sadly, men couldn't compete. The sailor and I managed quite well for amateurs and I came very close to suggesting we formed an original duo, the Dorsal Swimmers.

"Have you ever seen a *Domus*?"

"No."

"They're prehistoric buildings, very poetic. Fairy houses."

"I really don't care."

"Next time the ferry goes to Sardinia, get off and visit one. We need to open ourselves up to the world and to other civilizations, even very old ones."

I soon grasped that the sailor didn't want to talk to me until the launch reached us. He didn't say anything, even when I revisited the subject of the salesgirl in the shop or the young woman on deck who'd asked him a question just before I jumped. He was probably tired after his physical exertion. Or angry with me. Like Gavino and various members of my family, like Carlo when I didn't answer his calls, like Alessandra when I took her off to a beach surrounded by flames, like Jessica when I said "he" instead of "Ishmael". From my point of view, things were looking much better. In fact, so long as I was in the water, things would be better. Because water was better than emptiness.

The sound of the motor launch coming to help us grew increasingly insistent. There was considerable agitation on board, men talking loudly and waving their arms around. The Rimbaud book floated next to me. *Nina's Reply*, *A Winter Dream*, *The Drunken Boat* . . . They were there with me. I had nothing to fear.

* * *

Boats don't sink anymore. So the "What to do in the event of shipwreck" training has very little chance of being put into operation. We'd been brought back to quite a large room and the rescue team were eyeing us like weird sea creatures. My saviour was the hero, and I was the madman. The big blue woollen blankets that had been put over our shoulders were as scratchy as allergenic hair-shirts. The sailor wouldn't look at me, as if banishing me to the realms of an idea, transparent. We shivered even though it was midsummer, evidence that we weren't really okay after all. "Would you like a hot drink?" a member of the crew asked me. A hot drink in the middle of summer. I said I would. Someone in charge came over to me.

"Do you have a cabin?"

"Yes, number 1789. The Revolution!"

"Are you travelling alone?"

"With a friend."

"We'll inform them."

"If you like."

"Were you trying to end it all?"

"Not at all. I don't want to die."

"Well then, why jump overboard in the middle of the sea?"

"In the middle of the summer."

"Yes."

"Because your crewmate" – I pointed to the sailor – "said he'd dive in if a passenger fell in the water. I had to confirm that statement. I also do have some personal problems but I didn't want to die, I assure you."

"That's ridiculous! What if he was lying and he hadn't come to help you?"

"I'd have floated for a long time. Someone would have reached me eventually. I've got friends in the area."

"I'm not following you at all."

In the end the Captain appeared, his hair all awry and his eyes swollen from too long a siesta.

"Good God, Giacomo, what got into you?"

"I wanted to check what this sailor sitting next to me said."

"Committing suicide in the middle of the Mediterranean, that's so pathetic. Be a man, my boy. Use a handgun, it's the only way! You should have talked to me about it first."

"But I wasn't trying to kill myself. Nobody here seems to understand that."

"I've got the necessary in my bag . . ." the old soldier said under his breath. "I always have a weapon on me, you never know. And if I get an urge to die, I wouldn't have to ask anyone for permission. One bullet, just the one and then I'll be looking down at the earth from heaven."

We had to break off our conversation because the boat's doctor wanted to examine me. I was taken into a cabin that served as a consulting room where the doctor asked me to lie down on the examination table, and pulled out a length of disposable paper so that I didn't feel the chill of the leather. Then, on autopilot, he took my pulse and blood pressure. Silence reigned all powerful in there, enveloping the room. I could hear my heart, and the doctor's. *Two Hearts*, like in the Phil Collins song. Their beats were intermingled. You got the same distinctive intermingling during an ultrasound scan: the mother's heart and the baby's beating together. I could also feel the man's breath. Soft and warm. With a smell of peppermint. Next he checked my reflexes by striking my knees with a sort of rubber-tipped hammer. Well, thank goodness it wasn't a real hammer, the effects would be terrible for patients. Then it was time to look at my eyes and ears. The medical examination found nothing unusual. The doctor tried to maintain an overcooked kind of suspense before resentfully pronouncing that everything was "fine". I knew everything was fine because I wasn't in any pain. In fact I'd been feeling rather good since taking my dip. Contact with the chilly water had had a positive effect on my metabolism.

"You were lucky."

"Really?"

"Yes, you could have killed yourself diving in."

"That's why I went in feet first."

"Well played. Is this the first time?"

"That I've jumped like that?"

"That you've tried to take your life."

"I wasn't trying to kill myself."

"I'm sure you'll agree with me that what you did looked like a suicide attempt."

"If I'd wanted to die I wouldn't have taken Rimbaud with me!"

"You need to rest now. I won't have you helicoptered off because physically you're unharmed. I'm more worried about you psychologically."

"Don't worry about me, I won't do it again."

"You'll be kept under surveillance until we berth. Then I recommend you make an appointment straight away for psychological monitoring. Where do you live?"

"Marseille. Rimbaud was hospitalized there when he got back from Africa. But he didn't see any causal relationship between the two."

"Do you know a therapist in Marseille?"

"No."

"I'll give you the name of a friend. Tell him I gave you his contact details."

"Alright."

The doctor muttered a few words to a crew member and then turned back to me.

"Franco will stay with you for the last part of the journey. And I'm at your disposal should you need anything."

"One last thing, doctor."

"Yes?"

"Are you familiar with the *Domus de Janas*?"

"Yes, I'm very keen on them, vestiges of Nuragic civilization."

"You're the first person who knows about them! People don't usually know what they are."

"Anything's possible!"

"There's a legend that there are some at the bottom of the Mediterranean."

"And why not! There wasn't always seawater here. Montaigne said, 'The world is a perpetual see-saw' and he was right. Everything is on the move!"

"Thank you."

Madness depends on your viewpoint. I didn't tell the doctor that I jumped into the water in the hope of possibly being seen by Ishmael, snuggled down there in a *Domus de Janas*. Or by Ahab, back from the depths. Or by the whale, found at last. We always do things for someone. Thank you. I didn't add anything because there wasn't anything to add. I just needed to get on with the journey. To land and get off the ferry. Because I still had a long way to go.

Acknowledgements

Thank you to Michèle M. for her patience and our never-ending conversations.

Thank you to Giacomo, the real one!

Thank you to Giacomo, the other one, the one I've been trying to find for so long.